"A satisfying journey toward self-identity." **—USA TODAY**

"A riveting page-turner that will keep you hooked till the end."
—ENTERTAINMENT WEEKLY

"An exquisite coming-of-age story with a twist."
—FAMILY CIRCLE

"Fascinating . . . This novel evokes every possible emotion and will linger in your heart after you reach the end."
—ROMANTIC TIMES BOOK REVIEW, TOP PICK

"[A] suspenseful YA debut." **—THE BOSTON GLOBE**

"Gripping . . . We promise you won't see the end coming."
—HELLOGIGGLES

★ "Flora's resourcefulness in overcoming her disability, along with her determination to gain some measure of autonomy from overprotective parents, makes her a strong and appealing character. In her YA debut, Emily Barr does a terrific job portraying how disorienting life must be for someone who can't remember what she does for more than two or three hours at a time. Life is always a mystery, yet Flora persists."
—SHELF AWARENESS, STARRED REVIEW

Flora be brave

Flora be brave

Flora be brave

Flora be brave

Flora be brave

Tora be brave

Flora be brave

Flora be brave

Flora be brave

Flora be brave

Flora be brave

Flora be brave

Flora be brave

Flora be brave

Flora be brave

Flora be brave

brave

Flora be brave

Flora be brave

Flora b

Flora be brave

Flora be brave

Tora be brave

Can a kiss be the cure?

"You kissed him." Paige is not shouting, but it would be better if she were. She is quietly furious. She fixes me with intense eyes and says it again. "You kissed him. I *know* you did. You won't remember it, but you did it, and I know you did because . . ."

My head is ringing and I can't focus on her words. I know she is talking. I know she is angry. I know she is right to be angry. She is saying words, but I am not hearing them. I force myself to stop looking at yellow notes that tell me things I already know and make myself look at her. I have to tune back in.

She is breathing deeply. "And you've written it down!" One of my Post-it notes is in her hand, so I cannot, of course, pretend anything at all. The words are there, in my writing, and she knows that my notes are for facts. She knows this is real.

I know it is real too. I can remember it. I remember things from before I got sick, and now I remember kissing Drake. I know, now, that I am not a little girl, because I kissed a boy on a beach, and he asked me to spend the night with him. I am not ten. I am seventeen.

I was sitting on the beach, and he came over, and he sat beside me, and we kissed.

This is the only clear memory in my head apart from the ones from before I got sick. I cling to it, willing it to stay, living inside it as much as I can. I adore it. I need to keep it forever. If I remember this, I will remember other things. Drake's kiss will be the thing that heals me. I will remember something else, soon, though I hope it won't be this conversation.

OTHER BOOKS YOU MAY ENJOY

THE
ONE
MEMORY
OF
FLORA
BANKS

THE
ONE
MEMORY
OF
FLORA
BANKS

EMILY BARR

speak

SPEAK
An imprint of Penguin Random House LLC
375 Hudson Street
New York, New York 10014

First American edition published in the United States of America by Philomel Books,
an imprint of Penguin Random House LLC, 2017
Published in Great Britain by Puffin UK in 2017
Published by Speak, an imprint of Penguin Random House LLC, 2018

THE LIBRARY OF CONGRESS HAS CATALOGED THE PHILOMEL BOOKS EDITION AS FOLLOWS:
Names: Barr, Emily, author.
Title: The one memory of Flora Banks / Emily Barr.
Description: New York, NY : Philomel Books, [2017]
Summary: A girl with recurring memory loss chases down the boy
she loves based on the one memory she is able to hold on to.
Identifiers: LCCN 2016017680 | ISBN 9780399547010
Subjects: | CYAC: Memory—Fiction. | Amnesia—Fiction. | Love—Fiction.
Classification: LCC PZ7.1.B3726 On 2017 | DDC [Fic]—dc23
LC record available at https://lccn.loc.gov/2016017680

Speak ISBN 9780399547027

Printed in the United States of America

1 3 5 7 9 10 8 6 4 2

U.S. edition edited by Liza Kaplan
U.S. edition designed by Eric Ford
Text set in Trump Mediaeval

For Craig

THE
ONE
MEMORY
OF
FLORA
BANKS

Prologue

May

I am at the top of a hill, and although I know I have done something terrible, I have no idea what it is.

A minute or an hour ago I knew, but it has vanished from my mind, and I didn't have time to write it down, so now it is lost. I know that I need to stay away, but I don't know what I am hiding from.

I am standing on the ridge of a mountain in an impossibly beautiful icy place. Far below me on one side is a stretch of water, with two rowboats pulled up on the shore beside it. On the other side there is nothing: mountains stretch as far as I can see. The sky is the deepest blue, the sun dazzling. There is light snow on the ground, but I am hot because I am wearing a big fur coat. This is a bright, snowy place. It cannot be real. I am in a place inside my head, hiding.

When I look back, I see that there is a hut far below me, down near the boats: I have scrambled away from it, up the hill, away from whatever is inside it. I should not be out here on my own because I know that there is something dangerous.

I will take my chances in the wild rather than face the thing that is in the hut.

As there are no trees, I must cross the ridge before I can hide. As soon as I am over it, I will be in the wild. There will be just me and the mountains and the rocks and the snow.

I stand on the ridge and take two smooth stones from my coat pocket. I don't know why I am doing this, but I know it is essential. They are black, and together they fit neatly into the palm of my hand. I throw the stones, one after the other, as hard as I can, as far as I can. They disappear among the snow-covered rocks and I am pleased.

Soon I will be out of sight. I will find a place to hide, and I will not move until I remember what it is that I have done. I don't care how long it takes. I will probably stay here, in this cold place, for the rest of my life.

Part 1

Chapter One

The music is too loud, the room too crowded, and it feels as though there are more people in this house than any human being could possibly know. The low notes vibrate through my body. I have been standing in the corner for a while: I take a deep breath and start to push my way between strangers.

I look at my hand. PARTY, it tells me, in thick black letters.

"I can see that," I tell it, though I don't know why I am here.

The air is thick with sweat and alcohol and perfume, mingled together into something nauseating. I need to get out of here. I want to smell the outdoors. I want to lean on a railing and stare at the sea. The sea is outside this house.

"Hi, Flora," says someone. I don't recognize him. He is a tall skinny boy with no hair.

"Hello," I say back, with as much dignity as I can muster. The boy is wearing jeans. All the boys here, and most of the girls, are wearing jeans. I, on the other hand, am wearing a shiny white dress with a sticking-out skirt, and a pair of yellow shoes that aren't even nice and that don't fit me properly.

I imagine I dressed for what I thought a party was like: I stand out as the person who got it wrong.

I look at my hand. It says, I am 17. I look down at myself again. I look like a teenager, but I don't feel like one.

When I was younger, I loved dressing up to go to parties. I would put on a party dress, like I have tonight, and people would hug me and tell me I looked like a princess. But I am not young enough for that anymore. If I had a pen in my hand, I would write that on my arm to emphasize it: *I am older than I think I am.* I should not wear party dresses anymore. I should wear jeans.

"Drink?"

The boy is nodding toward a table that has plastic cups and bottles on it. I look at my wrist. Don't drink alcohol, it says. Everyone else here is drinking whatever is in the bottles. It might be alcohol.

"Yes, please," I say, to see what happens. My hand also informs me that Drake is leaving. P's boyfriend. This is a party that is happening because someone is leaving. *P* is for Paige. Paige's boyfriend. Poor Paige. "That red one, please."

I lick my finger and blur Don't drink alcohol until the words are no longer legible.

The tall boy hands me a plastic cup filled to the brim with wine. I wince at the first sip, but holding a cup of alcohol makes me feel that I belong here, and so I set off, looking for Paige.

I am seventeen. This is a party. Drake is leaving. Drake is Paige's boyfriend.

A woman puts a hand on my arm and stops me. I turn to face her. She has whitish blond hair cut in feathery shapes, and I can tell that she is older than everyone else because there are lines on her face. She is Paige's mom. I don't know why, but she doesn't like me.

"Flora," she shouts, to be heard above the music. She is smiling with her mouth but not with her eyes. I do the same back at her. "Flora. You're here and you're all right."

"Yes," I shout back, nodding vigorously.

"Well, I will inform your mother of that fact. She's only texted me three times so far to check up on you."

"OK," I say.

"Dave and I are going out now. Will you be all right? I know you always need a babysitter."

She is being a bit mean.

"Yes, of course."

She looks at me for a while, and then she turns and walks away. That woman is Paige's mom, and this is her house.

The music stops and I sigh in relief. It was loud and shouty. However, more music immediately starts up, and now the people around me are jumping around and doing the kind of dancing that I could not possibly copy. They are, clearly, pleased with the new, bouncier song.

"Put the Pixies back on!" yells someone, close to my ear. I jump and drip red wine down the front of my dress. It looks like blood.

A girl steps back and steps on my foot. She has very short hair and huge earrings and bright blurred lipstick that makes her mouth look like a wound.

"Oh, sorry," she says, and turns back to her conversation.

I need to leave. I have to get away from here. Parties are not the way I thought they were, with dresses and games and cake. I can't see Paige; I have no one to talk to.

I am heading for the door, and the smell of the sea and the sound of not-music, and my home, when something makes a tinging noise, and a "shhh" spreads across the room. Conversations grind to a halt and I stop in my tracks and turn my face in the direction of all the other faces.

He is standing on a chair. I think this is Drake. Drake is Paige's boyfriend, and Paige is my best friend. I am on solid ground with Paige; I met her for the first time when we were four years old and starting school. She had her hair in braids, and I did too, and we were both nervous. I remember jumping rope and playing on the playground. I remember learning to read alongside each other: I already knew how, and I helped her. As we grew up, I helped with her schoolwork, and she wrote little plays for us to perform and found us trees to climb. I remember starting our last year of primary school together, excited that soon we would be going to secondary school. I know Paige, and when I look at her, I am surprised to see that she is an adult. That means Drake is her real grown-up boyfriend.

I notice he has dark hair and black-framed glasses. He is wearing jeans, like everyone else.

He scans the crowd: when our eyes meet, he smiles for a moment and looks away. That means that, even though I don't recognize him, we know each other. There is a blond-haired girl standing next to his chair, gazing up at him. She is too close. I think I have seen her before. She should not be looking at him like that, not if he is Paige's boyfriend.

"Hey—thanks, guys, for, you know, coming," he tells this room full of people. "I never expected an actual party. I mean, I've only been in town for, like, five minutes. Or five months, to be more accurate. It's been amazing staying here, with Aunt Kate and Uncle Jon, and I never expected to make a whole pile of new friends while I was at it. I just thought Cornwall would be a little outpost of London and that I'd ride on double-decker buses and, y'know, eat terrible British food and become a soccer fanatic. Instead, I've had the greatest time. If any of you want to come to Svalbard and visit me in the most amazing landscape on earth, please do it. I've dreamed of living there forever, and I'm so lucky to have the opportunity."

Someone behind me says quietly, "He should go on about the Arctic a bit *more*," and someone else laughs.

I have a phone in my hand. I use it to take a photograph of him, to remind me of why I am here. I don't know what "Svalbard" means. It is a strange word. I can see that he likes it, though.

I drink the last of the wine, which is still horrible, and look around for more. I feel sick.

"Of course," he continues, "while I was here, I was lucky enough to meet the beautiful Paige." He pauses, and smiles, and goes a bit red.

The person behind me mutters, "*Way* out of his league," to a snort of agreement.

"And through her," Drake continues, "I met lots of you lovely people. I'll miss you. Anyway. Thanks, everyone. Look out for snowy pictures on Facebook. That's pretty much it, I think. Oh, and thanks to Paige and Yvonne and Dave for letting us take over the house, when I was planning just to go to the pub. Now keep drinking and try not to trash the place."

There is a little round of applause as he steps awkwardly off the chair, but it is a muted one as everyone is holding a drink and clapping in a strange, non-clappy way.

I try to piece together what he has just said. He is leaving. He is going somewhere snowy, and he is excited about it. He has been here in Penzance for five months, staying with Aunt Kate and Uncle Jon. Paige threw this party for him.

Paige is in a corner, with a group of people around her. She looks up and asks, using only her eyebrows, whether I am OK. I signal with a tiny nod that I am.

Paige is beautiful, with long black hair that is thick and slightly curly, and creamy skin, and cheeks that dimple when she smiles. She looks like a china doll. Today she is wearing a dress that is bright blue and short and figure hugging, and she is wearing it with thick tights and clumpy boots. I tug at my stupid white party dress, and try not to look at my horrible shoes, and feel all wrong.

I wonder what I would look like in a mirror. I can't see one anywhere.

There is a little note on the inside of my arm. Movies with Paige tomorrow, it says. Cheer her up.

I refill my plastic cup with red wine and slip out through the side door, as if anyone would notice or mind my leaving. The cool air hits me in the face, and the sea fills my ears and lungs. I close my eyes for a few seconds. Thank God I am out of there.

• • •

I am standing in the middle of the road, and it is nigh. around, trying to work it out. There is a white line under my fee. This is the exact middle of the road. A car comes toward me, fast, and honks its horn. I stare at the headlights as they come closer, but it swerves and keeps on going, its horn still sounding as it vanishes into the distance.

I should not be out on my own. I shouldn't stand in the middle of roads. I have only just been allowed to start crossing roads without a grown-up. Why am I out in the dark? Why am I alone? Where is my mom?

I am wearing a white dress and weird yellow shoes. The dress has a red stain down the front, but when I touch it, it doesn't hurt. In my hand there is a plastic cup filled with grape juice. I have spilled a bit onto the white line.

I am ten years old. I don't know why I am in a grown-up's body. I hate it and I want to go home. I run across the rest of the road and find I am on a strip of pavement beside the sea. There is the sound of music from somewhere. I lean on a railing and try not to panic.

I take a sip from the cup and wince. This is not grape juice, but the horrible taste is familiar to my mouth, so I must have been drinking it already.

I look at my hand. FLORA, it says, and that is me. Those marks on my hand spell out my name. I hang on to that. I am Flora. Under that word, it says: be brave. I close my eyes, take a deep breath, and gather myself. I don't know why I am here, but I will be all right. I am 17, it says under that.

My other hand says: PARTY and Drake is leaving. P's

boyfriend. Something else is blurred and impossible to read. On my arm it says: Movies with Paige tomorrow. Cheer her up. On my wrist it says: Mom & Dad: 3 Morrab Gardens.

I know who Paige is. She is my best friend. I met her when we started school, when we were four. Drake is her boyfriend, but he is leaving, and Paige needs cheering up.

I know I have parents and I know where I live. I live at 3 Morrab Gardens. I need to go home, and that is what I will do. It feels strange inside my head. I am dizzy.

I stare out at the moon's chopped-up reflection in the sea. There is a poster tied to the railing. MISSING CAT, it says. BLACK-AND-WHITE CAT WITH NO EARS. MISSING SINCE TUESDAY. There is a phone number to call if you've seen it. I take a photograph of the poster, and then another, and then another. I don't like the thought of a black-and-white cat with no ears wandering around lost. It will not be able to hear the traffic. I need to look for it.

I turn the phone around and take a photograph of my face. When I look at it, I see that I look different. I am older than I should be. I am not ten.

There was a party. Drake is leaving. Paige is sad. I am seventeen. I need to be brave.

The water is black; it is a huge expanse of blankness that stretches into the night. The moon's reflection glimmers off the darkness. The bright esplanade is where the land runs out.

I wonder whether I should go down to the beach and ruin these strange yellow shoes that I am not sure if I like or not by walking through boggy stones and sinking into patches of wet sand.

I could sit there and drink the cup of red stuff that I am hold-ing and stare at the water for a bit longer. I walk carefully down a set of steps that has been worn away to dips in the middle, and set off across the stones. My heels do not sink after all. The stony sand is more solid than it looks. I find a place to sit and stare out at the water.

The waves suck noisily at the stones as I hear footsteps coming up behind me. I don't turn around. Then someone is sitting next to me.

"Flora," says the boy, with a big smile, and he is beside me on the stones. Our shoulders are touching.

"Is that wine?" He takes the cup from my hand and sips from it. I look at him. He is wearing glasses, and he has dark hair, and he is wearing jeans.

I edge away a little.

"It's me," he says. "Drake. Flora, are you all right?"

"You're Drake?"

"Yes. Oh. Yes. I see what's happened. It's OK, Flora. I've known you for months. I was Paige's boyfriend."

I am not sure what to say to him.

"It's all right. Honestly. But drinking wine? That's not like you."

I want to say something, but I have absolutely no words. I want to try to pretend to be normal. This is Drake. He had a party, and now he's on the beach.

"What are you doing here?" I ask. "Here, on the beach?"

I look at the words on my left hand. I can just make them out by the light from the streetlamp, behind us. Drake is leaving, my left hand tells me again. The bit underneath it is unreadable. The right reminds me again: FLORA, be brave.

He takes my left hand and reads it. His hand is warm on mine.

"'*Drake is leaving,*'" he says. "'*P's boyfriend.*'" We stare at the words together. "'*Flora, be brave,*'" he says, reading the other hand. "I love the words on your hands. Does it work? Do they help you remember?"

I nod. He is holding both my hands.

He said, "I was Paige's boyfriend." I don't know why he is here. He is leaving. He's going somewhere else.

The night has turned colder, and there is a freezing wind blowing straight off the sea and into my face.

"What's it going to be like? Where you're going? Is it exciting?" I talk fast because I am uncomfortable.

He still has my hands. I like the way his warm hands feel on mine. I can see from the look in his eyes that I should already know the answer to my own question.

"It's going to be amazing," he says. "Cold. I've been once before. Like, a long time ago. We went on vacation to Svalbard to see the midnight sun. I was ten and I've wanted to live there ever since. Nine years later, I'm finally going to do it. It's going to be epic." He sighs. "My course is taught in English because people go there from all over the world. Which is lucky for me, really, because I'm shitty at languages."

He shifts a little so that we are touching all the way down our sides. He lets go of my left hand and holds my right hand tighter.

It is impossible to focus on what Drake is saying because all the skin on my body has developed a life of its own. It has become hypersensitive, and all it wants, every part of all of my skin, is for him to touch me.

He is Paige's boyfriend and I don't know what he is doing here.

"Lucky for you," I echo. I lean my head onto his shoulder, since I have nothing to lose. "You're nineteen," I say. "I'm seventeen." It seems important to remember that. I take my head away, because he is my friend's boyfriend.

Drake stretches up, puts his left arm around me, and pulls my head toward his shoulder. I lean on him, feeling his arm encircling me.

"Paige and I broke up," he says.

He turns his face to me and I turn mine to him. When his lips touch mine, I know this is the only thing in the world I can do.

Cars go by, above us. The waves crash in and out, close to our feet. I am kissing Drake. I want to sit on the beach with him forever. I have no idea how or why this is happening, but I know that it is the only good thing that has ever happened in my entire life. A bright light flashes. The rest of the world vanishes.

I manage to pull myself back to reality. A wave crashes to the shore and the wind blows my hair all over the place.

"Hey," he says. "Look. Do you want to go somewhere with me? Like, now? We could spend the night . . ."

I stare at him. *We could spend the night.* Everything inside me tenses. I want to spend the night with him. I would have no idea what to do. He wants me to spend the night with him. The night. This night.

I have to go home.

"But my mom—" I say. We stare at each other, and I can't finish my sentence. I cannot look away from his eyes. I lean in to kiss him again but he edges back.

"Your mom," he says. "Oh God. I'm sorry. That was a terrible idea. I mean. What the hell am I . . . I didn't—"

He stops. I cannot speak, so I nod. He is looking at me with an expression that is difficult to read.

"I'm OK," I tell him.

"Flora, I'm sorry. I . . . I'd . . . I never . . ."

I take a strand of hair and pull it into my mouth. I can't speak. I want to tell him that I never expected this to happen to me. That I am sure it never has before. That I am confused and still trying to pull myself into the moment. That I will love him forever for making me feel normal. That I would love to spend the night with him. Yet I cannot be this disloyal to my friend; and I cannot stay out all night, because I just can't.

"She'd call the police," I add, thinking of my mother.

"The police. Jesus. I am an *idiot*. Forget I said it."

The hairs on my arms are standing up with cold. The sea is choppy, blowing around, and the moon and all the stars have disappeared behind the clouds. The sky is as blank as the sea.

"The thing is," says Drake, "I can say this, because, like, what the hell? You won't remember anyway. I would be, like, out at a bar with you and Paige and looking at you, all pretty and blond and different from every other girl in the world, and wondering what it would be like to be with you. You're so different. And you always smiled at me. And I wanted to look after you and listen to the things you say because they're different from the things other people say."

He takes my face in his hands. "Will you be OK, Flora?"

I nod. I want to write down that I kissed him, right now. It would be weird to scrawl on my arm while he's talking. I want to write down that he wanted to take me somewhere for the night. I don't want to forget that. Maybe we could do it. I could find a way. I could have a night of being normal, like a grown-up.

"I'll be fine," I say. "Look. If we go somewhere now, I could. I'm sure I could. I could make it OK."

"No. Sorry. My fault. We can't. But you know—maybe we can keep in touch? Just—let me know you're all right? OK?"

"Keep in touch." I want to kiss him again. I want him to keep kissing me. Now that I have kissed him, I want to delete everything in the world around us until nothing exists but Drake, me, and a beach.

The water is close now, so we are edging back on an ever-smaller strip of beach. He takes a deep breath and squeezes my hand tightly.

"Flora Banks," he says. "Take care of yourself. Please don't tell Paige about this. Don't tell your mom. Don't write it on your hand." He picks up a stone from the beach and holds it out in the flat of his palm. It is a small stone, a smooth one. Even in the moonlight I can see that it is perfectly black, though most of these pebbles are slate gray.

"Here," he says. "Take it. This is for you." He puts the stone into the palm of my hand and closes my fingers around it.

"I'll keep it forever," I tell him.

I stand up. I am freezing, and stiff, and confused. I want to crawl into bed and relive these moments endlessly. Drake stands too, and we stretch and look at each other.

"Well," he says. "Well, I'll . . . Oh, I can't go back to Paige's tonight. Not now. I'll go, and in the morning I'll leave quietly."

He kisses me again, on the lips. I lean against him and feel his arms encircling me. I know I will never feel this way again.

"Want me to walk you home?" he asks, but I shake my head. I stand still on the beach and watch him leave. He reaches the steps and goes up to the real world. He stops and waves before he walks out of my life forever.

I kissed the man of my dreams. And he is moving to somewhere cold and far away, with a midnight sun. I look up at the dark sky.

When I get home, my mother is waiting, in her robe, her hair loose down her back, holding a cup of tea. She kisses my cheek.

"Did you have a good time?" she says.

"Yes." I beam at her. "Yes. It was great, actually. Absolutely completely wonderful."

She smiles, then looks me up and down, noticing the stain on my dress.

"You've been drinking."

"A little."

She sighs. "Did Paige walk you home?"

"Yes."

"Good. I'll have my shoes back, then."

I kick off the yellow shoes and go upstairs. In my bedroom I change into my pajamas, and write down every single detail of my encounter with Drake. I write it at the back of an old notebook so Mom won't think to look there, and hide the book under all the other stuff in the box under my bed. I write a Post-it note to remind myself that it's there, and in the morning I wake up and read it over and over again.

I read it, but I don't need to, because I can remember it.

The black stone sits on my bedside table. I can remember. I am seventeen.

Chapter Two

"You kissed him." Paige is not shouting, but it would be better if she were. She is quietly furious. She fixes me with intense eyes and says it again. "You kissed him. I *know* you did. You won't remember it, but you did it, and I know you did because . . ."

My head is ringing and I can't focus on her words. I know she is talking. I know she is angry. I know she is right to be angry. She is saying words, but I am not hearing them. I force myself to stop looking at yellow notes that tell me things I already know and make myself look at her. I have to tune back in.

She is breathing deeply. "And you've written it down!" One of my Post-it notes is in her hand, so I cannot, of course, pretend anything at all. The words are there, in my writing, and she knows that my notes are for facts. She knows this is real.

I know it is real too. I can remember it. I remember things from before I got sick, and now I remember kissing Drake. I know,

now, that I am not a little girl, because I kissed a boy on a beach, and he asked me to spend the night with him. I am not ten. I am seventeen.

I can remember it. The stone, or Drake, made me remember. Perhaps this is what it is to fall in love.

I cannot deny it to Paige. I remember kissing Drake. It might have fixed my memory, though at the moment I still cannot remember anything else that happened after I was ten. I look at the note Paige is holding, and see that I wrote the words as small as I possibly could around the edge of a yellow note. In the middle it says Buy milk in thick pen. Around the edge, in tiny letters, I wrote, I kissed Drake. I love Drake. I keep finding myself gazing at the words. I marvel at the fact that it happened. It makes me happy and it makes me cry.

I was sitting on the beach, and he came over, and he sat beside me, and we kissed.

This is the only clear memory in my head apart from the ones from before I got sick. I cling to it, willing it to stay, living inside it as much as I can. I adore it. I need to keep it forever. If I remember this, I will remember other things. Drake's kiss will be the thing that heals me. I will remember something else, soon, though I hope it won't be this conversation.

Paige is holding the note and staring at me with such hatred that I have to look at the floor. We are in a cheerful little tearoom, waiting for our order. Afterward we were going to go and do other things. Paige found the note because I sat down and took out my phone to text Mom and let her know that I got here OK. A shower of yellow notes tumbled from my bag. Paige reached down to pick them up for me, and I had forgotten that there could possibly be anything on any of them that I did not want her to see.

I had forgotten. Of course I had. I remember the kiss, but I had forgotten that I'd written about the kiss.

She saw his name at the edge of a note I picked up, and took it out of my hand. Now she is looking at me.

"You *love* him?" she says. "Not only did you kiss him—and I have no idea how many times that might have happened, any more than you do—but you actually think you *love* him. Now, that I wasn't expecting."

I don't know what to say to that. I know I love Drake, but I don't want Paige to know how passionate last night made me feel. All the same, I nod.

"And you did kiss him. Admit it. I *know* you did. I am absolutely one hundred percent certain."

I stare at the floor again, which looks like wood but isn't. Then I turn my head away from Paige and stare at some people at a larger table nearby. They are a family: two adults and two children, adults reading the newspaper and children kicking each other under the table, all four in jeans and blue fleeces.

"He went to the beach," she says quietly. "He never came back. You spent the whole night with him."

"I didn't! I went home. You can ask my mom. Paige—I can remember!"

I remember that he asked me to spend the night with him. I will not tell her that part.

"No, you can't. Your mom would cover for you. If you came home with my boyfriend, she'd be horrified, but she wouldn't tell me because she wouldn't want you to lose your only friend in the whole wide world. And by the way, you can tell her I've changed my mind about her little favor. I only agreed to get her off the phone. Tell her they can take you with them."

"No!" I can feel the panic rising. "No, honestly, Paige! We did sit on the beach. We did kiss. I'm sorry. I went home and he went . . . I don't know. I'm so sorry, Paige. I didn't mean it. But I remember it. I actually remember it. In my head."

I have no idea what the "little favor" is. Now is not the time to ask. I have probably been told it twelve thousand times already.

"You didn't mean it? Jesus. And, Flora, don't tell me you remember it. I know you don't."

"I didn't mean for *it to happen*. I didn't expect it. Not I didn't mean it. And I do remember. I don't know why, but—"

She interrupts. "You love him."

I shrug, embarrassed.

"Correction: you have written your little love story down, and every couple of hours when you forget everything, you read it and convince yourself you love him. It's pathetic. Of him, most of all. Go ahead and take him, if that behavior is what you look for in a boyfriend. For all I know, and for all you know, he might have seduced you over and over again over the past few months. Nice. A lot of good he'll be to you at the North Pole. You can have my boyfriend, but he's gone."

She stops and takes a deep breath. I can't say anything.

"And you know what else? I'm sick of taking care of you. I've been the only one looking out for you for years and years. I've taken you out when your mom would have kept you in a plastic bubble at home. I took you to the movies. I took you to Zumba. I took you gig rowing for an entire year. I looked after you better than your one-to-one woman did on the days you went to school. Every time you forget where you are, I help you. My mom always hated me doing it. She said I shouldn't have to be your caregiver. But sure—have my boyfriend. And for what it's worth—"

She breaks off as the waitress, who looks bored, appears with our tea on a round tray. She spends a long time putting a cup down in front of each of us, a little jug of milk between us, a container of sugar packets, and finally a shiny blue mini teapot.

Neither of us speaks or looks at each other while she is doing that. In the end Paige says a tight "Thanks."

I pour the tea for us both, doing hers first. Paige watches, and my hand trembles and then there is tea dripping onto the table, pooling and heading toward the edge. She does nothing, so I finish pouring and then go to the counter for a handful of napkins to wipe it up before it cascades to the floor.

Paige doesn't pick up her tea. She is dressed in skinny black pants and a tight T-shirt with a scooped neckline. Her hair is tied back and she has bright lipstick on. It says on my arm that we were going to the movies. She was probably going to talk about Drake and how she misses him.

Now we will be doing none of those things, ever again.

Paige draws a deep breath and continues from where she left off.

"For what it's worth, I always knew you had a thing for him. I could see it. Nobody is more transparent than you, Flora. I didn't imagine he would act on it, though, and God only knows how many times it's happened. I had no idea he noticed you at all, beyond your interesting medical history—you've never known the half of it. *For what it's worth,* there is nothing you could ever say that would convince me you didn't have sex with him. Nothing. *For what it's worth,* I cannot get my head around you doing anything with my boyfriend. Mine. I know you'll forget Drake, because you didn't know him before your so-called illness, but you wrote his name on your hand, and it said he was my boyfriend. I know"—she waves the note in the air—"you think you're in love with him. Were you secretly in love with him all along?"

I try to shake my head, but I cannot quite do it.

"I don't know," I say. My voice is tiny and shaky. "I can't remember."

"Hey. That's OK." She is smiling now, looking me straight in the eye. "You've written yourself a sweeping great love story and it's making you feel less childish. It's not a secret anymore, so you can update your silly little note. Here. I'll do it for you."

She stretches out an open hand. I push the blank Post-its across the table. She takes a pen out of her bag and starts writing, first on my original note and then covering one, two, three new ones. As she finishes each one, she slaps it onto the table in front of me. When she is done, she picks up her bag and walks away. She hasn't touched her tea.

She pauses in the doorway and looks back at me. I look at her. She opens her mouth as if she is about to say something. I start to stand up, but she shakes her head and leaves. The door slams closed behind her.

I read the array of yellow squares instead. The words Buy milk are crossed out. It now says: I kissed Drake. I love Drake. This is NOT a secret. I need to find a new best friend. The second note reads: Paige will never speak to me again. Remember not to contact her, ever. The third says: DO NOT PHONE OR TEXT PAIGE EVER AGAIN.

I drink my tea and stare at the words. The stone is in my pocket, looking after me.

"I do remember," I say to the place where she was sitting. "I do."

When I get home, the fight with Paige is in my head. There is a suitcase by the door. Mom is not waiting at the window for me. I can hear footsteps upstairs. It feels busy and different.

"Hello?" I call as I take off my shoes. I wonder if the suitcase means someone is coming or going. Maybe Drake is here. Maybe we are going away.

I pick up some junk mail from the doormat. There is a pizza menu and a brochure about the summer season at Flambards. Flambards is a place with roller coasters and a log flume and a carousel. I want to go there. I put that one in my back pocket, with my stone.

I am longing to tell my parents that I have a new memory, but I can't tell them I kissed Paige's boyfriend. Still, something is happening here, and I am terrified that Paige has called and told them my secret. Perhaps they know everything and they are sending me away.

Dad comes down the stairs two at a time.

"Flora!" he says. He turns to the stairs. "Annie!" he shouts. "It's Flora!" He turns back to me. "Let's get your mother."

My father is funny and wonderful. At work he is an accountant, but at home he wears patterned sweaters that he knits for himself. His hair sticks up in the air, when Mom hasn't patted it down. He says funny things. He would do anything for me, I know that, and I would do anything for him, if I were capable of doing anything.

Right now he is looking worried. I check my hands and arms, wondering what important thing I have forgotten.

"Are we moving?" I hazard.

He smiles weakly. "No. No, sweetie, we're not moving. Annie!"

My mother rushes down the stairs, almost falling on top of us, long cardigan trailing behind her, hair wild and frizzy.

"Flora, honey," she says. "Oh, Flora. How's Paige? OK. Why don't we have a cup of tea?" She is talking very fast.

She looks at my arms, and I hold them out to show her that there is nothing new. The yellow notes from Paige are in my bag and I am overwhelmed with relief that they don't know about Drake. They would panic and try to talk to Paige and smooth it over as if I were a tiny child, not responsible for my actions. I am not a tiny child anymore. I am seventeen.

Drake has made me remember. I open my mouth to tell them all about it, but then I close it. I don't want them to know that I kissed a boy on a beach. In this house I am a little girl. It would be wrong to kiss a boy.

I knew what I was doing. I cling to that fact. It was not nice of me, but the kiss is mine and it was real. It is still there. It is in my head. I can remember it because I love Drake. I hold the stone in my pocket, sure that if I lose the stone, I will lose the memory.

"I'll put the kettle on," I tell her.

"Thanks."

I put the kettle on the stove and make tea, using the spotted tea-pot that we have had since I was tiny. I put it on the table, the milk in its plastic bottle from the fridge, and everyone with their favorite mug. There is a poster on the fridge showing whose is whose: it is a printed-out piece of paper with photos on it and names below them. I imagine I made it myself. My favorite mug is apparently a pink spotted one, the dullest mug in the world. My mother's favorite says WORLD'S BEST MOM on it with a cartoon lady in an apron, and Dad's says WILLIAM SHAKESPEARE with a picture of a man with a beard. I bet those aren't their real favorites, but I get them out anyway.

I can feel Paige's words in my bag. I don't have to check to know exactly what they say. Not yet.

"Flora," says Dad, once we are sitting at the table. It is unusual for him to be the one to start a conversation. "Look. We need to talk to you about something. Something difficult."

I take out my notebook and pen, and my phone, because this feels like something I'll need to hang on to.

Mom is cradling her tea in both hands and not speaking. She has not said one word.

"You know Jacob?" Mom asks.

"I love Jacob! Jacob's my brother. Where is he?"

I follow my parents' gazes and look at the photographs on the wall.

There are printed-out pictures of me, Mom, and Dad, all stuck to the wall with tape. There is a photo of a boy in a frame beside them and under the boy's picture it says JACOB (BROTHER).

I know Jacob. He is the person I love most in the world. He is bigger than me. He used to pick me up and carry me around, and he let me sit on his lap to watch television, and I have a very clear memory of him allowing me to paint his toenails once.

"He's in France," says Mom, speaking quickly. "Jacob's older than you. Do you know that? He's twenty-four. He lives in France now and we don't see him very often, but he loves you very much. More than he loves us."

"Twenty-four?" I frown at the picture. That boy is skinny and dark-haired and handsome in a bony sort of way. He looks younger than twenty-four.

"That's an old photograph," says Dad. "Yes. He's twenty-four now. We haven't seen him for a while." He looks at me, checking my face, and then continues. "He called us yesterday, and then this morning we heard from his doctor. Sweetie, he's very sick. We have to go see him."

I am trying to keep up.

"If we haven't seen him for a while, how do you know he loves me? I know that I love him because I remember."

"We just do," says Mom. "That's not the important part. Flora, we have to go to visit him in the hospital."

"We're going to France? Is that why there's a suitcase? We're going away from home? We're going to see Jacob?" I have never been away from home. I have no concept of what France will be like. I know that the Eiffel Tower is there. That is all.

"No," Dad says, and Mom drinks half her tea in one gulp. She is stressed. "You're not. We're going, but we need you to stay here. This is the best place for you. France would be too much, and we'll have to focus on Jacob. The journey would be difficult, and then you'd have to deal with being in a new place, and we would be concentrating on Jacob. You're much better off here."

"But I want to see Jacob! I want to come with you!"

"You don't have a passport," says Mom. Her voice sounds strange. "If you stay here, you'll be safe. I spoke to Paige yesterday, just before you went to her party, and she's going to come and stay with you. She'll look after you."

My dad nods and Mom takes a deep breath and carries on talking.

"I've made up the spare room. Remember not to go next door if you need anything, because Mrs. Rowe is more confused than you are these days and God only knows what the two of you would cook up between you. Just rely on Paige and you'll be fine. We'll leave you money. I'll fill the fridge with meals and we won't be away long. I'll text you every day to see how you're doing and remind you to take your pills. You can take an extra pill each evening, to help you sleep and keep you calm. Whenever you forget where you are, Paige will tell you."

"Oh." I think about this. Paige will not be coming to stay and will not tell me where I am, because she is not speaking to me because I kissed her boyfriend. Our conversation is still in my head, but if I don't tell my parents about any of it, I will get to stay at home on my own.

I scrawl down everything they have told me, and then take a photograph of the page with my phone: Jacob is sick and I want to see him, but I don't have a passport, so I can't. France would be too much for me.

If I stay home on my own, I will be able to think about Drake, all day long. I will be able to sit in this house and remember our kiss. I will be able to walk down to the beach where it happened without anyone asking where I'm going. I have the kiss, an island in my memory, and I want to spend as much time with it as I possibly can in case it fades away.

The idea thrills me.

"How long are you going for?"

I watch Mom relax, slightly.

"We're booked for five days. Whatever's going on there, we should be able to work it out and get back in that time. If either of us needs to go again, then we will. I really hate to leave you, but this time, honey, I think we just have to."

I nod and drink my tea too.

"When you get back," I say, "can we go to Flambards?"

My mother leans back as if I have said something shocking. She closes her eyes. Dad reaches over and puts his hand on top of hers.

"We'll do something fun," he says. "I promise."

I am sitting at the table, in the house I know, with people who look like my parents but who are too old. I look at my hand: I am Flora. I must be brave. I don't know what is happening or what anyone is saying or what I was doing a moment ago.

I do know that I kissed Drake, on a beach. He asked me to spend the night with him. I am not a little girl. The waves were crashing onto the stones. It was dark, and the moonlight was reflected on the water. I love him. I am seventeen.

I reach into the back pocket of my jeans and find the magical stone that makes me remember. It is there. I don't take it out. I want to tell my parents that I have a new memory, and I open my mouth, but then I decide they shouldn't know that I kissed a boy, and so I close it again.

There is a brochure in my pocket too. I take it out and put it on the table. Dad reaches over, takes it, and puts it in the trash. I didn't even see what it said on it.

There is a piece of paper in front of me. I pick it up and read it. I read words in a notebook. I discover that I forget things. No one says anything. My mother has her arm around my shoulders.

"It's all right," she says. "You're home. We just told you that we need to go to Paris, to see Jacob. He is very sick and he needs us. You're going to stay here for a few days and Paige is going to come to keep you company."

Jacob is my brother. I love him. I remember him. He was kind to me when I was younger. Now he is sick and my parents are going to see him. Paige is going to come and stay here and look after me.

That will be nice.

"All right?" says Mom. "Are you back up to speed? So, we're leaving early tomorrow morning because we're flying to Paris from Exeter at eleven. Write that down, or I can if you want. We're driving to the airport." They don't like driving, although we have a car. It sits behind the house, never used. I don't know how I know this, but I do. This must be important, to make them drive. "I asked Paige to come over at nine. We'd better double-check that. You should give her a call now. Or I can?"

"No, it's OK," I say. "I'll call her. It'll be great having her here."

I kissed Paige's boyfriend. I mustn't tell Paige. I mustn't tell my mom.

"Promise to keep in touch."

"Yes," I say. "Yes. I promise."

"Text us," says Dad. "We only won't reply if we're on the plane, and that will only be because they make you turn your phones off."

"Or if we don't have reception," Mom adds. "But we have international coverage, so the phones will work fine in France. Just keep yours charged. Check your texts. And we'll be back in plenty of time for your birthday. We'd never miss that."

I stand up, pushing my chair back. It tips over and crashes to the floor, so I have to do an awkward turn to pick it up and put it back on its feet.

"I'll be OK," I tell them. "I'll be absolutely fine here on my own. With Paige. It'll be good for me. And," I add, "I'll call her now, OK? Don't worry about me. Paige and I will be fine."

Mom smiles. "Of course, honey. And I'm going to leave you notes all around the place before we go, OK? About everything. If you've got Paige, I won't need to worry so much."

"You worry about Jacob," I tell her. "Not about me. What's wrong with him?"

"We don't know," says Dad.

When I call Paige, she doesn't answer.

I find another photo of Jacob on my bedroom wall. The boy I remember is standing in a garden, wearing a T-shirt that says

ARIZONA GRAND CANYON STATE on it, and holding the hand of a little blond girl in a blue dress. According to the writing under the picture, that girl is me.

We are in a garden in that picture. It is the garden of this house, but there is a swing. I wish there was still a swing. Maybe I will ask Mom and Dad to get me one.

I take the picture down from the wall to look at it. I touch his face with the tip of my finger. That is my brother. That is Jacob, and he is older now, and sick. I turn the picture over and see that there is writing on the back of it. I did not expect there to be writing on it.

Call me. I love you. There is a string of numbers. I stare at them, and then I put it back.

Mom spends the rest of the day cooking, even though I should be able to feed myself. She is worried that I will leave the oven on, or somehow set gas flowing through the house, then light a match. She puts all the things she cooks into pots and foil-covered dishes, and labels each one with the day on which Paige and I are supposed to eat it. There is lasagna for tomorrow, chili for Tuesday, shepherd's pie for Wednesday, macaroni and cheese for Thursday, and pizza for Friday. They will be home on Saturday. The cabinet is full of bread and things to put on it, and Mom is making me an enormous pot of soup to keep on the stove for lunches.

I try to call Paige, but then I see that I have already called her five times. She doesn't answer. Then a text arrives from her:

Flora, stop calling. I don't want to talk to you. You kissed my boyfriend. Leave me alone.

I don't tell my parents.

I lose myself in the memory. I love Drake so much that he has made my brain work again. I sat on the beach. There were waves. He came and sat beside me. He said I was different from every other girl in the world. He said I was pretty. I can remember our conversation. I cling to it. I can remember. I go over every word, again and again and again.

I find Paige's yellow notes in my bag and take a photo of them all lined up, to remind me not to call her. I can't write it on my arm in thick pen like I want to, not until my parents have left.

Finally it is evening and everything is ready. My five days of food are lined up in the fridge. There are pills laid out in little boxes in the kitchen, with the right day of the week written on each box in capitals. The parents have a suitcase by the door, and they have checked and double-checked their passports. They don't have physical tickets because they booked the trip online, but I know they are flying to Paris from Exeter, and they will be leaving tomorrow morning at five. I know this because it is written on notes that are all over the kitchen, and more notes in the hall and the living room and probably everywhere else in the house direct me to the kitchen for when I forget.

Mom hangs up her apron, pulls out her hairband, and looks at me with a strained smile.

"Do you want to walk down to the beach, sweetie?" she says. "A blast of fresh Cornish air might be nice. I'd like that, before we go."

I put on my shoes and raincoat and stand on the porch, amid random things that have piled up there (tennis balls, a bat that looks very old, a cardboard box in the corner filled with my notebooks from primary school). I really hope we won't run into Paige. I will be all right on my own, but I know my parents will never leave me if they discover the truth. I want them to go to Jacob. I want to see how I can exist by myself. I want to be allowed to live inside my memory.

The front door is open a crack, and I can hear my parents talking to each other in the hushed way they do when they don't want me to hear. I am tempted to move closer and really eavesdrop, but as soon as I step toward the door, Mom says, "No, she clearly has no idea at all and let's keep it that way," and I freeze.

I clearly have no idea at all. That is going to change now, because I am going to remember things. There is something that my parents are keeping secret. I write that on a note and stuff it into my pocket. M&D have a secret from me. I can look through the house while they're away and try to figure out what it is.

I walk away, leave the porch, and set off down the garden path, and I look at the place where I'm sure we used to have a swing.

Mom comes out behind me, standing on the porch and breathing deeply. I pretend I don't know she's there; she waits half a minute or so before she says in her brightest voice: "Flora! OK. Let's walk down and look at that sea."

She clearly has no idea at all.

"OK," I say, but I hesitate. If I were to ask her what I clearly have no idea about, she wouldn't tell me, so for now I will let it go. I will figure it out later.

"What is the matter with Jacob?" I ask.

"We don't know." I think I have asked this many times before, because she sounds annoyed.

My mother is shorter than I am, wider, and her dark hair is wiry and thick and completely different from mine, which is horribly washed-out and pale with no body to it at all. I can see how upset she is about Jacob, and I want to take care of her.

I cannot begin to take care of her: she takes care of me and that is how we work.

The sea draws a flat horizon at the end of the street, but instead of going straight there, we walk through the gardens opposite. These are green and gorgeous, a happy place that wraps me up like a blanket.

"Why did you stop seeing him?" I say.

She jumps and looks at me. "Stop seeing who?" she asks, even though she knows exactly who I mean.

"My brother. Jacob."

"Oh, Flora," she says. "It was complicated. And long ago. He was young and stubborn and he thought he knew best. And it was . . ." She looks away.

"Was it because of me?" I ask, certain that it was. There is something in her face.

"Oh. Not exactly."

She walks away toward the exit gates, on which a sign announces that arson is a crime. I trot along after her. I know not to ask any more. If she told me, I would forget. She has probably told me a million times already. I must be annoying to live with.

We cross the road and stand leaning on the railings, looking out to sea. The air is chilly, but the evening sunlight picks out every detail of everything. Every stone on the beach casts its own shadow. The sea shines at us like a mirror, and the sky is clear and cold.

To the left is the outdoor swimming pool. It is pretty to look at, but although I remember taking swimming lessons when I was small, I wouldn't dare to try it now. Beyond it, there is a fairy-tale castle out in the water, and the land sticking out behind that makes this feel like its own world, a safe enclosed harbor. This is my world: it has always been my world.

To the right the land curves around again.

Drake is far away in a cold place that he has wanted to go to ever since he was ten. His course is being taught in English, which is good because he is shitty at languages.

I look down at my right hand. FLORA, be brave, it says. One day I will do something. One day.

"I'll miss you," says Mom.

"You will come back? Right?" I find myself saying, though I don't know why.

I feel her looking at me, but I keep staring out to sea. Drake and I kissed close to here, just a little way down to the left. The tide was high. It came up close to us. I remember the way his lips felt on mine, the smell of the seaweed. I sacrificed my friend-ship in that moment, and the shameful fact is I would do it again right now, a hundred times over. I reach into my jeans pocket. The stone is still there.

"Of course we'll come back," she says. "Flora. Look at me."

I do it slowly, reluctantly. She is gazing into my eyes, and I cannot read her expression.

"I promise you we will come back," she says, staring hard at me as she speaks. "We're doing what we have to do and then we will come home. All right? You sit tight and we will be back. Do not go anywhere. Don't get any ideas."

I attempt a joke. "I'll be very fat by the time you get home. You won't recognize me. All that food I've got to eat."

I want her to know that I remember the food. I can see she is pleased.

"Yes. Make sure you do. Eat three times a day, take your pills every morning and evening, and text me all the time."

"Of course. I will."

"Take care of yourself. *No going anywhere.*"

She looks hard into my face until I turn toward the sea. We stand side by side and stare out at the Atlantic. All I can think about is Drake.

Chapter Three

I am sitting on the floor of my bedroom, reading a book.

The book is black, with hard covers, and on the front is a white sticker which says:

FLORA'S STORY. READ THIS IF YOU FEEL CONFUSED.

It is not in my handwriting. I am almost certain it is Mom's. *You are Flora Banks*, it says.

You are ~~16~~ 17 years old and you live in Penzance in Cornwall. When you were ten, doctors discovered a tumor growing in your brain, and when you were eleven, they removed it. Part of your memory went with it. You can still remember how to do things (how to make a cup of tea, how to work the shower), and you can remember your life before the illness, but since it happened you have not been able to make new memories.

You have ANTEROGRADE AMNESIA. You are good at keeping things in your head for a couple of hours (sometimes less), and then you forget them. When you forget them, you feel confused. This is OK: it is normal for you.

When you feel confused, you have to look at your hand, your notes, your phone, and this book. These things help remind you of where you are and what is happening. You have become very, very good at writing things down. Your name on your hand makes you feel grounded, and you always follow your clues and remind yourself of what is going on.

You remember us, and you remember your best friend, Paige, and other people you used to know up until you were ten. Other people you forget, but that's OK because people around here know you and they understand.

You'll never live anywhere but Penzance, because this is the only place in which you're safe. This town is mapped in your mind, and it is your home. You will always live with us, and we will always take care of you and you will be fine.

You are brilliant and strong. You are not weird.

You are very good at reading and writing, and you are better at noticing things than lots of medically unremarkable people are.

We will always make sure you have everything you need. You take medication twice a day, and you always will.

We love you very much.

Mom and Dad xx

I close the book. How could I have forgotten that I have amnesia? How, though, could I possibly remember?

I know I am seventeen. I kissed Drake. Every detail of our kiss is still in my head. I was sitting on the beach. He came and sat down with me. I was seventeen then, and I am seventeen now.

My bedroom is the same as it was when I was ten. It is decorated in pink and white, with frills and dolls and children's toys. There are Barbies and teddies and Legos.

The words in that book are not true anymore. I can remember something now, and it's not from before I was ten. It is from a day that feels like yesterday. I decide to do a test.

I put a row of toys on the bed. A brown-haired Barbie, then a Lego ambulance, then a soft squishy doll named Phyllis, then a gray Buckbeak the hippogriff. I stare at them. Barbie, Lego, doll, hippogriff. I throw a thin pink blanket over them and write in my notebook: Barbie, Lego ambulance, Phyllis doll, Buckbeak. I take it off and check, but I know I am right, because it has only been thirty seconds. I need to leave the room and come back hours later and see if I remember them then.

I cover the toys again and tear a page from the back of the notebook.

What toys are on the bed? I write, and leave it on the floor, just inside the door, with a pen so I can write the answer when I come back in.

I have kissed a boy and I am in love. I am seventeen and I do not need a little girl's bedroom. That is ridiculous. I gather the teddies and dolls in my arms, push them into the toy box, and shove it all into the corner of the room. I cover the box with a sheet from the laundry basket. Those toys belong to a child, and I am not a child.

I could paint this room. If I were going to paint it, I would make it white. It would be plain and blank, like a normal room, and anything would be able to happen in it.

I sit on the floor, staring at the covered lump that is the toy box, and revisit my memories.

I was sitting on the floor (probably this floor) playing with a Lego ambulance. I was a normal tiny girl. I was chattering away to someone big who was sitting on the floor with me. He was helping me whisk a little Lego girl to the hospital. I was happy. He was my brother, Jacob.

It was my first day of school. I was scared and excited and I got up when it was still dark and put my uniform on and my backpack on my back and waited as long as I could before I went to wake my parents and my brother. They were all grumpy because it was still early.

I was getting ready for a day out. It was exciting because we were going to a place with amusement park rides. I could not wait. I was dancing around impatiently, asking everyone whether I could get into the car yet. I couldn't wait to get there. They laughed at me and told me we had to have breakfast first. I can't remember the day out at the place with the rides: I wish I could . . . Flambards. The place was called Flambards.

. . .

"Mom?" I shout, wondering where she is, whether it's time for a cup of tea. She doesn't answer. I run all the way down to the kitchen to put the kettle on anyway, and when I look at the notes all over the walls, I discover why. They have gone away, to see Jacob, who is the big person in my first memory, who is my brother, who is sick.

I start to panic. I can't be here on my own. I don't want to be alone. I need someone. I need my mom. I need my dad. I need people around me. If Jacob is sick, he should have come home to be taken care of.

I can remember kissing Drake on the beach, but I can't remember anything else. I run back up the stairs to my bedroom, not looking at my parents' door because I don't want to see that they're not there.

There is a note in my writing saying: What toys are on the bed? I lift the blanket and see that there is a Barbie, a Lego ambulance, a squishy doll named Phyllis, and a hippogriff. I write them down because there was a pen beside the question, but I have no idea why I needed to. This is so frustrating that it makes me cry.

If I'm going to manage on my own, I'm going to have to leave myself better notes than that. I turn to a new page in my notebook and write: Flora's Rules for Life. I underline it. I try to think of one, but all I can come up with right now is: don't panic. I write it down.

Don't panic, because everything is probably all right, and if it's not, panicking will make it worse.

I look at it. That looks sensible.

• • •

I walk from room to room looking at things. I write longer and longer notes and put them in strange places, telling myself why I am alone and how long it will last, wondering why I don't remember this too. I stick notes around Jacob's photograph: Mom and Dad are with Jacob because he is sick, I write. I don't know how sick he is, but it is serious.

Mom texts: Hi sweetie. Reminder to take your pills.

I reply: Can we go to Flambards when you get back?

She doesn't answer.

I log every text I have with my parents, copying them onto Post-it notes and sticking them in a line on the kitchen wall. I take my pills.

I decide to send a message to Paige, because she is supposed to be here with me and I can't find her in the house. However, when I pull up her name on my phone, a list of texts comes up from her. All of them tell me that I must stop calling her because I kissed her boyfriend. I stare at them. I feel scared all over again. If my parents aren't here, and Jacob is sick, and Paige hates me, and Drake is in Svalbard, I have no one.

Paige is not my friend anymore. I kissed her boyfriend on the beach: I remember. I know that is true. Of course she doesn't want to see me. I stare and stare at her words. I met Paige on our first day of school, when we were four. We both had our hair in braids.

I stare at a note beside my bed that says Drake on it. I have written his name and drawn a heart around it. I find the black stone. I stand by my bedroom window and hold the stone to my lips. He gave me the stone. I remember him giving it to me. I remember.

47

•   •   •

Monday passes, and I do not go out at all. I remember the kiss. It might vanish from my head at any moment, and so I immerse myself in it again and again until it is more real than the house around me. When I find myself confused, with no idea why I am alone, I have the memory, and I remind myself of the rest of it with the notes that are everywhere.

Jacob is sick, they say. Parents are in Paris with him. THEY THINK PAIGE IS HERE BUT SHE IS NOT HERE BECAUSE SHE IS VERY ANGRY WITH ME. PAIGE IS NOT MY FRIEND ANYMORE. That fact is everywhere I look, and it crowds into my head and makes me cry. Paige is not my friend. I must let my parents think that she is here so they don't worry about me, but she is not here because she is not my friend. I deserve that.

In between thoughts of Drake and memories of the kiss, I play "Twinkle Twinkle Little Star" on the piano. I turn it into the alphabet song, and then into "Baa Baa Black Sheep." I take a bath and try to read a book while I am there. I stand still in the middles of rooms and listen to the quiet.

I find a can of white paint in the cabinet under the stairs and start to paint my bedroom. I want it to be white because that's a normal, grown-up color, and I would like to be a normal grown-up. I pull the bed and the toy box into the middle of the room and use a sheet and a thin pink blanket to protect the floorboards. I am covered with paint splatters, and I only paint half the room, but I am pleased with how it looks.

I reply carefully to the texts my parents send from the airport, and then from France, and note down what time they arrived and what they said. I remember to tell them that Paige is with me. I pretend we are watching TV. They are pleased to hear it. I take my pills. The extra evening one makes me very sleepy indeed.

I find a note that says: M&D have a secret from me. I don't like that. I stick it to the wall and stare at it for a while. Then I go into their room and look through their things, in case I can find out what the secret is, but they have nothing interesting at all, as far as I can tell. I flip through the pages of their books in case something is hidden. I look in their drawers. I find a stash of cards at the back of one of Mom's drawers, held together with an elastic band, and it turns out to be a collection of seventeen Mother's Day cards, all from me. The first one has my footprint on it. The fourth has my name written in massive childish letters, by me. The next six are written by me with increasingly legible *To Mommy*s and *Love Flora*s. The one after that is written by Dad. After that they're from me again.

These cannot be the secret. I will keep looking.

I eat the soup Mom made for lunch and half the lasagna for dinner, and both times I fill the sink with hot soapy water and wash up and put everything away. I drink coffee, then tea, then water, and go to bed in my half-white room, feeling like I have been so busy I had no time to go out, enjoying the smell of the paint. I must remember to finish the job.

Living on my own is going to be all right.

I lie in bed and read everything I have written about Drake.

He has left the country. He is in the Arctic. I try to imagine him there, but all I see is snow. I wonder if there are shops. In my head, the North Pole does not have shops or buildings of any sort, but he is not really at the North Pole. He is at a university in Svalbard, and at a university there must be food, and there must be beds.

His course is taught in English. I know that because he told me so, and I remember.

I drift off to sleep imagining what it must be to be normal. I imagine my head filled with clear pictures of all the things that have actually happened, just filed away so I could look back on them whenever I wanted. I cannot imagine how luxurious it would be, and I go to sleep crying at everything I have been missing. I hope that I will wake up and still be able to remember.

I wake up in the middle of the night with a start. My heart is pounding and I sit up in bed, looking around. The house is so perfectly quiet that the silence is a smothering thing, a presence in itself.

My hand shakes as I reach for the bedside light. I kissed Drake on the beach, and I am seventeen, but there is something else. I fumble for my bedside light. Something is wrong. I can't find the light, so I get out of bed, too jumpy to stay in the dark for another moment. My bed is in the middle of the room, which is why I couldn't find the switch. The room smells of paint. The soles of my feet stick to the bedroom floorboards. I am on the landing, feeling the old carpet under my feet, then running and jumping down the stairs and pushing open the door of my parents' room. I know that the sight of either one of them will soothe me. I walk slowly into the room, not wanting to wake them. A narrow beam of light is falling through the gap between the curtains and landing on their bed, which is perfectly made, smooth and undisturbed.

They are not here.

The panic rises, ready to crash over me, and I run for the light switch on the wall, blink in the sudden harsh light, and look around. They are not here. It is the middle of the night, but my parents are not in their bed. They are the people who take care of me and they are not here. They are always in their bed at night and I don't know what to do if they are not. They are everything. I cannot manage without them.

I am breathing fast. There is a note on Dad's pillow. I walk slowly to the bed and pick it up. It is written on a lined piece of paper torn from a notebook, in Dad's writing.

Darling Flora, it says. **We're away because Jacob is sick. Paige is with you. Everything is explained in the notes in the kitchen.**

In the kitchen I piece it all together. Paige is not here because I kissed her boyfriend, and I remember doing it. I am at home on my own. There is no chance of my going back to sleep. I am on my own and there is no one in this country who knows or cares.

I could do anything.

I decide to make a cup of tea, take it back to bed, and try to read a book. I could do anything, but staring at a book, with a cup of tea, is the only activity I can think of.

I could leave the house and go wherever I want. I could, but I won't.

I switch lights on as I go and look at the notes that my parents have left around the house. On their instructions I first check that the front door is locked (it is, with the chain on) and then the back door (this is locked too). I put the kettle on the stove and, while I wait for it to boil, walk around reading more notes. Many of the ones in my handwriting are about Drake. I know that I kissed Drake. It is shining in my head, clear and defined and real, standing out against the fuzziness of everything else.

It is two fifteen. Most people in Penzance are asleep. I have the house, and the world, to myself. I sit down in front of the big computer, the one my parents use, and stare at it, half in a trance, wondering what to do.

I must doze briefly, because I jerk awake, sitting in front of the computer, and I have to remember all over again. It feels like time to go back to bed, so I pick up the little laptop on the desk, because it has a sticker on it saying, Flora's laptop, and take it upstairs, holding it under one arm and my mug of lukewarm tea with the other hand.

The bedroom walls are partly pink and partly white, and the floor is varnished wood covered with a sheet and a blanket, splattered with paint. A board of labeled photographs takes up most of one still-pink wall.

There is a strange lumpy shape beside the bed, covered by a blanket. I lift the blanket and find a box of toys. I don't want a box of toys: I kissed a boy on a beach, and I am seventeen. I pick it up and put it out on the landing. I am going to paint the rest of this bedroom tomorrow. I want it to be white, like normal rooms. I approve of my past self's actions, assuming that it was me that started it.

• • •

I am looking at the Wikipedia page for Svalbard when I notice an e-mail. I didn't know I had an e-mail account on this computer. The red "1" next to the envelope icon makes me click; when I see the name, I can hardly breathe.

It is a message from Drake. All it says is:

Flora—I can't stop thinking about you.

I read it over and over again. It is seven words long, but they are the best seven words in the world. I copy it out many times and stick notes to myself all around my bedroom.

Drake has made me remember things: perhaps, now, I will remember this too.

I am glad I am on my own, because if my parents were here, everything would feel safe and constrained, and I would never have been on the computer at two forty in the morning.

I read the seven words again and again. I love Drake, and now he has written me this message. He can't stop thinking about me. And I can't stop thinking about him. I can hardly type my reply, because I am so desperate to tell him that he has made me remember.

When I have managed to get the right kind of words out, in the right kind of order, I send it, even though I know I should really wait until the morning. As soon as it is sent, I lie down and dream of Drake in his new weird home. I picture him in a snowy, bleak place with houses made of snow and ice, and a spartan, cold life, and I wonder whether I could send him anything that would help. Perhaps I will make him up a care package of things he might need from Cornwall.

In the morning I will go to the beach and find a second black stone and send him that.

I wake up late, the sun coming straight through the thin curtains and onto my bed. I roll over, wrapped in a pink duvet, and yawn. The walls are half-painted white and my bed is in the middle of the room. It is a quarter to eleven.

I am utterly disoriented and my heart starts pounding. I don't know why I am in a bed in the middle of the room. I read my hand. I read the notebook that is beside the bed. I read everything that is on the walls that are still pink. I am Flora. I am seventeen. I was sick when I was ten and I have anterograde amnesia. I kissed Drake on the beach. Paige hates me. I am on my own.

Drake wrote to me. *Flora—I can't stop thinking about you.*

The laptop is on the floor. Within seconds I am sitting up in bed staring at it. I reread the reply I wrote him in the middle of the night. It is not too long, which I suppose is good, but it is still much longer than his message to me. I push my hair behind my ears and start reading.

Dear Drake, the three-in-the-morning me has written.

I am so happy to hear from you. I never thought that would happen. I can't stop thinking about you either! And this is the amazing thing: I can remember it! I remember us sitting side by side on the beach, with the tide coming up. I can remember every word either of us said. I can remember kissing you. All of it. Everything else goes right out of my head, but the kiss is still there. I can't stop thinking about you.

I should have gone with you for the whole night, I wish I could go back and change it. (See? I really do remember.)

Paige doesn't want to be my friend anymore because she knows about it. I forgot that, but I wrote it down. It made me sad, but I don't blame her.

My parents have gone to France because my brother, Jacob, who lives there, is sick. I'm at home on my own. It's just me, until Saturday. That's why I'm on the computer in the middle of the night.

Tell me more about Svalbard. I remember you telling me how you went there when you were ten to see the midnight sun and now that you're nineteen you finally get to live there. Tell me everything else.

Flora

I wish he had replied during the night. I stare at the inbox, willing an e-mail to land. I have scared him off. I have no idea what time it is at the North Pole. Perhaps I will ask him. Whatever time it is, nine hours have passed since I sent that message, so he has probably seen it by now, and he has not replied.

I carry the laptop downstairs to make coffee and toast. I make sure the sound is turned right up so that the moment an e-mail arrives, it will ping as loudly as it can. I do not turn the radio on, even though with my parents away I can listen to whatever music I want.

I can put on music as loudly as I want, and I do want to, now. I want to turn it up loudly and dance around the kitchen. Even though he is at the North Pole and not answering, nothing can change the fact that Drake said he can't stop thinking about me.

Drake is, right now, the only person in the world. Drake's

North Pole course is maybe a year long, or maybe two or three. I don't know. After that he could come back. Or he and I could go somewhere else. We could live together. We could get married. I could be his wife. He is nineteen and I am seventeen, and that makes us old enough. He could take care of me, and I could, in my way, take care of him. I would remember everything, if I was with Drake.

Drake has made me remember. I am going to be normal, because of him. I have to spend my life with him, because he makes my memory work.

I don't feel like a child.

I make coffee, put some slices of bread into the toaster, and stare at the laptop screen, attempting to make it ping with a new e-mail, just by using the power of my mind.

My mom has called me twice, but I missed her. She sends a text that says: Morning darling. How are you and Paige? Remember your pills.

I reply: Hi. We are OK. I will, and I take them. The landline rings, and when I pick it up, a girl's voice says: "Checking you haven't gassed yourself."

"Paige!" I say, but she has hung up.

Nothing else happens. After a while I lie on the sofa and put the TV on, drifting off to sleep.

I jump awake and realize over an hour has passed. I am at the laptop in seconds. Drake has replied. A new e-mail is waiting.

For a moment I do not allow myself to read it. Then I sit down in front of the laptop and devour it.

Flora,

Seriously? You remember? That's crazy and amazing.

Have you spoken to a doctor? Does it mean you could be starting to recover?

Are you OK on your own? That sounds surprising—your mom was always so overprotective of you. She left you alone? I hope your brother will be OK.

Your message has made me imagine things that might have happened, but didn't. I wish I'd asked you again to come with me, that night. We could have worked it out. I spend more time than you might imagine thinking of what you would look like naked.

Is that a terrible thing to have said? It is, isn't it? I am so sorry. I am thinking of you constantly and I cannot even see you. I never expected this to happen. And if your memory is coming back— then anything could happen.

Take care of yourself. Remember to eat and things like that. Keep remembering!

Drake

I read it over and over, and I am shocked each time by the fact that he wants to see me naked. That makes me blush all over my body even though I am alone. I don't know how to deal with him saying a thing like that. I attempt to commit the e-mail to my memory (this feels possible), and then I print out our correspondence and put it carefully into a folder.

He spends more time than I might imagine thinking of what I would look like naked. I close my eyes and try to take that in. It's scary. I am not ten anymore.

The house changes. It is no longer empty even with the suffocating silence. It becomes a magical place. Every surface seems to glitter. There is enchantment in the air. I exchange messages with Drake as day becomes night and night becomes day. Drake has to work at his satellite station, but whenever he can, he rushes to a computer and writes to me. I write back over and over again, letting the messages pile up for when he has a chance to read them. His replies are sparkling and golden.

Our messages escalate. In one he is thinking of me naked. In the next he is telling me what he would like to do to my naked body, and I am doing my best to write the right kind of replies. I have no idea how a conversation like this is supposed to go, so I just write what I think and hope that is OK. The things he is saying are strange and new, but I love them. My words pop up on his screen, in the snowy place, and, as soon as he can, he answers them. It is intoxicating. I am, somehow, doing it right.

There is nothing, I find myself typing, that people do together that I wouldn't do with you, if you wanted to.

As soon as I have written that I want to qualify it, because I immediately start to imagine people doing terrible things to each other and I don't mean that at all. However, following it up with an e-mail saying "aside from . . ." would not be romantic, so although I start to write it, I stop and delete. I hope that Drake will understand what I mean.

Sometimes I find myself sitting in front of my parents' big computer, looking at random web pages, wondering what I'm doing there. My e-mails are on the laptop. I think I migrate to the big computer without even noticing it, when I'm worried about my parents. They text sometimes and tell me they're fine, but that Jacob is very sick and that it is a difficult time for everyone. I reply telling them happily not to worry about me. They ask about Paige, but I know Paige hates me because it is written everywhere, so I tell them she has lost her phone, and pass on messages from her instead.

I find a note that says: I told Mom Paige lost her phone. This is so they won't call her. I have told them at least twice, then. I have probably told them many times over.

My memory is not better. But I remember the kiss. I cling to that.

On Tuesday I don't eat the chili that is in a Tupperware box in the fridge marked with the words: EAT THIS ON TUESDAY. I have a few slices of toast and then a banana, and I don't leave the house because leaving the house would involve leaving the computer: even if I took the laptop outside, I wouldn't get Wi-Fi. I sit and stare at it, and when I am not staring at it, I run to the bathroom or make tea. I take pills when Mom reminds me to. Paige calls on the landline and says: "You haven't burned the house down? Brilliant."

It is Wednesday. I should shower. However, showering would mean leaving the laptop somewhere dry. I cannot leave it. I carry it from room to room, and wear my pajamas all day, and stare at the screen. I compose long messages and edit and send them, and I write short messages off the top of my head too. I love Drake, and

I tell him that I love him, and he says that he loves me too. *I love you too.* I look at myself naked in front of the mirror and picture myself through his eyes.

I remember the kiss. It is there, in my head. It stays there. It does not go away. Other things come and go, but the kiss stays.

On Wednesday we talk more about sex. Until I had my memory, I would not have been capable of the kind of relationship other people have. Drake asked me to spend the night, and I immediately said I couldn't because of my mom. I regret that. Regret is a strange feeling.

I would give anything, **I write**, for the chance to kiss you again, and to touch you and to feel your hands on my body. **The words** tumble out of me, uncensored and joyous.

Something I never imagined was inside me is unleashed.

I wish, **I tell him**, that I'd said the right thing when you asked me to spend the night. I would give anything to have you with me, here in my bed where I am right now. Anything.

And I would give anything to be there, **he replies.** To wake up by your side and reach for you. Your body is perfect. I know it is. If it wasn't such a creepy thing to do, I would ask you to send me a picture.

I cannot do that: taking a picture of myself naked is an impossible idea, and I tell him so. I would never take a picture of myself and attach it to an e-mail: I couldn't.

You will just have to imagine, **I add**. Perhaps one day . . . you know.

I hope so, **he says, later.** When do your parents come home? Saturday?

That's what they said. What day it is now? Wednesday?

• • •

Hours pass.

Thursday. You have two more days before someone is going to ask you what exactly you're doing on that computer all the time.

I reply straightaway. They like me on the computer. It means I'm safe.

I can hear his amusement when, sometime later, he writes back: They do know about the internet, right? Most parents don't want their daughters hanging out online, talking to men.

That's ten-year-olds, I remind him. And I'm seventeen.

I wake up with the words "I kissed Drake" in my head. I kissed Drake. I hold it in my head. I kissed him on the beach, and even though I have been to sleep since then, every detail is fresh in my mind and I want to stay in it and live there forever. I feel warm and glowing all over. I love Drake.

He said: "Maybe we could spend the night."

I said: "My mom."

I reach for a pen to write it down before it disappears. I kissed Drake: there is no way I am losing this.

My bed is in the middle of the room, and the walls are partly painted white.

I look at the notes that I have left out beside the bed.

I discover that: even though I can remember the kiss, I cannot remember any of the many things that appear to have happened since. This is crushing.

Mom and Dad are in France.

My brother, Jacob, is very sick.

I decided to paint my bedroom white.

Paige is not my friend anymore. She knows I kissed Drake.

Drake is in the Arctic. We are e-mailing each other.

I look at the pictures on my phone. I read everything again. I open the laptop to read the e-mails Drake has sent to me. As I look at them, a new e-mail arrives.

Sorry, Flora 🌺

Got to get out of town and out to the North Pole satellite base and do the research, or I'll be thrown off the course almost before it's started. The satellites are way out of town and I won't get any reception, let alone Wi-Fi. You should get ready for your parents, anyway. I'll e-mail tomorrow, in the middle of the night, your time?

OK, I tell him, choosing my words carefully, hoping they are right. Be careful. I love you.

I close the laptop and look around. According to everything I've just read, this house has been an enchanted haven of love for days and days. It has been a gorgeous place, a glowing new universe. Everything has been flawless and perfect.

I kissed Drake days and days ago, but it is still in my head. I don't know why, but I want to know why. It must be because I love him. It could be because of the stone. I need to ask a doctor: perhaps this is the beginning of me getting better. I will try to find a doctor and ask. I write a note to myself about that.

I walk downstairs, trying to make sense of my reality. I am in love. I write love letters on the computer, and I get love letters back. This is a magical place. I am seventeen and I love a boy. Before that I was ten, and now I have grown up.

That is what I am thinking as I step into the kitchen, and stop, unable to move, unable to breathe.

We have been robbed. I have been robbed, while I was asleep. Someone has come into my perfect happy dream world and ransacked it.

Thoughts run through my mind but vanish before I can hold on to them. This room does not look the way it should look. The kitchen is dirty, with everything everywhere. It smells. All the plates are out and there are trails of crumbs. The used plates are all around the kitchen, not stacked in the sink but just put down in random places.

There is coffee all over the place: it has left little dried stains, and there are brown rings on almost every surface.

My heart gradually slows down as I look at the details. I did this. It was me. I wrote that this place was enchanted and magical, but actually it isn't.

I should never write things that aren't true.

I can't find anything to suggest that I have left the house since Sunday, when, apparently, I walked to the beach with Mom. I run

back to the hallway and look at myself in the large mirror. The
girl in the reflection gapes at the unkempt stranger staring back at
her: my hair is lanker than I thought it was, and sticks to my head.
I might have been wearing these pajamas for quite a long time. I
can smell myself: the neighbors probably can too. My parents can
probably smell me in (I check the wall) France.

I read the kitchen-wall Post-it notes, and check the food in the
fridge. Tuesday's, Wednesday's, Thursday's, and Friday's dishes
are all still there, yet I know this does not mean it is Monday.
I seem to have taken approximately the right amounts of pills. I
need to find out for sure what day it is, and I do not dare open the
laptop again because I will write to Drake, and "What day is it?"
is a silly reason for restarting a conversation. Also, I have just read
that he is working and out of range of e-mail. He would not be able
to reply and that would make me sad.

I remember the kiss. I remember our conversation. I remember
the waves crashing on the pebbles, and the smell of the sea, and
the moonlight. I remember the stone. I look down and find that it
is in my hand.

Drake said he will not have Wi-Fi. I know he will have his
phone because people always bring their phones. I will text him
instead.

I text Drake, I miss you. I think it's Friday. I stare
at the phone for a while, but nothing happens.

I call a number on the phone, a number I read from a business
card that is stuck on the fridge.

"Hello," says a man's voice. "Pete's Taxis?"

"Hi," I say. "Is it Friday?"

"Today?" he says. "Yes, love. It's Friday. Do you need a taxi?"

"No, thanks. Bye."

I put the phone down. My parents are coming home tomorrow, and I have a lot of work to do.

The house is more disgusting everywhere I look. There are letters piled on the mat by the front door and a SORRY WE MISSED YOU card from UPS. I take pictures of everything, of the mess and the devastation and myself, so that I will remember this.

All the windows are shut, but when I stand beside one of them, I see the sun shining outside. The house needs fresh air. I open every window.

There are Post-it notes everywhere, and lots of them say things like: I LOVE HIM and He wants to see me naked. I gather them all up and put them in an envelope and put the envelope under my bed.

I will deal with myself first. I start to run a bath and tip a huge amount of bubble bath into the water. While the room is steaming up, I stare into the mirror, running my fingers through my hair and looking myself in the eye.

I am a different person.

The mirror fogs up. I write his name with a fingertip: DRAKE. Then I write FLORA and then I write be brave. I put a heart around the whole thing.

I stare for a long time at my naked body, wondering whether he would be disappointed if he saw it. I run my hands over myself, down my waist, trying to feel my skin through his fingertips.

When I smell the air, I wonder why the oven is on, but when I

65

go downstairs in just a towel, it turns out I have switched it on, at some point, but have not put anything inside it. The smell in the air is the smell of the charred pieces that have dropped off other things inside the oven, in the past.

I turn the oven off and go back to the bathroom. The water is hot and deep, and I am delighted to see that I have not let it overflow.

Drake asked for a picture of me naked in one of his e-mails. I said no. That, I decide as I step into the too-hot water, is a good thing. Drake has a strange beautiful girl in his head: if he saw the real me now, he would be disappointed. It was dark on the beach.

I lie back in the bath and check my hands and arms. This is important because I don't want to wash away significant things; and I cannot write a note on my hand to remind me to check the notes on my hands. Right now there is nothing written there that isn't currently in my head.

I wash my hair with shampoo and conditioner. I scrub myself properly and shave my armpits and legs. When I get out, I am pink like a lobster and far more fragrant than either a lobster or my recent self.

With the windows open, the house starts to breathe again. The smell that has been hanging thick in the air fades, and the air that comes in from the outside world reminds me that there is a world outside. It smells of the sea, the fresh air that has blown across the Atlantic.

I stand wrapped in a towel and look out the window and

discover I am crying. I am not sure whether the e-mail exchange with Drake actually happened, whether my parents are really away, whether my brother, Jacob, is so sick in France that they had to leave me behind and rush to see him. I don't believe that Paige isn't speaking to me, because she is my best friend and we met when we were four, on the first day of school. I only know about any of that because I have read it, but I could have written anything. Is there a boy at the North Pole who loves me as much as I love him? Did I really kiss a boy? Did he ask me to spend the night with him?

Yes. Yes, he did. I know that, because I can remember it. I kissed Drake on the beach: that is the only thing I know.

The world starts to go white around the edges. I walk shakily to my bedroom and sit on the bed. I lie down and close my eyes.

When I wake up, it is dark. The windows are all open and the evening air that is blowing in my face is cold.

I have not closed the curtains. The light in my bedroom is on. The bed is in the middle of the room and the walls are partly white. I read the notes and work it all out. My parents will be home on Saturday. I find a clean pair of pajamas in my drawer. They are white and cotton, and I am cold in them, so I add a sweatshirt and a pair of thick socks. The house is quiet.

I kissed a boy on the beach in the moonlight. All the hairs stood up on my arms.

Every single window is open as wide as it will go, and I shiver as I walk around closing each one. I can hear distant shouting down by the seafront, but those are sounds from a different universe. The living room is deathly quiet: the TV stands gray and mute, accusing me of not watching it as instructed. The sofa is pristine, one cushion dented but otherwise untouched. I sit down just to make it look as if I have been there.

I clean the kitchen before I notice that it is two in the morning. By that point the plates are in the dishwasher, the floor is swept but not mopped, and I have wiped a ridiculous number of crumbs into my hand and dropped them into the trash.

I should go back to bed, but instead I make a cup of peppermint tea and open the laptop with no idea whatsoever of what I am going to find. There might or might not be a breathtaking stream of e-mails between me and Drake: I don't entirely believe the Flora who wrote that it happened. I am scared I will just find my side of them. I do not want to have been e-mailing him like a poor little damaged girl. That would be unbearable.

But no: it is all here, on the screen. I read through it with increasing amazement and excitement.

It ended, twelve hours ago, with us both saying we were going to go and do things.

Drake is probably asleep, by his remote satellite dishes. I go all the way back upstairs and lie down and go back to sleep too.

Chapter Four

"Pete's Taxis?"

"What day is it, please?"

"Saturday. Need a taxi?"

The house is nice and clean. I have mopped and sprayed and wiped and dusted. I have thrown away most of the food and taken the trash out so they won't find the perfectly good food. I have photographed the house clean, so that I know I have done it. They will be landing on Saturday afternoon, and this is Saturday morning, so I decide to brave the outside world and replace all the bread I have eaten.

The air feels strange on my face: I don't think I've been outside for a long time. It is a warm day, and I go out in a cotton dress and cardigan with bare legs and flip-flops. As I edge out the front door, I feel like an interloper: I walk up the road, pass a big office building, and let my legs take me to Chapel Street, where there is a small grocery store. The fresh air burns my lungs. I feel color returning to my cheeks. I think of Drake in his cold snowy place, and there is a spring in my step.

I am away from the computer. When I get home, there might be an e-mail. Meanwhile I have read his other e-mails saying wonderful things to me. He said he adores me. I have a boy, hundreds of miles away, who loves me. He wants me. He replies to my messages. His kiss made me remember.

I want to go to the North Pole to find him.

I look at my hand. FLORA, be brave.

I buy three loaves of bread and some cookies and a cake. I buy milk even though I don't know whether we need any or not, because buying milk at the store feels like the kind of thing people do. I remember Mom buying milk there when I was little. I get a box of chocolates for my parents because that feels like a nice thing to do. I buy an expensive box, because if they cost a lot, they must be good ones.

When I smile at people, they smile back. This is so encouraging that I decide to walk through town as well, to feel the sunshine on my skin and to smile at some more people and to swing my bag of groceries and to feel happy and normal and desired. Drake wants me. He kissed me on the beach.

I wander around and Penzance encloses me. I duck into shops and stalls: there is a huge amount of secondhand stuff for sale. I look down at myself. I am seventeen. I am wearing a little girl's dress and flip-flops, and I look like I did when I was ten, but bigger. I see a girl about my age walking down the street toward me. She is wearing a red-and-white dress with a swishy skirt and bright red shoes. I would like to look like her, not like me. There is a woman across the road who is wearing a long coat with a furry collar. She looks like a person who could go to the North Pole. I don't.

In a cave-like secondhand shop I find a huge fake-fur coat and pull it on over my boring dress. It is as warm as wearing a duvet, but it makes me look like a spy. It is slightly too big. The woman looking back at me from the mirror is mysterious, poised for adventure: she would probably have a gun concealed in a pocket, and she would definitely not be wearing a little girly dress underneath.

She would have a boyfriend.

"How much is this?" I ask the salesclerk, who has been repeatedly pressing a button on a contraption of some sort that I have not seen, something that mystifyingly asks, "Shall we check the wireless, Gromit?" again and again.

"Should be on the label," she calls back, and I check the label. Thirty-five pounds.

"Could you do it any cheaper than thirty-five?" I ask, feeling my cheeks flush as I do.

The woman shrugs. She is small and brown-haired, and looks distracted. "Thirty? Summer coming up. Sure."

I take the huge coat off and lay it on the counter, pausing to wonder whether I could also buy an old typewriter. I flatten three ten-pound notes from my purse while the salesclerk folds my new coat as small as she can get it and pushes it into a huge and very crumpled brown paper bag with handles.

"It's not a great bag," she concedes as she hands it over, "but it *is* a great coat. Really nice. Cheers, Flora."

I am trying to work out the words to say something about preferring a great coat in a crappy bag to its opposite, but am brought up short by her knowing my name. I look at her. She has a round face and short dark hair and I don't recognize her at all. I hate not knowing my own past. I hate it that she knows me and I don't know her.

"Thanks," I say, and I leave.

I stop on the corner and wonder whether to put my new coat on. I would be much too hot, but it would be nice to be wearing it rather than carrying it in a ripped brown paper bag. I rearrange my things, and reach into my dress pocket, checking for my keys.

Instead, I find a piece of paper, folded up lots of times, which opens up into a map. It is not a hand-drawn map, but a printed one, with yellow streets with their names marked on it. Someone has put an X on Morrab Gardens and written HOME next to it, and that is, indeed, where I live. I live at 3 Morrab Gardens. Someone has also put an X on the other side of the town, and written DRAKE beside it.

I look at the notes on my arms and try to compare the handwriting. I cannot tell whether I wrote the things on the map or not.

It takes me a while to look at the street names and figure out where I am currently standing, but when I do, I mark it on the map and draw a line from here to the place that is called DRAKE, because that is the only place in the world I want to go. Drake is in the Arctic, and this is a map of Penzance, so unless there is something else I forgot to write down, I don't think I will find him there, but I have to go and see, because he might have come back.

He might have come back. His name is on this map.

The journey is a straight line and I follow it quite easily. I walk past lots of shops, and then past the train station, keeping the map in my hand. By the time I turn off the main road and start walking up a steep hill, my bags are heavy and awkward and I am wishing that I'd dropped everything off at home before setting off on this journey to a place called *DRAKE*. The bag with the coat in it has such a huge rip that I may as well stop and put it in the next trash can I see and wear the coat. The bag with milk and chocolates and bread and cookies and cake in it is much heavier than it should be, but I struggle on up the hill, because I want to know what is here and why I have the map. It feels like a message from the universe. It feels like a mission. I wanted an adventure, and here is one, given to me.

I might be walking toward Drake. He might be here.

It is a gray stone house, at the top of the hill, with three floors. I walk up to the door and ring the bell.

I know what Drake looks like. He has brown hair and glasses. I know what his kisses feel like. If he is here, he will kiss me now, and I will kiss him back.

Nothing happens for a while. I ring the bell again and then there are footsteps inside, and then someone is fiddling with the other side of the door, and then it is open and a man is standing there. He has no hair at all, but he has smiley eyes, and he nods at me.

He is not Drake. But if thirty years had gone by without my noticing it, he could, possibly, be Drake. That thought scares me, and I look down at myself to check that I am still seventeen. It is hard to tell from my clothes, so I lean slightly sideways to look at myself in the bay window.

I am still seventeen, and this is not Drake.

"Hello, Flora," says the man.

"Hello," I reply. I try to have smiley eyes too. I don't know him, but he knows me.

"Drake sent you?" he says, and I nod.

"Great," he says. "He said someone would be here for his stuff. I wasn't expecting it to be you, but come on in."

I swallow hard. Drake is not here. That would have been too wonderful. However, this is a man who knows Drake, and knows me, and he wants to give me "stuff."

"Thanks."

"Come in, Flora. It looks like you're carrying a lot. You're not actually going to be able to take all the junk away today, are you? Or is someone coming to pick you up?"

I shake my head. "I can't take it today. Sorry."

This man is going to give me Drake's stuff. I will have things that belong to Drake. I will make sure I take something, at least, away from here.

He sighs. "It was too much to ask, I suppose, that the boy would sort his room out before heading off to the North Pole. He just didn't bother. Why should he when he can get a nice girlfriend to come and do it for him, right?"

"Right." I try to file away the words "nice girlfriend." I like them.

I don't know how else to reply to that, so I just follow the man into the house, which smells of intense things like food and perfume, and up some stairs. I follow him to a door, but he just looks around the edge of it and says, "Kate? Drake's friend's here. She's going to sort his stuff out, but for today she's just here to see what the damage is."

Even though I can't see into the room, I nod because what he said seems to make sense. A cat rubs against my legs. It is a white cat with very long hair. I check its ears but they are there. Of course they are there. I have no idea why I might expect them not to be.

"Wonderful," says a voice from inside, and then a woman is in front of me. She has gray hair that is as long as her chin, and she's wearing a tight pink dress and a leopard-print scarf. "Oh," she says. "Hello, Flora. I thought it would be Paige." My heart pounds. I hold my breath and wait to be asked to leave. "That's OK. Come on up."

"Are you Drake's aunt?" I ask.

"I certainly am, my dear," she says. "Kate Apperley. This is my husband, Jon; I'm sure he won't have thought to introduce himself to you again."

Then, at the top of another flight of stairs, I am actually standing in Drake's bedroom.

This is miraculous. Paige must have been here. I might have been here. This is the room he would have brought me to if I had said yes to spending the night with him. There is the bed we would have slept in. This is our place.

He said: "Hey. Look. Do you want to go somewhere with me? Like, now? We could spend the night . . ."

I said: "But my mom."

The stupidest three words I could have possibly said.

● ● ●

Drake's room has a sloping ceiling and a window, and there is a double bed and a dresser, and a closet with some empty hangers in it. I breathe in the air that was breathed out by Drake before he left. There are books on a table, and clothes, most of them T-shirts, on the floor. Bits and pieces are scattered all over the place. The bed is the only thing that is bare: a white duvet and two pillows are piled on the mattress. I wish his sheets were still there. I would get into his bed if they were. It would still be too late, but I would have gotten there in the end.

Kate is looking at me. I look back at her and smile.

"I know!" she says. "Boys! I'm joking, but I do wish I'd checked it before he left. I just assumed he'd tidied up after himself. Silly me."

"Wow."

"If he was a girl, of course, he'd have been a little more house-trained. You'd never walk out of a house and leave it like this, would you? He wasn't so bad when he was living here. I mean, he put things in the dishwasher and did his share of cooking. Ah well. We still miss him, you know. Even if he has left us all these lovely reminders."

"I miss him too."

"Well, just have a look around. Organize it however you want. You can come back later with a box or two. There's nothing major. It's just the bits of crap that he couldn't be bothered to deal with, if you'll pardon the expression."

"I will," I tell her, and she leaves the room, and I am alone with Drake's things.

I pick up a red T-shirt and smell it. I am instantly back on the beach.

• • •

He said: "Your mom. Oh God. I'm sorry. That was a terrible idea. I mean. What the hell am I . . . I didn't—"

I said: "I'm OK."

He said: "Flora, I'm sorry. I . . . I'd . . . I never . . ."

"She'd call the police," I said.

"The police. Jesus. I am an *idiot*. Forget I said it."

I ruined everything.

I hold the T-shirt to my nose. This is what Drake smelled like, on the beach. I want to breathe nothing but this for the rest of my life. It is the only thing I want. I was so close to him then that all I could smell was Drake.

I write it on my hand first. I am in Drake's room. Then I pick up all the clothes from the floor and smell each one in turn. I fold the red T-shirt carefully and push it into my bag with the milk and the chocolate. There are random things on top of the dresser—a scrap of paper with a number on it, a row of stones arranged in size order, a bowl with some shells in it. I straighten it all up, like the nice woman asked me to, and grab as much as I can fit into my bag. I take all the stones and all the shells. I take the piece of paper.

I will come back for the rest of it. I will just come along with a suitcase and take it all away. I will keep it forever. It will help me hold on to my memory.

I stand at the window and look out. I know that I must be looking at Penzance, but this makes no sense. I live in Penzance and it does not look like this. I know that from my window at home I see treetops and the tops of buildings across the park. That has always been what I see from my window. The place spread out before me is beautiful, and Penzance is ordinary. I am looking at a sweep of ocean over to the left, rows upon rows of houses, palm trees, all of them lit by a bright sun that is shining upon everything and bleaching it all white.

I clutch the windowsill. I am not in Penzance at all. I have gone somewhere else. This is not the same place. I am somewhere new. I can't remember getting here but I am here.

It says on my hand that I am in Drake's room. Does that mean I am in the cold place? Svalbard? But this place does not look cold.

I stand and stare, trying to make sense of it all.

The door opens and a woman comes in. "Are you all right, Flora?" she asks, and I stare at her.

I want to ask her where I am, who she is, where Drake is. I want to ask which country we're in and where my parents are and what is happening and how I can get home.

"Yes," I say, instead. "Yes, I'm fine, thank you. I think I need to go."

Chapter Five

I am sitting at the kitchen table with my phone. My parents will text or call, because it is two twenty and, according to everything I have read, there is a plane that is due to be landing exactly now, and that plane has my parents on it. They went to France because my brother was sick. Now they are coming back, so maybe he is better.

The house is spotless. Nobody would look at it and suspect for one moment that I had been anything other than clean living and responsible this week. I would not believe it myself, except for some pictures on my phone that show me exactly how bad it was. Now everything is clean: the floors are Swiffered and mopped, the dishes are clean and put away. The back door is open and spring air, scented by things that are growing and blooming and unfurling, is creeping through the house.

It looks exactly like it should look. If I didn't have the words and the pictures, I would not suspect a thing.

I kissed Drake on the beach. I am alive in that memory. Having it, owning it in its crystal clarity, carrying it in my head rather than on my skin—all of that makes me feel like a human being. I live in it as much as I can, and the rest of the time I discover (again and again, I suspect) that our relationship is ongoing. We have written e-mails to each other, and they are wonderful e-mails. I love him and he loves me. He has made me remember and I need to see him again, to make my memory work again.

I have gathered up all my notes about what has happened this week: they are ordered in a file, and that file is hidden in a box under my bed. File under bed, written on the inside of my left wrist, is the only evidence. When my parents get home, they will only see normality. I have read everything: right now, I am fairly confident that I know most of it.

I put on a CD and wait, still looking at the phone. It is an album by David Bowie, *Hunky Dory*, and I find that I know all the words to it, without knowing how I know. They will hear it in the background when they call me to say they're on the way back.

I am wearing a red T-shirt that is too big for me. It smells of Drake.

The album is over. I put on a CD by the Beatles and discover that I love it. The album is called *Abbey Road*, and I wonder whether I have listened to it before or whether this is me hearing it for the first time. I write on a Post-it note: I love Abbey Road.

They must have landed by now. I have probably never been on a plane, but I know, because I have written it down, that you're not allowed to use your phone on one.

I call Mom's cell phone. She does not answer. "Sorry," says a robot lady. "No one is available to take your call. Please leave a message after the tone. To rerecord your message, press one at any time."

I decide to leave my mom a message. "Hi," I say. "It's me, Flora. Call me when you can. See you soon!" I press one, and then I say it again. I call my dad. He doesn't answer either.

I write on a lined piece of paper that is next to the phone: Left a message on Mom's phone. I add up the number of times I have already written this on the piece of paper and see that I have left my parents thirty-four messages. They will certainly know that I am thinking of them.

Phones can die. They can break, and they can get lost, and they can slip down the sides of seats and be left behind.

There are many things that could happen to a little phone.

My parents should be driving back from the airport, but they hate driving.

I renew my preparations for their return, with the kettle set again on the stove, and the teapot out ready with bags in it, and the chocolate cake sliced on a white plate in the middle of the table, and plates and cups set out for the three of us. I look at the phone, and I wait.

The chocolate cake is hardening around the edges. My parents have not come home. I must have done something wrong.

I take my pills and start yawning. They still do not come home.

There are no notes that offer any guidance at all. There is

nothing interesting on my hand: all my notes are about phone calls I have made, timetables I have checked, messages I have left. I find a number for Exeter airport and check that the plane landed safely, because websites can get things wrong and the thought of a plane crashed into the sea while I leave message after message with the robot lady makes me tremble.

I cannot find a real person to speak to, but I do find a recorded message that assures me that all flights from France have landed as normal. It occurs to me that if an airplane had crashed other people would want to know about it, so I check on the TV and again on the internet, and there is nothing about any plane at all.

I think I have called Exeter airport before. I think I am doing it over and over again.

On my wrist it says File under bed. I look under my bed and become distracted, absorbed in the visit I made to Drake's aunt's house. I take my phone and look through all the pictures I took there, and back to the photos of the clean house and before that the dirty house. I look at the picture of the poster of the missing cat, and of Drake, standing on a chair.

I don't remember taking that, but I have a photograph of Drake on my phone, and when I find it, I stare at it for a long time.

I take out everything I took from his bedroom and line it up. I put the stones next to each other, in size order, like they are in the picture I took at his aunt's house. I put the shells in a long row on my bedroom windowsill so I can look at every single one of them. I take off the red T-shirt and bury my face in it, remembering.

82

When I come back to the present, my parents are still not here.

Something bad could have happened on the journey. I read a note that says they have a secret from me. Perhaps the secret involves them never coming home.

I wish Paige were here. I need someone who knows how to take charge. There must be something I am missing, something obvious, something that will make it instantly all OK. I get out the phone to text her, and then I see how many times she has told me to leave her alone. That makes me cry.

Mom's last text says: Can't wait to see you, Flora darling. Take care of yourself! Remember—macaroni and cheese today. Mom & Dad xx

I replied saying: Yes, macaroni! Paige and I are doing great. That is the last text on the thread.

I need to find someone to help me now.

I look at everything in my room and find some numbers on the back of a photograph of Jacob. It says, Call me. I love you, so I dial the numbers. Someone answers with a strange foreign voice. It cannot be Jacob, so I hang up.

Mrs. Rowe lives next door. I remember her giving me sweets, and swapping our used jam jars for bars of chocolate. I remember climbing the wall and talking to her as I balanced on our back garden wall on my tummy. I remember that she had grown-up twins who were a boy and a girl, and that her boy twin had twins too. In those memories I am smaller. She might still live there, or she might not. Her twin's twins might have had more twins by now.

I go out, carefully leaving the porch door a little bit open, and walk up our garden path and down Mrs. Rowe's. When I ring her bell, which makes a buzzing sound that I remember, the door is open before the noise has even finished.

"There you are!" she says. "At last. Have you got me the . . ." She pauses. She looks at me. Her eyes are cloudy and she is much older than she used to be. She looks so old that she must be almost dead. "Have you got anything for me?" she says, in the end.

"No," I say. "Do you know where my parents are?"

"Do you like strawberry jam?"

"You used to take the jam jars."

"Come in!"

It feels as if I have passed some sort of test, and I follow her into her house, which matches ours but is the other way around. There are pictures of her children on the walls, starting from when they were babies. Every bit of wall has a photograph on it. I stand in front of one.

"Look!" I say. "Look, Mrs. Rowe. This is me! And this is my brother, Jacob. Those are your twins. Your boy and girl twins. And those are your other twins. Your grandchild ones."

Her grandchild twins are about Jacob's age. They are both boys. I look at the three big boys, and me. I am wearing a pair of orange shorts and a yellow vest, and we are all in our back garden. I try to remember the picture being taken. It's not fair, because I am only about seven in that picture, so I should be able to remember it, but I can't.

"Yes, yes," she says, but I know she isn't listening.

The house smells a bit funny.

"Here you go," she says. "Jam."

I stand in the kitchen doorway and stare. There are jars of jam all over the table, and all over the countertops, and on a lot of the floor. There must be hundreds of them.

"Wow," I say.

"Have some jam, dear," she says.

"Flora," I tell her. "I'm Flora. Have you seen my parents?"

She doesn't reply. I don't think she even hears. I take the jam, and kiss her on the cheek because I know what it's like, and I go home.

The jam is moldy on top but I don't want to throw it away, so I put it at the back of the cabinet.

I e-mail Drake and tell him about my parents, what should have happened and when, and what actually happened (nothing). I tell him about Mrs. Rowe's jam. As soon as I have sent it, I realize it must be an odd message to receive. He does not reply, even though I stare at my inbox, making it check for new messages every few seconds. There is nothing from him, and there is nothing from my parents.

I find a number on the back of a photograph. I call it on my phone, but it won't ring: it says NUMBER BLOCKED.

I think I have forgotten something. I can't remember what it is. I pull at my hair in frustration and enjoy the sudden pain. I pull again. I bang my head on the white wall of this stupid half-pink bedroom. I stare at the window, longing to smash the glass, to cut my skin, to throw myself through it. I want to make myself feel something so intensely that I will remember it.

I stand beside the window. It would be easy to do. Nobody is here to stop me.

• • •

Drake pulls me back. I remember Drake. I remember him asking me to spend the night with him, and I lie on my bed and run away into the memory. I live it again and again. I go back to the beach, as a ghostly extra presence, and tiptoe around, watching us as we sit side by side.

"Cold," he says. "I've been once before."

"Lucky for you."

"Spend the night?"

"My mom."

I pull a chair to the bedroom window so I am looking out at the trees opposite. No cars go by, because the street at the front of the house is not big enough for cars. A few people walk past. We must have neighbors on the other side too, but I don't dare bang on their door. I don't know if I know them.

Nothing happens. No one comes. The house is quiet. I start to feel sick. There is something I have missed. If I didn't know that I had been outside today, I would think it was something to do with the whole world rather than my parents in particular. There has, however, been no apocalypse, as far as I can tell.

I open the laptop to check everything again, and the presence of two messages from Drake takes me by surprise. I gasp out loud and burst into tears before I have even read them.

His name is there at the top of the screen: Drake Andreasson. I settle down to read the oldest one first, my heart pounding.

The house closes in on me as I stare at his words.

Flora,

Well, it's Saturday, and here I am back from work, and your parents must be home. Hope all is OK with your brother.

It's magical here, but I'm missing you. Working out at the satellite dishes was awesome but I didn't stop thinking about you.

Did you get your house all cleaned up? Are your parents impressed? I wish I could see you. I can't stop thinking about all the things we talked about. How would you feel if, over the holidays, I came to see you?

Drake

His second message says:

F—Sorry. I wrote that message offline when the internet was down. Then I saw your next one. Are they back? Have you checked to make sure there's no message? Maybe they stayed longer with your brother? It's weird that they haven't called you. How long has it been?

I hope they've returned since you wrote that message. Let me know.

D

They have not come back. I write and tell him so. Then I write again, and again, and again.

Chapter Six

"They said they were coming back," I tell the policeman, "but they didn't. And they always do what they say. It says in my book that I've called them sixty-seven times."

The police station is a gray building with an orange tiled roof. It is boring on the outside, and inside it is boring too. The reception area is small, with a little row of three blue chairs by the window.

The man who is sitting at the reception desk is being polite, but he doesn't think my problem is the most interesting thing that will happen to him today. He has a bald head, which is shining under the electric light. There is a piece of paper in his hand and he keeps trying to read it. I know it has nothing to do with me.

"Sixty-seven?" he echoes. He looks up at me with a little frown. "Seriously?"

"They always tell me what they're doing. Always."

"Your parents are visiting your brother and have not come home when you thought they would?"

"That's right."

"Have you contacted your brother?"

"I don't think so."

"And they are fully functioning grown-ups?"

"Yes."

"As are you?"

I see him looking at the words on my hand, trying to read them. He looks at my face. He stares into my eyes for a few seconds, and his manner changes. He pushes his papers away.

"Oh. I know who you are."

I don't know what to say to that, so I say nothing.

"What are you?" he says. "Sixteen or so?"

"I'm seventeen and I kissed a boy on a beach. Before that I was ten and I was going to the amusement park. I met Paige when we were four."

I only meant to say the first two words out loud. The rest of it was supposed to be in my head. He looks as if he wants to laugh at me, and I hate that.

"Yeah. You've been here before. You've met my colleagues. OK. I'll call someone for you. Have a seat. Do you have a friend? Neighbor? Any other family around?"

"Paige is my friend."

"Let's have Paige's number, then. I'll get her to come and pick you up. Maybe you can stay at her place."

I look at my phone, searching for Paige's name and number.

Paige will pick me up and take care of me. But I know as I say the words in my head that they are not right.

There are texts on my phone, but they are all from me. All of them say things like: `Hello Paige. Are you going to be back soon?` She has not replied. I hope she is OK. I scroll up and up until I find her last text to me. It is from a few days ago, and it says: `Flora. This is the last time I'm going to answer. I am not your friend anymore, not since you kissed my boyfriend. WE ARE NOT FRIENDS. Leave me alone.`

I stare at the words. I did kiss her boyfriend. That happened: I can remember it. I kissed a boy on the beach. He was Drake. I love him. That means Paige and I are not friends.

I look up. I am in the police station because my parents haven't come home, and there is a man with a shiny head and a pen and a yellow Post-it note in front of him. He is waiting for me to tell him Paige's phone number so he can ask her to come and get me.

I stand up.

"It's OK, actually," I tell him, and I walk to the door, and then through it, and then I run down the road, all the way home. I am on my own. It is suddenly exciting. I skip down the road. I dance. I can do anything.

I scrawl the words on my arm. Contact Jacob. Maybe Jacob might help me.

If the policeman called Paige, she might try to help me in spite of everything. I could go and bang on her door and she would probably let me in. Yet I cannot do that because I would not be able to tell her about my e-mails with Drake, and she would find out instantly because his name is everywhere in my world. It is on my hands and arms and a hundred new little notes perching around the house like butterflies.

I need to take the new notes down in case my parents get back. I must remember to do it.

There is too much to remember.

"Hello?" I call. There are no extra shoes on the porch, no coats, no luggage, no voices. I want my parents to be here. "I'm home!" I add, and stand and wait.

Contact Jacob.

My parents keep paperwork in a filing cabinet and in teetering piles in a bedroom that has a single bed without any sheets on it. I start with the teetering piles.

I write a note—Looking for Jacob's phone number—and stick it onto the edge of the table with tape.

There is nothing about my parents' trip. There are no travel details, no hotel booking, no letters. I would probably find them if I looked harder, on the big computer.

I open the filing cabinets and look for traces of my big brother. This involves plowing through lots of boring pieces of old paper, checking each one for his name. I find an envelope that says FLORA on the front, and take out a sheaf of papers from inside, but words like "temporal lobe," "associated confabulation," and "GCS 8" jump out and make me nervous. I write down some of the strange words and put the piece of paper in my pocket. Then I shove everything back in its envelope and push it down into the cabinet.

There is a postcard with a picture of the Eiffel Tower on it. That is in Paris. I turn it over and see that it is addressed to me, in messy handwriting. It says: Looking at this right now and thinking of you. You're amazing. Jacob xx.

I stare at it. I take a photo of it. It doesn't have his phone number or his address on it. I put it on top of the filing cabinet. Jacob was thinking of me, in Paris. I must have seen this card before. I screw my eyes shut tight and tell him that I am thinking of him too. I hope he knows.

I find a passport, and oddly it turns out to be mine. It was issued two years ago and is valid for another eight years. I leave that out on the side, just in case, and write I HAVE A PASSPORT! in big letters down the inside of my left arm.

I think of Drake. He makes me remember. I can remember kissing him. The smell of the sea.

The black stone.

"We could spend the night."

"My mom."

He is far away. I put the passport into the back pocket of my jeans.

After a long time I find a piece of paper with a handwritten address on it, topped with the word *Jacob*. It says *Paris*, but it does not have a phone number.

It does not look like a new piece of paper. It looks like the kind of piece of paper that would fall out of an old book. It says: *Jacob, Apt. 3, 25 Rue Charlot, 75003, Paris, FRANCE.*

When I type the address into the computer, it appears on a map: it really is in Paris, the capital of France, and it could be where he lives, or it could be a place he lived in once. There must be a better way of getting ahold of him, but since I can't think what it would be, I write him a card saying who I am and that I am worried because our parents haven't come home, and I ask him to call me if he's well enough, or to get our parents to call me, as soon as he can if he gets this. I add my e-mail address, just in case.

I read it over. It sounds all right, I think. It sounds normal.

I find three first-class stamps in the drawer with the tape and semi-working pens, and I run outside and mail it.

I report it all back to Drake and write it in my notebook. Time passes, and then Drake replies.

He's probably on Facebook, he advises. Have you looked? But there must be tons of Jacob Bankses.

I try to look him up, but I can't log in, because I don't have an account. I follow the instructions to make one, but when I put in my e-mail address, it says I do have an account after all. The laptop fills in the password with a row of dots, so I click "OK" and look at a part of me that I had no idea existed.

There is a photograph of Paige and me. We are cheek to cheek, smiling at the camera. I miss Paige. She is not my friend anymore, though she is listed as being one of my friends on Facebook. I only have five friends on here, and they are people I remember from primary school. My page has nothing written on it. I don't know how this works. I remember Jacob being on Facebook when I was little, and I remember pestering him to get off the computer and come play with me. The website was blue then, and it is blue now.

I type "Jacob Banks" into a box, but then it comes up as my status, so I know I entered it in the wrong place. I type it in a different box and see what happens.

Many Jacob Bankses show up in a long list. Except it is impossible to see anything about most of the people who appear, and I have no idea what my brother looks like now. In my memories he is big and wonderful. In the photos in this house he is still a teenager, but I think now he is much older than that. Some of these profiles say things like "San Diego" underneath them, so I know they're the wrong Jacob Bankses, while others show teenagers in their photographs (teenagers who do not look like my pictures), so I know they're not him either. There is a photo of a man with a big red scar all down the side of his face. I don't click on that, because that's not my brother, and also it says that he lives in Gay Paree, wherever that is.

Whenever I click on a likely photo, I get: "Do you know Jacob? To see what he shares with friends, send him a friend request," and a suggestion to "add friend." I do that with everyone who I think could possibly be my brother, and the "friend request sent" messages pile up until there is nothing more I can do but wait.

I search the internet to find out where else you might find people. This leads me to a website called Twitter. There are lots of people with his name there too, but hardly any of them have privacy settings. This is easier, and I plow through until I have eliminated every single one of them. I try to do the same with a few other websites, but it is suddenly all too hard. When I check back in with Drake, he thinks it's funny that I have asked all the Jacob Bankses to be my friends, and we agree that we have explored the obvious social media connections.

All we can do is wait. I decide to sleep.

Although it's not actually night, I turn the corner of my parents' duvet back and leave the chain off the door, because I might sleep until morning. I curl up on the sofa and close my eyes.

When I wake up, it is light and I am scared. I read everything in my notebook and all the notes I can find, and get it into my head, and it makes me more scared, though my only rule for life appears to be that I mustn't panic. I go to my room and read everything I have stuffed under the bed.

I sent Jacob a letter. My parents have not come home. Drake is in the Arctic and I love him.

My parents' bedroom door is ajar, and I give a polite little tap before I push it open. The bed has not been disturbed.

I need help. I run up our garden path and down Mrs. Rowe's. She opens the door at once. "There you are at last. Have you got me the . . ." She pauses. Her eyes are cloudy and she is much older. "Have you got anything for me?"

"No," I say. "Do you know where my parents are?"

"Do you like strawberry jam?"

"You used to take the jam jars."

"Come in!"

The house smells funny.

"I must give you some jam."

I stand in the kitchen doorway and stare at all the jam.

"Flora," I tell her. "I'm Flora. Have you seen my parents?"

She doesn't reply. I take the jam and kiss her on the cheek because I know what it's like for her. The jam is moldy on top but I don't want to throw it away, so I put it at the back of the cabinet. There are already two like it there.

There is no one in Penzance who can help me. I turn on my phone and the computer. There is one new e-mail from Drake, and a string of messages from Facebook. I have eleven "friends": six of them are named Jacob Banks and the rest are people I used to know.

According to my notes, I sent requests to more than twenty Jacobs. If any of them is the right one, he will know who I am. I make tea in what a note on the fridge tells me is Mom's favorite mug (WORLD'S BEST MOM!) and sit at the table, which is covered in junk. There are yellow notes everywhere. They are scrawled with Jacob, Mom, Dad, France, and Drake, Drake, Drake. As I start to make my way through the six Jacob profiles that are now open to me, my phone pings with a text.

I read it. Then I read it again. I copy it out to make it more real, and I read it again.

Darling, so sorry we're late! Are you all right? Please text back immediately. We can't use our phones in here. We missed our plane. We missed all your calls. I left you a message yesterday—did you get it? There was an emergency at the hospital and we couldn't go anywhere. Jacob took a turn for the worse and for a couple of days we had to trust that you were OK and just focus on him. Stick with Paige. Emergency money is in a box at the back of Dad's sock drawer, and a credit card, PIN 5827. Please reply. Jacob is now v. sick but we're going to come home as soon as we can for a while at least. Will let you know more once we book a new flight. Thinking of you always. LOTS of love, Mom and Dad xxxxxxx

I read it again and again. They are all right. There is an explanation. It is not like them to forget me (I forget things, not them). They have me with them all the time, like a pet. I bet they are enjoying being away from me.

They are not enjoying it. There was a dire emergency. Jacob is very sick. He is probably about to die. He might be dead already. She might not have wanted to say it in a text.

I write 5827 on the inside of my wrist, and I go and find the money and the card and put it all in the middle of the table, where I can look at it.

I write to Drake and tell him that my parents missed their plane, so everything is fine.

Everything is fine for me. My parents are still alive and they are still in France. Everything is not fine for Jacob and it is not fine for Mom and Dad either.

Jacob is my brother, and I have no idea what he is like now, why he went away and never came back. I know that I have looked at every piece of paper in this house, and I still don't know. I cannot even miss him when he dies, because the only memories I have of him are from when I was very small.

But I do miss him. He let me paint his toenails. He picked me up when I was crying. I love him.

I am sad for my parents, sitting at their son's deathbed. No wonder they forgot me.

I wander around, sit in different places, make some tea. All the time I am waiting for Drake's reply. It arrives. Drake is the most dependable thing in my life. I have no idea what I would do without him.

He kissed me on the beach. He gave me a memory. He gave me a stone.

Hey, **he writes.** Have you noticed something? You're living independently. You've been in that house on your own for days. You've been to the police, done some investigating, set up a FB account, and made friends with people mainly named Jacob Banks. You can do anything. You are brave.

I am brave. The thought is intoxicating.

I call Mom's cell. It goes to voicemail and I leave her a message. "Don't come rushing back," I say. "Stay with Jacob because he needs you. I'm all right. Paige and I are fine here. Honestly we are."

The house is beginning to close in, so I put on my shoes and a denim jacket, as it is too warm for the beautiful furry coat that is hanging up with my name written on its label, and walk down to the seafront. The water is huge and splashy, the clouds low and bruised: I can see a storm approaching from the west, from beyond Newlyn. I turn my back on it and walk away, to the Jubilee Pool, where some people are doing laps and others are just splashing around with dry hair.

There are people sitting at the café drinking coffee, some of them eating pastries or sandwiches. I stop to look. I yearn for Drake. I need him to be walking along here holding my hand.

He thinks I can do anything.

He can't come to me because of his studying.

I look at a note on my arm. I HAVE A PASSPORT, it says.

When I get home, there is a message on our answering machine from my mother.

"Darling," she says. "Are you all right? Please call us back again. If you and Paige really are OK, then we will stay a couple more days. But I'm not doing it without speaking to you first. We love you. I so wanted to hear your voice." Her voice cracks at the end and she hangs up abruptly.

I look at my cell and see there is a missed call from her. I cannot believe I missed the chance to talk to her. My eyes fill with tears, and for a moment I want to go to France so I can hug my family.

I want to go to France, but I want to go to Svalbard more.

Drake would meet me at the other end. I have a passport. And no one is here to stop me.

I call my mother back and carefully say all the right things.

Chapter Seven

I take the stone out of my pocket and look at it. I forget everything, but I will not forget the story of this stone. It is small and smooth in my hand.

If I could kiss Drake now, in the Arctic, the kiss would be different. It would be intense and wild. It would not just be a kiss. I imagine it day and night. I would remember it again: I am certain I would. I remembered it once and I would remember it twice. I would remember it three times. I would remember it to infinity.

I tidy the house. I vacuum, even though there is nothing at all to vacuum away. There is rain falling outside, splattering on the windows. I put some music on, the Beatles, something called *Abbey Road*, and I find I like it.

My parents are safe, and they are coming back soon and everything will be normal again, depending on Jacob.

I find pictures of Svalbard on the internet. I stare at the place, the real place, where Drake is.

I look at the pictures on my phone and see that I took a photograph of him at a party. As soon as I find it, I set it as the home screen, and I stare at it for a long time, wondering what it is about his face that makes my cheeks glow pink, my skin tingle all over, and my body start to melt. I look at his dark hair, his prominent cheekbones, his heavy glasses.

He kissed me and made me remember. I remember it all. I remember his smell. I remember the way his lips felt on mine. When I took that picture, I might not have known that we were about to kiss. I took a photo of a missing cat poster too, but I have forgotten to go out looking for the poor missing cat with no ears.

I put my shoes on and step outside, checking that the keys are in my hand before slamming the front door behind me. Then I am running straight down the road toward the sea. I cross the main road, dodging between a couple of cars. I cannot be bothered to wait until there is a break in traffic. They beep and are annoyed, but no one is actually going to run me over. They don't point their cars at me and drive, like they would if I were a cat with no ears.

The tide is halfway out. That flat line of water at the edge of the earth is the edge of my world. I cannot imagine anything beyond it. I can remember a trip to a theme park when I was ten: that is the only sense I have of ever having been away from here.

I look at my left hand. STONE, it says, but I knew that anyway. I run down to the beach. It does not take me long to find a black one. It is not exactly the same as mine but it is close enough: it is smooth and it fits into the palm of my hand. I hold the new stone, the stone for Drake, to my lips and kiss it again and again and again. The warm breeze runs through my hair. A man with a dog looks at me but I don't care.

I walk back home looking at cats, but they all have ears. There are more posters for the missing one. I take more photographs of them.

When I get home, there is an e-mail from Drake. I put the laptop on the kitchen table, his stone beside it, and put the kettle on: I force myself to make a cup of tea before I read it. I jump from one foot to the other as I take out my favorite mug and put a tea bag into it. Together, we can start to make some plans.

When I sit down with my tea and finally allow myself to open the e-mail, I am tingling, ready to devour his words.

Hey Flora,

Look—I'm sorry. If you were here, things would be different, but you're not. We both got carried away and I think we need to cool it off, because this can't work from this distance, and you can't come over here, can you?

I'm happy that you remember our time together. That means the world. Let's leave it at that. Sorry for everything.

Love, Drake

I read it again to check, but it still says the same thing.

I don't know how far away Svalbard is, but I know it must be a long way.

I sit with the two stones together in my hand. I am not going to lose Drake.

My fingers press keys on the laptop. I find a flight, and a place is saved for me on an airplane.

I look up places to stay in Svalbard and book myself into the cheapest one. I book a room for five nights because that will give me time to work it all out and find Drake.

It is easy to do. I pay with a credit card I found in a box on the table, and then I get my passport and double-check it. I cannot believe that it exists. It has my photograph in it. It is valid for another eight years. It feels like magic, but I have to trust that it is real.

Drake said, "You can't come over here, can you?" That is a question, and my reply is: "Actually I can." I'm going to surprise him.

I will put the stone into his hand, and we will kiss and we will go to wherever he lives and talk and kiss some more, and do all the things we have talked about doing together. The world in my head will become my reality. I will start to remember everything.

If you were here, things would be different.

My stomach is in knots thinking about it. I have to go to Drake because he made me remember. I have to go to him because I adore him. His e-mail said that for this to work we need to be together, and we do. He is right.

I write things down as I pack them. There are two pairs of jeans, all my sweaters, some pajamas, and my new fake-fur coat. I add underwear and my toothbrush and some makeup so I can look nice. I find a red T-shirt that looks way too big for me and am about to push it aside when I look at the label and see that I have pinned a note into it that says, THIS IS DRAKE'S T-SHIRT, so I smell it, and remember that smell, and fold it carefully into my suitcase. All my other clothes have my name written on the labels, and I check that everything I am packing belongs to me, not to Mom. I am going to be myself on this trip.

I put in the notes and books I need to remind me of who I am, and write a long message to my future self about where I am going and why and what I need to do when I get there. I read an account I have written about going to Drake's aunt and uncle's house and taking lots of his things. I find all those things and pack every one of them. I pack stones and shells, with a note telling me why.

I print out the e-mails so I can read them wherever I am.

I don't print the one that just arrived.

I write notes of times and flight numbers. I write down my passport number.

I check my e-mails again and again but nothing changes. I type out a text to Paige saying that I'm going away for a while and I like the way the words "I am going away" look on the screen. I met Paige when we were four. She is not my friend anymore. I don't send the text. I delete it.

I leave my parents a note telling them that I am fine. I text them to say that Paige and I are going to the movies.

I pop next door to tell Mrs. Rowe that the house will be empty but that my parents will be home in a few days. Mrs. Rowe has twins who are grown up, and one of her twins has twins too. She gives me some jam but it's moldy. I put it in the cupboard. There are three other jars like it, right there.

• • •

I step out of the house with my suitcase and lock everything behind me. Mrs. Rowe waves to me from her upstairs window, and I wave back.

The suitcase has wheels, and it makes a rumbling noise as I pull it along. Nobody else looks at me. I am doing something momentous, setting off to travel to the Arctic to find the man who has made me remember, and no one knows at all.

I am wearing a cotton dress and a cardigan, leggings and sneakers and the big furry coat that I apparently bought in Penzance on the day I went to Drake's aunt's house, because if I pack it in the suitcase, nothing else will fit. It is ridiculous, but it's the only way I can take it. I am hot and I feel silly, but it is a coat I must have bought for this trip, and the North Pole is cold, so I have to take it.

I walk through the middle of town, past shops and shoppers, and just as I am waiting at the pedestrian crossing at the top of the hill down to the train station, somebody taps me on the shoulder.

I jump and turn around.

"Hey, Flora," she says, and I turn and look into her dark eyes.

"Hi." The green man comes up and I start to cross the road, pulling my case behind me. Paige walks with me. I wish she wouldn't. I pick up my pace.

"Nice coat," she says. "Going somewhere?" She catches up, striding easily alongside me, even though she is shorter than I am. I look at her, trying to figure out how much she hates me.

"I liked the coat, so I bought it."

"Where are you going?"

I cannot tell her the truth. "My parents went to France," I say, "because my brother. Jacob. You know. He lives there, and he's really sick and they went to visit him. They didn't think they'd be away for long, but he's worse than they realized and so they've stayed longer."

"I know that. I know they went to see him. I was going to come and babysit you, but then I didn't because you kissed my boyfriend. Remember? I guess I can stop checking up on you now if you're off to France. Are you going to Paris?"

I want to say "Svalbard," but instead I say: "Yes. I'm going to Paris."

"On your own? Are your parents meeting you?"

"Yes," I say.

"Good. Be safe. Are you sure you can do this?"

"Yes."

Paige looks at me hard for a minute or so, then turns and walks away. Cars are speeding by, taking the corners fast, on their way out of town. I watch her go. She does not look back.

My hands are covered with notes. The word Spitsbergen is clearly written there in black ink, and I wonder whether she knows that that is the name of the island where Drake lives. Of course she does. All the same, I think she believed me about Paris.

I walk behind her, far enough behind for it not to feel as if I am following her. She knows I am there, but she doesn't turn around. I walk into the station, and she carries on past the parking lot.

The train is waiting at the platform that is outside the station building. It is long and scary-looking. I check my sheet of instructions again. I need to get onto this train and stay on it all the way to London Paddington, which is the last stop. That is how my journey will begin. One thing at a time.

Part 2

Chapter Eight

I am looking out the window, and everything is white because all of it, whatever is down there, is covered in snow. I have no real concept of snow. I know that it is white and cold, but I don't know what it looks like up close, or how it feels to touch it, or how it gets there.

I check my hand. FLORA, it says, be brave.

This snow stretches as far as I can see, and it has its own sweeping patterns and swirls and peaks and valleys, all of it perfectly white. Nothing made by humans is anywhere in this landscape apart from the shadow of an airplane, and I am on that airplane, with my nose pressed to the window, looking down.

You should always try to get a window seat, because that way you can tell where you are. I write that down in my notebook and see that it becomes my second rule for life.

I look at the world outside. We must be nearly there, because the snowy wilderness down there is the surface of Spitsbergen, and

Spitsbergen is the biggest island in the archipelago of Svalbard, and this is the island where I am going, and Drake is here, actually here, on this island below me.

I am doing the bravest thing of my life. I have been reading my notes without stopping, so I feel as if, right now, I know what I am doing. I am sitting on a plane, on my way to Svalbard, to find Drake. He said, "You can't come over here, can you?" That is practically an invitation. My answer is "Yes, I can."

I look at the piece of paper that got me onto this plane. It has a date on it, but when I look at it closely, I see it must be wrong. According to this, today is Sunday. That would mean my parents were due back yesterday. I am sure I waited for them for a while. Perhaps I let the time stretch out and become longer than its real self.

Perhaps I panicked and went to the police for no reason at all.

Sometimes I think I see a flicker of movement on the surface of the snow, and think it might be an animal, but I have no sense of scale, so I don't know whether I could make out an animal, or any running thing, from this height.

I have made it to this point (almost to the town of Longyearbyen, almost to Drake). I have done it. I have no idea how I got to the airport in London, but I was suddenly standing there, surrounded by people. I took deep terrified breaths and sat down on the floor and tried to find my mom, but then I read everything and found out that I was on my way to visit Drake at the North Pole. I had no idea how to get there from the big smelly place with no windows, with TV screens, with lots of people brushing past me, to the place where Drake was.

I stood and stared around, and the panic built inside me until I started to cry, but they still all ignored me. I wanted my mom and dad, but they weren't there. I wanted Drake, but he wasn't there either. I had to go to a woman who had the word INFORMATION on a sign above her head, and she made me hand her all the pieces of paper I had, and told me exactly where to go and what to do, and when I went to the right places and showed the right things, I found that I was on an airplane, and it took me to a place called Oslo.

Traveling is exciting, as long as you do exactly as you're told.

There was a moment of panic when I realized I had six hours to wait at Oslo airport: I wanted to ask someone if I could just sit and wait, but when I realized no one cared, I decided I would. That airport was clean and easy to get around, and I bought a Lonely Planet guide to Norway in English, because it had a big section about Svalbard in it, and I sat in cafés for a bit and had strange food with fish and herbs, and a few people spoke to me in Norwegian, but when they realized I didn't speak it, they looked surprised and then went to ask someone else. I bought a bright red lipstick because it was there. I will wear it in Svalbard, because that is the sort of thing a girl with a boyfriend would do.

I have managed, so far. I changed all the money from the box on the table into the right sort of money for Norway, so at the moment I feel I have lots of money, plus a credit card. I have coins now that have holes in the middle of them. You could thread them onto a necklace.

• • •

When I got onto this plane, I was so excited I could hardly click my seat belt into place. This is the plane that will take me to Drake, and I am almost there. I am by the window and the seat next to mine is empty, and I am watching the wild white landscape below me for signs of the town and an airport.

We landed in a place called Tromsø on the way, and that was confusing, because everyone got off the plane and stood on the tarmac in the pale sunshine, and I had no idea what I was meant to do because some people were ending their journeys here and going into the airport and off to their unimaginable Tromsø things. Others were not. I stood with the crowd, looked at the few small planes on the runways, and at the sign saying TROMSØ LUFTHAVN and at the cold sunshine, and I marveled at the bald fact that I had already gotten myself to the actual Arctic. Then I asked a woman what I should do. She told me, and I did it: everyone, she said, had to go through more security inside the airport, and so I did, and it was easy. I stood and waited my turn, showed a man my passport, and went back outside. Soon we were on the plane again, and suddenly everyone looked different.

Drake is right. I am capable of more than I imagined.

All of these people, apart from me, look like people who are going to Svalbard. Many of them are boys who look a little like Drake. They are strong and clever and comfortable. They belong.

Some of them, like Drake, are scientists. I know this because one got on the plane at Tromsø wearing a T-shirt that had the words IT'S SCIENCE, BITCHES written on it, and others greeted him raucously.

None of them have a fake-fur coat stashed, with difficulty,

into the overhead compartment. None of them are wearing a cotton dress and leggings. None of them are nearing the end of a secret journey to meet the great love of their life.

None of them look as if they are chasing the only memory they have managed to hold on to since they had a part of their brain cut out.

I hold the two stones in my hand. I know I'm going to forget very soon. I hope I'm not too scared.

The seat-belt signs click on, and an announcement starts up. It is in Norwegian, but I know it will be saying we are about to land because I can see that the plane is getting lower in the sky, and although I can't see a place yet, I know we must be getting close to one.

I push my face back against the window and look. Drake is out there somewhere, and I am coming from the sky to find him.

"We could spend the night."

"My mom."

My mom is not here now.

This is an enchanted land. It is a fairy-tale place, a place in which a princess can meet a handsome prince. There is snow falling from the sky in fat flakes, landing in my hair, on my coat, all over the road and the buildings and the mountains. It is drifting through the air like feathers. I had no idea snow did that.

I have no idea what time it is.

The sky has clouded over since I was up in its blueness,

staring down at the glittering white, and now there is snow everywhere around me. The snow on the ground is dark gray rather than white, and nothing is quite as it was in my mind. It must be almost nighttime because it feels as if it is getting dark.

There are mountains on all sides of me, covered in snow. The town seemed to be small as the airport bus drove me through it, and I am now standing at its very edge. The mountains reach up, disappearing in the snow clouds, and the island stretches away. I have come to the top of the planet, the end of the earth, to find the man I love, the man who makes me remember. I am here. I remind myself of it, again and again. I take a pen, push up my sleeve a little way, and write it on my wrist: I am in Svalbard.

I underline it three times.

A figure is walking up the road, toward me, through the snow. Details come into focus as it comes closer. I stare, hardly daring to hope. I see that it is a man, that he is wearing a big weatherproof jacket like everyone else here, and clumpy snow boots. He has a wooly hat on.

He could be Drake.

He really could be Drake.

I must have told him I'm coming after all, and forgotten. He has come to find me. I smile, and my smile turns into a laugh. I start to walk toward him, and then I break into a run. I will run into his arms. This is the end of my journey.

This is it: I came to the magical snowy place, and I have found my happy ending. It has happened. I made it happen. I have done a brave thing and it worked. I must always be brave. This should definitely be one of my rules.

We will talk and laugh together. He will see that he has cured me. Before I kissed him, I would never have been able to get myself on trains and planes. Now we will go wherever he lives.

I am way too close to this person when I stop and look at the man's face. I realize that no amount of wishing could make this man be Drake. He has red cheeks and light blue eyes.

"Sorry," I say, forcing myself not to look away and running my fingers through my hair, which is wet with melted snow. "I thought you were . . ." My voice trails off. I cannot even say the word.

"That's OK."

This man, the one talking to me, looks nothing like Drake. He is older, fatter, and he is not even wearing glasses.

"Sorry I am not who you expected. Is everything OK?"

He is walking toward a one-story building behind me, talking to me over his shoulder. I run a little to catch up.

"Yes. I think so."

"Staying here? You just arrived?"

"Yes." It said in my book that I was going to stay here. I hope it was right. If this is right and they have a room saved for me, I will be wildly impressed with myself. I will be astonished. I will be capable of anything.

"Have you checked in?"

"No." I follow him inside the building and through a large hallway in which he sits down and starts taking off his snow boots. I do the same, though as I am wearing a horrible old pair of sneakers, I kick them off quickly while he takes much longer. The building is warm and comfortable on the inside, boxy on the outside. The man walks behind a reception desk and smiles at me.

"Welcome to the Arctic Guesthouse," he says. He taps some keys on his computer. "Miss Banks, yes?"

"Yes!" I agree. It worked! I am brilliant. I can make things happen. No one did that for me. I did it myself.

He pushes a little key on a plastic key ring across the desk. There are leaflets everywhere, signs offering excursions, suggestions of things to do here. I see the words HUSKY-DRAWN SLEIGH, BOAT TRIP, KAYAKS, CROSS-COUNTRY SKIING. It is too much. All I want is Drake.

"You are booked for five nights?" he says. "Could I have your credit card, please?"

I pass it to him. I am pleased that he said I have booked five nights. It will be too many, but it was sensible of me because I don't know when I will find Drake or when my parents will be coming back. Now they are in Paris. Jacob is going to die.

That fact fills my head. I push it away. Not now.

"I might not stay the whole five nights. My boyfriend . . ." I pause to let the word drift deliciously through the air. "Is studying here. I'm going to meet him. But anyway, I'll pay for the five nights, of course."

Drake is my boyfriend. I kissed him on the beach.

"Your boyfriend?" He nods. "I should have known. Is he at UNIS?"

"If that's where people study . . ." I look at the man's face. "Yes. He goes to a science place with satellite things. Do you know him? His name is Drake Andreasson."

"Drake Andreasson. No, I don't think so. Has he been here long?"

"Um." My sense of time slips away. I have no idea how long he has been here. "I don't know. Not long."

"Ah, well, that is why. People come and go all the time. Where is he living? At Nybyen?"

I do not have his address. "In a flat," I say firmly, and I pick up the key the man gave me and then carefully type in the four numbers from the inside of my wrist when he hands me the little keypad. They are the only numbers I have to use, and it turns out that they work.

"And he didn't come to the airport to meet you? You're not staying with him? If he has a flat, that would be easy, no?"

I cannot think of any answer but the truth.

"He doesn't know I'm coming," I tell him. The man nods and looks into my face.

"You'll be OK, I hope," he says. "Spitsbergen is very safe. Come right here and tell us if you have any problems. Yes? I will tell my colleagues. We can all help you if you need it."

"Yes, but I won't," I say.

"Of course. But if you do . . ."

He tells me I have to go outside again and cross the road to building five, and climb the stairs to the first floor, where I will find my bedroom, which is bedroom number five. Since they are both numbered five, it should be easy to remember. If anything would be easy for me to remember, this would be it. I don't write the big five on my arm in front of him, because I want him to think I'm normal.

"Good luck," he says. "Breakfast is in here, starting at seven thirty."

I put my sneakers back on and step out into the snow, exhilarated.

Chapter Nine

I am standing at a window, and outside it there is a snowy mountain. Snow is falling out there, tiny flakes drifting sideways past the window, blown by the wind. When I look straight out, there is nothing but white mountainside dotted with black where rocks poke through. When I move sideways and look diagonally, I see the mountain slope downward, an expanse of gray sky, another mountain beginning to slope up. There are wooden poles sticking out of the ground, and everything else is mountain.

This is not the view from my bedroom window. I should be looking at treetops. There should be a park. This is not my room. This room is small, with two beds, a desk, and a window. It is not a room I know. My bedroom is pink. Here, the beds have white sheets and nothing is pink. There is a row of stones in size order on the desk.

I look at my hand and my arm. The word *Svalbard* is written several times. Drake said "Svalbard" on the beach. He was going to Svalbard. His course is taught in English, which is lucky for him because he's shitty at languages. There are some numbers on my wrist: 5827. Underneath them it says: I am in Svalbard. The word Drake appears several times.

Drake lives in Svalbard now. "It's going to be amazing." That's what he said about it. "Cold. I've been once before. Like, a long time ago. We went on vacation to Svalbard to see the midnight sun."

There is a suitcase on one of the beds, and a huge fur coat that has my name on its label. I look through the bag and find other things that are mine. I take out a guidebook to Norway and lots of warm clothes, and a red T-shirt that is way too big. At last I find a notebook with a sticker on the front that says:

FLORA'S STORY. READ THIS IF YOU FEEL CONFUSED.

I open it to the first page. *You are Flora Banks*, it says, probably in Mom's handwriting.

You are ~~16~~ 17 years old and you live in Penzance in Cornwall. When you were ten, doctors discovered a tumor growing in your brain, and when you were eleven, they removed it. Part of your memory went with it. You can still remember how to do things (how to make a cup of tea, how to work the shower), and you can remember your life before the illness, but since it happened you have not been able to make new memories.

121

You have ANTEROGRADE AMNESIA. You are good at keeping things in your head for a couple of hours (sometimes less), and then you forget them. When you forget them, you feel confused. This is OK: it is normal for you.

Then a lot of things are crossed out and impossible to read. There are new things written overtop, in my handwriting:

You have a boyfriend, Drake. You kissed him on the beach and he made you remember. You are going to Svalbard to find him, because that is where he lives, and going to Svalbard will fix your memory problems. You can do more things than anyone but Drake has ever believed you could do. He is your magical future. When you get to Svalbard, all you have to do is find him and everything will be happy. You're going to travel on an airplane.

You are pretty sure that Jacob is going to die. He is very sick in France and your parents are with him. You keep forgetting that he's sick and so it makes you sad every time you remember. There is nothing you can do about it except keep out of the way so your parents can concentrate on him. You have to find Drake very quickly, before your parents realize you've left home.

Your brother is sick and is probably going to die, and you will miss him even though you only knew him when you were small. Your parents do not know that you are here. When you find Drake, your mind will work again.

I came here on an airplane: that fact takes my breath away. I love Drake and he loves me. I read through the printouts of our e-mail correspondence, which are all tucked into my notebook, and I find myself crying uncontrollably with love and sadness. Jacob is very sick. I love Jacob. I came here to find Drake. I love Drake. Drake asked me to come.

This might be the first time I have ever slept in a room that is not my pink bedroom in Penzance. That room is safe. I miss it with a sudden pang. That room was safe and this one is strange. I have gotten myself to the Arctic. That explains the snowy mountain outside the window.

It is broad daylight, and I have no idea what time it is. I look at my phone. It claims that it is 12:30 a.m., but I don't believe that. If it was after midnight, it would be dark. The words "midnight sun" come into my head. Perhaps I am looking at the midnight sun. That idea is thrilling beyond belief.

There is a text from Mom.

All OK at home? Tried to call the landline but no answer. Busy here but we are trying to get home tomorrow. xx

I type, I seem to be in the Arctic!!!, then stare at the words, knowing that they are wrong. I delete them and write instead:

Yes, all absolutely fine thanks! Don't worry. Hope you are all OK. Love xx

I send it, then worry that it sounds odd. However, I am odd. That text is probably normal for me.

Mom texts back at once. Have you taken your pills?

Yes, I tell her firmly.

I look around but can't see any pills. It is best, I decide, if I find Drake first, and worry about that later.

People are talking outside my room. It is not English, but I like the sound of their words. They have a nice rhythm.

I open the door and find two men in the corridor. They both nod to me and say hi, and continue their conversation. One is wearing a blue T-shirt and baggy shorts, the other a pair of loose trousers and a vest.

They don't seem to find me weird in the slightest.

"Hi," I say back. "Is there a bathroom?"

"Down there," says the one in shorts. His hair is black and glossy and he has friendly eyes. "On the right."

"On the right," I echo. There are many doors on the right. I will just try some until I find the right one.

"All four doors," says the other man. "All are bathrooms, but not all will work."

"Usually only two are working at any time," says his friend. "Different reasons. It rotates."

I have no idea what these people are talking about.

"It rotates?"

"Sometimes one is working, sometimes another. A lightbulb, a defective lock. You know."

"Oh. Thanks." I should brush my teeth and things like that. In fact, I should shower. I bet I haven't showered in ages.

When I reemerge from my bedroom clutching my toiletries and towel and with ROOM 5 written up my arm in waterproof marker, the dark-haired man has gone. Farther along the corridor people have put sleds, packed with brightly colored things, outside their doors. In fact, almost every room but mine has a sled outside it. I wonder whether I should have one too. I jump up and down in excitement (on the inside) at the prospect of sledding. It never snows in Penzance.

Then I remember that I kissed a boy. I am seventeen. I am probably too old to be excited about sledding.

"Do I need one of those?" I ask the fair-haired man, pointing. He laughs.

"Not unless you plan to come on our expedition tomorrow. I'm sure we could make room."

"What's your expedition?"

"Arctic guides. We are training to be Arctic wilderness guides. Tomorrow we go out camping for three nights."

I know I should be impressed, and I hope that I look it, because I cannot imagine what being an Arctic wilderness guide would involve and how brave and cold you would have to be.

"What time is it?" I ask him. "Do you know?"

He shrugs. "One, I think? It's hard to go to bed here, isn't it?"

"One in the morning?"

"Yes."

"Really?"

"You're British?"

"Yes," I say. "I live in Penzance. Where are you from?"

"Me? From Norway. Most of us on the course are. But we all speak English, of course. We study in English."

"Have you met a boy named Drake since you've been here?" I say. "He speaks English. His course is taught in English, which is lucky for him because he's shitty at languages."

He shrugs. "No, not that I know of. Who is he?"

"My boyfriend." I smile. "I've come here to find him."

The first bathroom I try has a door that does not lock. The second is locked, with scented steam puffing out around its edges. The third has a light that does not work, and as it has no window, that makes it impossible to use. I am relieved to claim the last bathroom in the row. Its light works, its door locks, and when I turn the shower on, it is quickly hot. I wash away the dirt that has accumulated since whenever it was that I last did something like this, being sure to leave traces of the ROOM 5 and the I am in Svalbard and the 5827 written on my arm. I shampoo my hair and wonder how on earth I managed to get here. I have been to other places, I think. I have been to France. I have been in a shower in France.

No, my parents are in France. Not me. I have only been in showers in Penzance, until this one.

I put on my pink pajamas and wrap a towel around my wet hair. Back in my room I stare at the snow. It is definitely not dark outside.

I am here to find Drake. I put his name into my phone to see what happens and discover that I have a phone number saved under Drake / Paige. The last text I sent that number says: I miss you. I think it's Friday. The one before that says: hi, it's paige on drake's phone. dropped mine. we're in lamp and whistle. come soon?

I replied to that one saying: Will come in 20 mins.

I don't like any of that, and so I delete it all.

Hello Drake. Could you text me your address? I write to the number, instead. Or e-mail it? I have something I'd like to send you. Flora xx.

I want to find him and let him see me, standing in the snow. I want us to walk down a long road, toward each other, and I want us to recognize each other gradually as we get closer. I picture us running toward each other, speeding up as we hurtle toward each other's arms.

I press the button, and the text goes straight to his phone. I spend some time figuring out how to access my e-mails, but in the end I think I have it working. When Drake replies, by text or by e-mail, I will get it right away.

It is still light, but it has stopped snowing. The snow is glistening: the sun must be out, though I cannot see it. I could go for a walk, though I am a little tired.

I check the time again. My phone now tells me it is three in the morning.

I listen. Nothing is happening along my corridor. Nobody is talking anymore. The Arctic wilderness guides are now quiet.

It is broad daylight. I remember Drake saying: "We went on vacation to Svalbard to see the midnight sun. I was ten and I've wanted to live there ever since." This is it. This must be the midnight sun.

I am not tired. I am tired. I have no idea. I don't want to sleep. I have to sleep. My hair dried a long time ago. Tomorrow I must find Drake. If all else fails, I will ask around until I find out where the satellite place is, and I will go there and sit next to a satellite until he arrives.

I want to go to Flambards.

That is a stupid thought. I am in the Arctic.

With a supreme effort, I walk to the window. All I want to do is sit here and wait until people start getting up. However, it is night, and so I need to go to sleep. I have to sleep at night, or everything will be wrong and I will be too tired to find Drake.

I reach out and pull the cord that lowers the blinds. Light still comes in around the edges, but it is dark enough, and soon I am on the bed and my eyes are closing.

Chapter Ten

There are people shouting. I have no idea how they got into our house. I keep my eyes tightly closed. Mom and Dad will make them go away. I will stay here and wait for it to go quiet.

Things scrape. Feet stamp. Doors bang. Things rustle and move and I don't know what any of it is.

I open my eyes. I am lying on my back, staring at a strange ceiling, and I try for a long, long time to stay calm. I am seventeen and I kissed a boy on a beach.

Sunlight is streaming around the edges of the blinds. It is daytime. I am in a narrow single bed and I am wearing a pair of pink pajamas that I know are mine. They are the only familiar thing. I have woken in a strange new world.

I reach for my notebook.

Then I am on my feet. This is Svalbard. It is scary but that doesn't matter, because today I am going to surprise Drake. I have to find him immediately because my parents will notice that I'm miss-ing. I have come here on my own, and I am here now, and starving, and breakfast, according to my notes, is sometime around now. My phone says it is eight thirty and that seems like the right sort of time to have breakfast. I will have breakfast, and then I will find my boyfriend. After that I will start to remember everything.

I get up and open the blinds. The air outside is glittering with cold, because I am in the Arctic—the actual Arctic—and when I look sideways, I can see deep blue sky. Everything is shiny and clean and I am filled with an energy that makes me want to dance and sing.

Soon I am wearing jeans and a T-shirt and a sweater and thick socks. I am not going to bother to put on that huge coat to cross the road to the other building. I will save it for when I go out and find the love of my life.

Drake will love my coat. I cannot wait for him to see it. I wasn't wearing it when I kissed him on the beach. I was wearing a white dress and yellow shoes.

I can see on my phone that I sent him a text. I can see that he has not replied. Not yet. I write a careful text to Mom and say: All is fine here in Penzance! Love from Flora and Paige xx. That sounds right, I think.

There are a few boys locking their doors and shouting to one another. One of them says, "Good morning," to me as he passes my door and takes the stairs at least two at a time, yelling, "Wait for me, folks!"

The other building is clattering with breakfast. I take off my sneakers because a sign tells me to, shivering because that walk was short but very, very cold. I look through the window to the breakfast place at the end of the big room, where hearty, confident people are eating in a hearty, confident way. I try to fix a hearty, confident expression onto my face so I blend in, then I walk through, in my socks, to join them.

I want to sit with people so I can feel normal. However, no one else is alone, and nobody looks up at me, and so I put my bag at an empty table and go get some food.

This is a weird breakfast, but all the same I think I could eat all of it twice. There is dark brown bread, and there are slices of fish and cheese. There are a few vegetables, and something in a red, yellow, and green striped wrapper called KVIKK LUNSJ that I take because I want to know what it is. It has a line drawing of a hardy-looking man in a bobble hat on the back, so it must be something good.

I manage, with much fumbling, to extract what I think is coffee from a dispenser, and only spill a little bit. I pour a glass of juice, and when I see some cereal, I take a bowl of that too and put milk and yogurt and canned fruit on top. It takes me a while to figure out what is milk and what is some strange kind of gloopy yogurt that comes out of a container that looks as if it should have milk in it, but I do OK in the end. I feel as if I haven't eaten for a long time, so I am determined to eat my fill while there is free food right here.

Nobody looks at me. I sit down and start off with a sip of watery coffee and stare at my phone. There is no text. I open up my e-mails. Every part of me is craving Drake.

I have almost finished the cereal when I realize somebody is standing opposite me.

"May I?" she says, nodding at the seat. I am pleased, so I nod back, and she puts her stuff on it and goes to get some breakfast. She has obviously been here before: she comes back with a plate of dark bread and smoked fish and cucumber and egg, with black coffee and orange juice, in a matter of seconds.

She has frizzy hair and little round glasses and is dressed for the outdoors. Everyone but me is dressed for the outdoors. I am the only one who is wearing bad jeans that her mother bought her.

"Hi," the girl says, in English. "I am Agi."

"I'm Flora," I tell her. She slices a hard-boiled egg and layers it over her fish.

"From England?" she asks. "Australia maybe?"

"England. You're Norwegian?"

"No, no. I am from Finland. Close but no cigar." She looks at me. "This is right? 'Close but no cigar'? This works in context?"

"Umm," I say, though I don't understand. "Maybe. Yes."

"Good. So, you are on Spitsbergen alone? Why is this? Me too, you see, and there are not so many of us. And you, I think, are very young."

"I'm here to visit someone." I check my hand. I am in Svalbard. It feels like a dream, but I really am here.

"Oh, so you are not properly alone. Oh."

"Well, I am really," I say.

Agi looks so dejected that I want to cheer her up.

"You see, I didn't tell him I was coming. This morning I'm going to go out and find him. I have to find him today."

Her eyes are big with exaggerated surprise. "You came all this way as a surprise? And now you do not know where to find this boy?"

Agi, I notice, has beautiful creamy skin. It is like Paige's skin. Paige and I met when we were four, on the first day of school. Paige isn't my friend anymore: I read that in my book and I keep thinking about it. Paige is not my friend. Jacob is very sick. My parents think I'm in Penzance. Drake is my boyfriend. I must find him right now. There are a lot of things to try to remember.

"That's right," I say. "Anyway, what about you?"

I am attempting to act normal, and I think I am getting away with it. This is beyond thrilling.

"Oh, you know, I love to travel on my own. I write a blog, but as it is in my own language, it has not so many readers. For this reason I wish to improve my English until I will be able to write in the world language and gain many international followers."

I am not sure what a blog is.

"Do you write about travel?" I say carefully.

"Yes! It is a travel blog! That is why I am here, of course. I travel alone and I write my adventures. 'Adventures of a Chick on the Road,' I call it. Maybe it will need a different title in English. Today I go on a tour on a minibus because I wish to see everything that can be reached in Longyearbyen by road. The roads go only around the town. Nowhere else because there is no place to drive to. So I will see the global seed vault, the little church, the old mines. The *whole shebang.*"

Agi looks at me questioningly. I am not really the best person to tell her whether her phrases work, but I like that she is talking to me, so I nod.

"Well," I say. "That sounds good. I would go too, but I'm going to go and find Drake today. It has to be today. I kissed him on the beach. I fell completely in love with him. I'm going to find him and I love him. All I want from the whole of the rest of my life is to be with him. So I'm going to find him and maybe I won't go home. Maybe I'll stay here, with him, forever."

I stop and take a breath. That did not come out sounding rational. It was not normal. I wish I hadn't said any of it.

Agi is eating her breakfast and watching me. She looks at my face for a long time. She looks at my hands, at the FLORA, be brave and the I am in Svalbard and the other words and numbers. She chews a mouthful of bread and fish. I look down at my name on the back of my hand too, feeling silly.

"Wow," she says when, eventually, she swallows. "You are an interesting girl. You like this boy, then."

"I love him."

"So you will do what?"

"I suppose," I tell her, "that I'll walk into the town and ask people about him. I'll find out where he lives."

"His name?"

"Drake. Drake Andreasson. He's nineteen."

"Drake Andreasson. Teenage Drake Andreasson. I will ask too. I will ask on the minibus tour. Where is his study?"

I shrug. "Here."

"If you don't find him, I will perhaps see you back here tonight."

"I have to find him. I have to find him today."

"I hope you find him. This is a romantic story. You must find him today, so you *will* find him today."

"Yes."

"He will be pleased to see you."

I pick up my phone and look at it again. I am connected to Wi-Fi, but there is no e-mail. Some boring e-mails have downloaded themselves, but not the one I want.

Agi drinks the last of her coffee and stands up, with her tray.

"Have a super-duper day, Flora," she says.

"Thanks," I say. "You too."

"See you later, alligator?"

I know there is a proper reply to this, but I can't remember what it is, so I just nod.

The guesthouse is at the edge of the town. I know I should be scared and confused, but I am not. I am about to see Drake. He makes me remember.

In my room I write Agi's name on my hand, and in my notebook I write: Look for Agi at the hotel this evening if I am there. Though I am sure I will not be, it is good to remember that I have a new friend.

I put on the big coat and my sneakers, and I bring all my money with me, because in addition to finding Drake, I am going to buy a pair of boots like the ones everyone else wears. I might, after all, be staying here forever. Drake has said that he loves me and he asked me to come here. I should probably live here with him. I will have lots of memories then, and be like a normal person, and that new life is going to start today.

I have my room key, and the word key on my hand to remind me to keep checking it. I am carrying my little bag, and it has my notebook in it.

• • •

The sky is deeply blue without a single cloud. Longyearbyen, which is the name of this town, is in a valley, with mountains on either side and an expanse of water, also backed by mountains, straight ahead. There are mountains all around. They are snowy, but the snow is not thick, and the landscape is full of black rock poking through.

"It's going to be amazing," Drake said. "Cold. I've been once before. Like, a long time ago. We went on vacation to Svalbard to see the midnight sun. I was ten and I've wanted to live there ever since. It's going to be epic."

It *is* epic. It is huge and breathtaking. The air is cold and clear. Breathing here feels different from breathing at home. The air polishes my lungs. Every step I take makes me giddy. This is me, Flora Banks, walking down a road in the Arctic. Each step I take is a triumph.

I have looked at the map and worked out the way I'm going to go. I am going to go to the place where Drake must be, and find him, and I have to do it this morning because no one knows I am here and soon they will start to look for me.

It seems so weird that this is not even scary. It could be a different universe. It's so different from anything else that is in my head that I push away all my worry and fear. I know that Jacob is sick, but I can't do anything because I'm in the Arctic. Nothing matters right now, aside from finding Drake.

I walk faster and faster, already too hot in my fur coat. I love feeling the muscles in my legs as they take me to my boyfriend. I love the way my face tingles as the cold from the outside and the heat from the inside meet each other. I know there is going to be an art gallery on the left, and there is one, just as the guidebook said. I want to go into it, and I put it on the constantly shifting, vanishing, and re-forming list of things I would like to do with Drake. I would like to see Spitsbergen with him. I would like to walk around hand in hand. I would like to go to his apartment with him and get into bed and hug him and kiss him and be with him.

I cannot wait to see his face when he discovers I am here.

I walk past a school, a few other buildings, and a road that goes off to the left where there are other buildings, including a little church. I look around in case Drake might live over there, but there is no sign of houses. I keep going. Metal pipes that look old but important run alongside the road. A road sign shows a silhouette of a man in a stylish hat, perhaps as a warning to cars, though there are only a few cars here.

I don't know how they got here. The roads in Longyearbyen go nowhere, that woman said. The woman I was just talking to. I check my hand: Agi. Agi said that. They take you to things in and just outside Longyearbyen, but they don't go anywhere else because this town is surrounded by Arctic wilderness. There is nowhere to drive to when the town's roads run out. Cars must come from somewhere else, and so must gas, and in fact so must everything.

It takes me twenty minutes to get to town. Even I cannot get lost when there is only one road.

I walk into a shop that sells things to wear in cold weather.

The walls and floor are wooden and it is so warm that I want to take off my coat, but I can't because I would have to carry it and that would be annoying.

I check my phone again. I have full reception, but nothing has happened. I call Mom's cell, but it goes straight to voicemail and I leave her the right sort of message.

A woman with rosy cheeks comes over to me and says something in a language I don't understand. I say I'm looking for a pair of boots to wear, and then wonder whether she understands. She immediately starts to show me things.

"The three Ws," she says, slipping easily into English. "That's what you need."

"The three Ws?"

"Wool, windproof, and waterproof," she says. "That is the Arctic way. Though in the summer, not so much, and if you're not going off hiking, then also not so much."

"I like these ones." I point at a pair of brown boots with furry linings and laces all the way up. She examines my feet, then goes off to look for the boots in the right size, and I sit down and open my e-mail. I don't care about the three Ws: I just want something better than sneakers.

I have written, very small, on my wrist: Drake said, "If you were here, things would be different." And: "You can't come over here, can you?"

I speak those words aloud. I can come here. Yes. I can.

As I am paying cash for the boots, which fit me perfectly, I say to the woman, "Do you know a boy named Drake Andreasson?"

She looks hard at me for a second. "Drake?" she says.

"He studies at the North Pole. There's a satellite thing."

"A satellite thing? Try asking at UNIS or the Polar Institute. I think they would know."

"Thanks. Can I wear the boots now?"

"Of course, my dear. Let me give you a bag for your sneakers."

I lace up my boots, put my old shoes in the bag the woman gave me, and set off in search of the Polar Institute. I type the words into my phone as I go and reach for a pen to write it on my arm too. This is better than wandering around hoping to run into Drake. This is how I will find him.

Chapter Eleven

I am sitting on a rock, and there is snow around me in patches, with black stones poking through. I seem to be wearing a big fur coat and a pair of warm boots, and jeans, and probably, if I opened my coat, I would find that I have a sweater on underneath.

So I am warmly dressed, and sitting on a rock, and looking at a hillside that is stretching out in front of me, covered in snow. There is nobody around. The air is cold on my cheeks. The sun is bright in a deep blue sky.

I live in a warm place where there is the sea, and where things are green. This is somewhere different. This place is cold and clear. It cannot be real. I do not worry at all about where I am, because I know I am inside my head. It is magical here and I don't want to wake up.

I sat on a beach and kissed Drake. That was real. This is not.

I look at my hands. One of them says FLORA, be brave. I am Flora.

My left hand bears the words: looking for Drake. On the inside of my wrist it says 5827 and I am in Svalbard. The words Polar Institute? are on my arm, and it says Arctic, and it says notebook and Agi and things about a passport.

There is a notebook on my lap. I open it and start to read. It tells me that I have anterograde amnesia and that Drake is my magical future.

I flip to the last pages with writing on them.

Do NOT leave town, because polar bears live there and they eat people. If you leave town, you have to have a gun and know how to use it, and that means I AM ONLY ALLOWED TO LEAVE THE TOWN IF I'M WITH SOMEONE ELSE WHO HAS A GUN. DO NOT HEAD OUT OF TOWN EVEN IF IT LOOKS PRETTY. ALWAYS BE IN A PLACE WITH BUILDINGS.

I scan the hillside in front of me. There are no buildings. There is a rocky path leading up something that looks to me like a mountain. There is a second path across the snow made of parallel lines, but there is definitely no town. I am sitting on a big black rock.

I leap to my feet.

I have broken a rule I don't remember learning, and even though this is a dream, I don't want to be eaten by polar bears in it. Polar bears are white: the snow around me is also white. There could be hundreds of them, camouflaged, all around. They could be about to pounce, to tear me limb from limb, to share me so everyone gets a piece and the winner runs off with my broken brain between his jaws.

I need to get to a safe place. The sun is shining into my eyes. I have no idea how to get to where the buildings are. I could walk all day and be farther and farther into the bears' territory. If I think hard about buildings, perhaps I could make them appear.

My heart is beating so fast that my whole body drums in time to it. I stand up, even though my legs are wobbling so much that I can hardly support myself.

I kissed Drake and I need to find him.

Instead of finding him, I have come to a place in which the first rule is "Don't leave town without a gun," and I have left town without a gun. I have come to feed the polar bears some fresh human meat. I could be ten miles from town—whatever the town is. I don't feel hungry or thirsty, so I might not have been out here for long. I turn on the spot, scanning the area, ready to figure out the most likely path back to safety.

Then I stop. I turn back to the hillside, which looks snowy and remote. I turn back the other way again, and laugh. I laugh and laugh, loudly, uncontrollably, and I cannot stop. I am the most stupid human being who has ever lived.

I was sitting on a big black rock looking at the mountain, in a still, cold place where polar bears live. But the rock was beside the road, and the road was in a town, and the only reason I didn't hear anything going on behind me was because there aren't any cars going past. As soon as I turn around, I see that I was sitting beside houses and roads and wonderful signs that this is a place of humans, and not a place of bears.

My journey to town takes five paces. I made the buildings appear by thinking about them, because all of this is inside my head.

Do not stray into polar bears' territory. That is now one of my rules for life. I stop and write it into my book.

I pick a direction and walk along the road. There are two stones in my pocket, and I hold them both in my hand as I walk. They are special stones. One is mine and the other is about to be Drake's. We kissed on the beach, as the tide crept up. I am going to find him and we are going to kiss again, in the snow. We are going to kiss again and again, and I am going to remember every single kiss. Even though I do not remember most of the things in my notebook.

The people I pass are all wearing nylon jackets, rather than big fur coats like me. They have ruddy rosy cheeks and they smile and say hi, so I do the same to them. This seems to be the way it works in this place, which is nowhere near Penzance because it's the town of Longyearbyen, on the island of Spitsbergen, in the archipelago of Svalbard, surrounded by the Arctic Sea. That list of difficult names makes me triumphant.

My parents don't know that I have left. If they come home and find I'm not there, they will call the police, and then I will be taken home without ever seeing Drake again.

I find my way to the Polar Institute by looking at my map and asking a nice man, but it is locked. I look at the doors for a while before I decide to walk up and push and pull them. They move a little bit, but they definitely don't open. I have no idea what day or what time it is, so it might or might not be the right time for it to be closed. The museum next door is open, but the university place is shut.

I stand and stare at those doors. I need them to open. This is the place where Drake studies, and I have come all the way to the door, but he is not here. I look through my bag and take my notebook out so I can write this down. I sit on a step.

A woman is standing a little ways off, looking at me.

"Is this the university?" I call over to her. She looks as if she might be a student.

She frowns, so I say it again, and then I remember to say, "Do you speak English?" too.

"I try," she says. She has long black hair and a grumpy face. "This is the Norsk Polarinstitutt, yes. UNIS is the university, just over there."

I follow her finger and see that she is pointing to another part of the same building. None of the buildings here are very pretty, but I like them because I am as sure as I can possibly be that Drake works inside them.

"Do you know Drake Andreasson?"

She shrugs. "Maybe. I don't know. You're looking for him?"

"Yes."

"He's a student here? Have you been to Nybyen?"

I frown. "I don't think so. What is Nybyen?"

"University accommodations."

I decide to write that down too. My phone makes a text noise from inside my bag, and by the time I have taken it out, the woman is gone.

The sun shines brightly on my face. A few people wander by. The horizon is a line of mountains. The sun is high in the sky, and although there are some clouds catching on the tops of the hills, the sky is mainly deep blue.

This is not a real place. It cannot be a real place. The people do not look normal. Nothing is how I think it should be; and Drake is not here. I know what Drake looks like, and none of these people are him.

I stare at the picture of him on my phone before I look at the texts.

When I see the word Mom I am happy, but her message is confusing.

Darling, your messages made me smile, and we needed that. I hope you and Paige are OK. We are still here. Are you all right? Please keep texting us. The whole thing with Jacob is awful. Perhaps you could come to Paris? Would Paige bring you? I'll call later to make a plan. Mom and Dad xxxxxxx
Paris. Jacob.

I check through my notebook. Jacob is in Paris and he is very sick. My parents are with him and I am pretending to be with Paige in Penzance.

I live in Penzance. I will always live in Penzance, but today I am not in Penzance. Today I am in the Arctic, and I got here by myself.

My remembering Jacob brings him into my phone: when I look at my e-mails, the words Jacob Banks jump out of it and punch me in the face.

He has, somehow, sent me an e-mail.

Dear Flora,

Thanks for the card, which my Jacques brought me. Luckily our parents didn't see it—envelope next time please! My little sister. You introduced yourself so formally with no idea that we know each other—that gets me every single time. Are you OK? You sound very worried about Mom and Dad not coming home—my fault. Sorry. I was whisked away with an emergency when they were trying to leave. Don't worry. They're fine. You're in Penzance with your friend? Or are you? Is it all going as planned, or have you dashed off for an adventure? If you're having an adventure that doesn't involve coming to see me, I will be HIGHLY offended. It's you I need, to keep me entertained through this tiresome illness. Take care of yourself. Please reply as soon as you can. Ask me all the questions, like you always do.

Your brother, Jacob xx

I read it again and again. Things do not make sense. There are always things that do not make sense.

You introduced yourself so formally with no idea that we know each other . . . have you dashed off for an adventure?

I look around, almost expecting to see him standing there,

laughing at me. We knew each other when we were young. We don't know each other anymore.

I am only briefly surprised by the fact that I am in a snowy landscape with bright glittery air and a jagged horizon of mountains. I have gone off for an adventure, like Jacob said. I don't know how he knew that. I can't have done it before. I have never left Penzance. I decide to find somewhere warm to sit, and to attempt to write a sensible reply to my brother. I love Jacob. He let me paint his toenails once. He told me to ask him questions, and so I will. I have a lot of questions.

I feel the stones in my pocket as I walk. They clink together. I scan every face I pass, but none of them belongs to Drake.

Chapter Twelve

The room has a cream carpet, and I am sitting on it, staring at it, picking at it with my fingers. There is a smell of food cooking, but I don't like the smell and I'm not hungry. There are sparkly bits in the carpet, as if glitter had been spilled here. I reach down to try to pick up the pieces, but I can't. The frustration of it makes me cry.

I am crying and crying. My whole body is racked with sobs. I have no idea what I am doing trying to pick pieces of glitter out of the carpet. I don't know why I want them.

Someone comes into the room and looks down at me on the floor and laughs, and then I am swinging through the air.

A person is holding me. I look at his face, and I know that this is my brother, Jacob.

He says: "What's the matter, you silly thing?" and I point down at the carpet and try to say "glittery," before I realize that this is not a baffling thing happening to me, but a memory.

I have woken up inside one of my own memories. I can smell the smells and hear the sounds. I can touch Jacob's hair and feel its texture. I am really here. Yet I know I am not. I am inside something that must be buried in my head. I am layers deep in my own brain.

I am trapped inside a tiny dark space. I can't move. My ears are ringing. I screw my eyes tight shut and try to make that one go away. I do not want it.

My heart pounds as I force myself back into the present. I am seventeen, and I am in a café that is warm and steamy, sitting at a table, and a man is standing in front of me, looking as if he's waiting for me to say something.

"I want to go to Flambards."

"Excuse me?" he says.

That is not the right thought. I push it away.

The other people here have healthy complexions and little chubby children, and they are all talking loudly and laughing. I shrink away from them, and focus only on the man.

"A coffee?" I try, because that feels like the sort of thing he is expecting me to say. "With milk? Please?"

"Sure thing," he says. He has a brown spot on the side of his face, and hair that points up, and a beard that points down. "Anything else?"

I consider whether I might be hungry.

"No," I say. "No, thanks." I look at my hand. FLORA, be bRave. I am in Svalbard. "Just one question?"

"Yes?"

"Am I in Svalbard?" Drake is in Svalbard. He went when he was ten for the midnight sun, and now he's nineteen and he has the chance to go back.

The man laughs. "Yes, you are! This is Svalbard. You are indeed in Svalbard."

"Do you know my friend?"

I take out my phone and show him a photograph of Drake. He is standing on a chair, wearing his glasses, the fringe of his hair slightly flopping into his face. He is wearing a blue shirt and jeans. I have no idea when or where I took it, but I know it is Drake because I kissed him on a beach and I remember him.

I stare at it for a second before I show the man. I love Drake. I adore him. This is Drake, the love of my life, and I love him and he loves me. He is my boyfriend. This is why I am here. I need to find him because he made me remember.

The man looks at it.

"Yes. I think I have seen him," he says. "Are you OK? You showed me this a few minutes ago. But yes, like I said, I am sure he has been here. If I see him again, I will say a young lady is seeking him."

"You've seen him?"

"Yes." He looks surprised by my excitement.

"Thank you. Oh, thank you! Could you tell him Flora is here?"

"Flora. Yes, of course."

I frown. "Actually, don't tell him it's me. Just say someone's looking for him. I want it to be a surprise."

I look down at my phone and flip to the next picture. I thought it might show Drake again, but it's a poster of a cat instead. A missing cat. Everyone is missing.

"Have you seen this cat?" I say, and I show him that picture too. He laughs.

"No. Not the cat. We don't have many cats around here."

Drake is here. That man recognized him: I have not made it up. I came here, to the right place, to find Drake, who is the right person. I am doing it right. I came all this way, and now I have found someone who knows Drake's face. That means I am almost there. It means I will find him before the police come to get me. I must write down every word the beardy man said at once. I dig in my bag and find my notebook, and fill pages and pages with my neatest handwriting, telling myself everything that is currently in my brain. I don't notice my drink arriving, but at one point I look up from my writing and see a wide cup of milky coffee beside me, so I begin to drink it. It is still warm and the best coffee in the world.

I think I have been sitting in this café for a long time.

I find a strange e-mail from Jacob on my phone, and read it. I need to reply to that. I see a text from Mom that asks me to come to Paris with Paige. That must be so that Jacob and I can see each other again. I loved him. When he came in and picked me up from the carpet, every part of my body surged with love. He was the person I most wanted to see when I was a little girl. When I was normal, he was my world.

I would like him to be a part of my world again now.

I write Jacob an e-mail that says everything that is currently in my head. I don't censor myself at all. I tell him that I kissed Drake on a beach and that I remember it. I type out every word we said to each other as the waves sucked at the pebbles and the moonlight shone on the water. I tell him that I am in Svalbard and I ask what he thinks I should do. I say that I am not sure what is happening in my head. I tell him that I remembered being tiny and crying and him picking me up and taking care of me. I ask why he went away. I ask lots and lots of questions. The e-mail is very long.

I send it without reading it through, even though I know that it is filled with spelling mistakes and that it must sound bizarre.

I see a text on the phone from Mom, and I reply to it telling her that I'm fine and not to worry about me. I don't mention coming to Paris.

I send her a second text saying: When you get back, can we go to Flambards?

When I look up, my coffee is still half there, and freezing cold, and everyone has left the café, and a man with a beard and a spot on his face is smiling at me in the manner of a person who would like me to leave. He is holding a set of keys.

"I'll pay my bill," I tell him. He waves his hand.

"Don't worry, Flora," he says. "You look serious. Your coffee is free."

I thank him and wonder how he knows my name.

It is brightly sunny outside, and I am exhilarated. Every single person in Svalbard thinks that I am normal.

I am walking through a sparkling wonderland where the air glistens and the people all smile. The buildings are not beautiful, but the wilderness stretches away in every direction. It is magical. I have left the place where I used to live, and the people who used to keep me there, and I have come to this new cold place in which I am free.

This place might be inside my head, but I don't care if it is. It is a wonderful place, and Drake lives in it.

I walk down the road, but then I stop. I don't know where to go. The house that is my home is a long way from here. I want to go to Flambards, but that is far away too, I think. I read my arms, which don't tell me anything that isn't already in my head, and then reach for my notebook.

My bag is not there. I don't have it.

I cannot do anything without it. I always have my bag, and in my bag I have my notes. I keep them in my bag. They are always together. I look at my hands and my arms and then I look in my bag for my notes. That is what I do.

There is nothing on my arms to tell me how to get back to the place where I am going, and even as I try to think of everything I can about that place, it slips away from me. I was going to a place, but I don't know why. I don't know where to go. I am here for Drake. That is the only thing that matters. I have to find him today, but I can't do it if I am lost.

If I have no bag, I have no money. I have no phone. I have no key. I have no books. I have no idea what I am doing and no one will be able to help me.

I kissed Drake. That is the only fact I have. There is nothing else in the world.

It bubbles and overflows. This is a cold place. I have no friends. I want my mom. I want my dad. I want my brother. I long for them with all my heart.

Tears are running down my cheeks. I have no idea what I am doing.

"Drake," I say aloud. I need to hang on to his name. Drake. I need to find Drake. He will find my bag. He will take care of me.

I need to remember his name. I don't have a pen, but I have to remember it. I am drifting now, and if I forget Drake, I forget everything.

I look around. This is the most urgent thing that has ever happened. I am the only person in the universe. I run up the road a little ways and stop. I don't have a pen, and I don't have any money. It says "Drake" on my arm, but that will come off.

There is a pen half-buried in snow at the edge of the road. I pick it up and roll up my sleeve. If I write his name again and again and again, that will make me remember.

The pen doesn't work. I must use it anyway, so I scrape the word into my arm with it. I scratch DRAKE so deeply into my flesh that it starts to bleed. That is good, and I work harder, deliberately puncturing my skin so that his name is written on me in beads of blood that will stay forever. I go over and over and over the letters. I like the pain of it. It makes me feel alive.

DRAKE

That is all I have to go on. I am lost, but I have Drake's name written on my body. Maybe I will cut it deeper, when I can find a knife. I want it there forever.

I start to walk. I will walk around and something will happen, because if I stay still nothing will happen. I walk and walk. My legs are tired, but it is still daylight. I walk to an expanse of water. It is bigger than a river but smaller than the sea, because I can see mountains and a little house on the other side. I stand on a jetty and look at the boats docked there. I turn back, because I can't go any farther without walking into the water, and walk past old machinery with cables and buckets. I go to a little church, hoping that some god or other might help me out.

I will just walk. When I see Drake, I will know him.

Some hours have passed. I have walked around and around. I have been into the church more than once, I am sure. There was a woman there who smiled at me. I went to write my name into the visitors' book, but it was already there, twice, on the line above the one I was about to write on, and the line above that. Flora Banks, it says, the first time. Penzance. Flora Banks, it says, the second time. From the cold place. I went into a shop, but I had no money, so I left. I have taken quick breaths and kept moving. I have walked and walked and walked. The shops are closed now. I see some steps outside a museum and decide to sit on them to rest my feet.

A man says, "Flora." I look at him. He has hair that sticks up and a beard that sticks down and a brown spot on his face. He is not Drake.

"Hello," I say. I look at him closely, peering into his face. He laughs. He looks a little uncomfortable. I don't say anything else because I can't think of any words that would be right.

"Flora—are you OK?"

He knows my name. He sits next to me and puts a hand on my shoulder. I don't know what to do, so I lean on his shoulder and cry. I am sobbing and his coat is getting slimy on the outside. I want to say sorry, but I don't even seem able to do that.

"Flora. What is it?"

I still can't speak, although I want to. I try to take deep breaths and calm myself down, and I say: "I haven't got any . . ."

"No. You haven't got anything, have you? Maybe you left your bag in the café?"

I nod. I have no idea.

"I have the keys. Shall we go back and look?"

I gaze at him. "Yes. Yes, please."

There is a bag on the floor under a table. I run to it and snatch it up and hug it close.

There is a notebook inside the bag, and on the outside it says: *FLORA'S STORY. READ THIS IF YOU FEEL CONFUSED.* I look at my hand, which says FLORA, *be brave.*

I open the book and start to read. I had an operation when I was eleven and I have amnesia. I have come to Svalbard to find Drake because he knows how to fix me. My brother, Jacob, is very sick. My parents are in Paris. Paige is not my friend.

"Thank you," I tell the man. "Thank you. You've saved me. Thank you."

"That's all right." He looks awkward again. I must be acting very weird, but I don't care. "You're welcome. Hey, I was about to go for a beer with some friends. Why don't I take you back to your hotel first?"

"No, thank you. I'm fine. I really am. Thank you. I need to go now. I need to go."

Chapter Thirteen

I follow the map and walk down a straight road that takes me past a school and an art gallery and a lot of other buildings. Away to the right there is a little wooden church. There are mountains all around. The clouds are moving fast across the sky.

I know exactly where I am (Longyearbyen) and why I am here (Drake) and where I am going (the Arctic Guesthouse). I am walking in the right direction. I am taking deep breaths, relishing every second of this overwhelming relief.

Someone is walking behind me. It is the man who helped me find my bag. When I look around, he waves. He doesn't catch up with me, so I just keep walking.

As I walk, I watch a dark line moving across the landscape. The line brings gray behind it, and when it reaches me, and passes me, this world, this place in which I am an ordinary human, is transformed.

The light disappears. Nothing sparkles. The magical land becomes gray and drab, and the cloud is a ceiling over my head. The sky is gray. The snow is unglittery and gray. Every single thing is tinged with gray. The cloud becomes lower and lower as I watch, and I feel rain in the air, the sudden change in the atmosphere that means things are about to get wet. When something falls onto my cheek, however, it is not rain. It is snow.

Drake lives in a snowy place. I am here. I am right inside the snowy place, like him.

The sky behind me is blue, in the distance. There, it is sunny and bright. Here, it is snowing thicker and faster, covering the road, everything turning white even as I look at it.

I don't know where I was going, but that doesn't matter. I am happy, right here and right now. I am a girl standing in the snow, marveling at the flakes of whiteness dancing in the air around me. I am in a beautiful place and a wonderful thing is happening. Nothing else matters.

I am in the moment. Living in the moment when I can must be one of my rules for life. You don't need a memory for that.

When the flakes become smaller and the clouds start to blow away to snow in a different magical place, I feel as if I've been asleep for a full night. I am full of energy and ready for anything.

The hotel is where the map said it would be. I have a key and a note telling me to go to room five, and a map to inform me which building room five is in (it is in building five, pleasingly).

The building is made from corrugated metal and has bikes and skis leaning up against it and a set of concrete steps leading up to the door. When I turn to go up the steps, I see that a man with a beard has followed me here. I wave to him and he gives me a little salute and turns and walks away. As soon as I walk through the door, I am assaulted by a smell of dirty socks and cooking. It is warm in here, and I take my coat off as soon as I have closed the door behind me. A sign tells me to take off my shoes too, and so I do. I sit on the bottom step of the staircase and unlace my boots, which have magically appeared on my feet as precisely the correct footwear for this location. My old sneakers are in a plastic bag, inside my shoulder bag, somehow.

The kitchen is neat and has cabinets in it with signs telling people not to use certain things, and not to steal each other's milk. That gives me an idea, so I put the kettle on, find a mug, and steal a tea bag from a box of them and find the best-looking milk in the fridge. No one, I am sure, would mind me taking a tiny bit.

There is a kitchen at home, and it has both more and less in it than this one. I close my eyes tight and try to think. It has more, because there is a teapot. It has fewer boxes of tea bags: just one. More, and less. The woman in the kitchen at home is my mother. The man is my father. I am Flora, and I am not ten. I am seventeen: I know that because I can remember kissing a boy on a beach.

Everyone has a favorite mug in our kitchen. Mine is pink and white. Mom's says WORLD'S BEST MOM! Dad's has a man on it.

I am delighted with myself, and swap the white mug I had picked for one with a pink pattern on it. I make the cup of tea and look around for people to talk to.

I want to go to Flambards.

That thought pops into my head, and it is odd. Flambards is a long way away. I write a text to Mom. Can we go to Flambards?

I have written a text to Drake, but he hasn't replied.

There is nobody here. I wonder what they are all doing: snowy things, I suppose. Cold things. Things that people do in places like this.

If I did see anyone, I would show them the photograph on my phone and ask them if they had seen Drake. I have come to find him because I kissed him on the beach.

Even if this place is all in my head, I am here, on my own, and I am living. This is real.

My key opens room five, and I lock the door behind me and sit on the bed. My head is spinning. I stretch my hands out in front of me, flexing my fingers and reading the words. FLORA, be brave. I am being brave. I have followed my hand's instruction. My arm stings, and when I roll up my sleeves I discover that this is because I carved Drake's name into my skin with what looks like some kind of blunt blade. I stare at it for a long time. It feels scary and exciting and terrible that I have carved a word into my arm.

I am in a strange place that must be a very long way away from my usual place. This is not my room, and yet these things in it are so familiar that they must be mine. This is my new room. This is the place I have made for myself: my very own home. I find every handwritten thing I can, and stay sitting on the bed, and start to read everything all over again.

• • •

"Medication" and "pills" are the words that leap out. I take pills and medication, and that gets me through the days. If I have taken anything lately, I have not written it down. I feel dizzy.

There is a big bag on one of the beds. I put my notebooks down and unpack it, taking out every single thing and lining it up so that I can look at the stuff I brought with me. It is nearly all clothes. I pick up a red T-shirt and smell it, though I don't know why.

There don't seem to be any pills. I need to do something about that, but I have no idea how to start.

My hands are shaking, and I get up and stand at the window, putting my hands onto the glass to steady them. It was snowing—I am sure it was snowing—but it isn't snowing now. There is a steep hillside behind my window, and I can see my reflection, in a faded and translucent way, in the glass, superimposed on the snowy rocks.

Even in this crappy reflection I can see that I don't look right. The girl in the window has strange eyes and odd skin. I lift a hand to touch my face. It is bumpy, when I am sure that it used to be smooth. A mirror materializes on the wall, and I look at myself properly.

That is not at all what I thought I looked like. I do not recognize my face. It is splotchy and red, the face of someone else. There are lumps all over it: they are yellowish at the tips, and red in the dips. The girl in the mirror is ugly. Mom says I am beautiful.

When I brush my fingertips over my face, it does not usually feel disgusting like this. I don't think skin is a thing I've ever worried about. I take my pen and carefully write What has happened to my skin? down the inside of my arm. I write it on a yellow note and stick it to the mirror. I write it in my notebook.

I hear a door open somewhere in the building. I'm glad people are starting to come back. Maybe I'll go back down to the kitchen and see what people do for dinner here. I am hungry.

When people are talking right outside the door, I decide to go out and join them. I have my picture of Drake, and I repeat, under my breath, the words I need to say. My horrible face makes me self-conscious, so I put on some makeup that I find on the desk. I smear myself in foundation cream, draw a line along the top of my eyes with black pencil, put on a bit of clumpy mascara, and finally try out a bright red lipstick that I cannot have worn before. It is brand-new, with a pointed end, and I color my lips in as if it were a crayon. I don't think I have done very well, but I smooth out the edges with a fingertip, and I think it will do.

If you have bad skin, you can stop people from looking at it by wearing bright lipstick. That is a rule.

I take off my blue sweater and put on a nice pink one, pick up the coat from the spare bed and set off down the hall, ready to spend the evening asking people about Drake. My notes tell me that I have a friend who is called Agi, so I will see if I can pretend to recognize her if she approaches me. I say her name in my head over and over again: *Agi, Agi, Agi.* I send Mom a text saying that I'm fine in Penzance. I sent Drake a text. I can see it on the phone. He has not replied.

It is still light. Even though it is the evening, it is as bright as midday. That is the magic of this place.

"Hi!" The man in the corridor is wearing pajama bottoms and has a towel slung over his shoulder.

It is only seven o'clock, but I suppose everything works differently here. If you have been out in the snowy mountains all day, you'd want to put your pajamas on.

I have a bedroom here. This fact thrills me, and for a second all I do is congratulate myself. I have a bedroom in the Arctic. It is a snowy, sunlit evening and Drake and I are both here, in Svalbard.

"You look smart," the man says. "What are your plans?"

"Oh." I cast around for an answer. "Nothing. I mean, I don't know. Nothing in particular. But my skin is being a bit gross, so I thought I'd put on some lipstick. So my zits don't show so much."

He nods. "Off on a trip? What did you do yesterday?"

"Yesterday?"

He does not know me, or he would never ask what I did yesterday. People tell me what I did yesterday: they do not ask. If he asked what I had done today, however, I would have said that I seem to have bought some boots, and I looked for Drake and carved his name into my skin.

"I don't really know," I say, and he doesn't ask why.

"And today? Any plans? You look very polished for someone on her way to breakfast."

I open my mouth to correct him.

Then I close it.

If he thinks I am on the way to breakfast, then I must be on the way to breakfast. That would make it breakfast time. I am not on my way to find evening entertainment and dinner. I am on my way to breakfast.

That would mean that a night had come and gone without my noticing it. I try to get my head around this most bizarre of possibilities. A day went past—the day on which I had to find Drake—and I did not find Drake.

"Did it get dark?" I ask.

"Not at all. At the end of August, maybe. Three months from now."

"Three months."

I did not realize that "the midnight sun" meant it would not get dark at all.

"You have to pull down the blinds. Just make yourself do it. If you let the daylight in all night, you'll never sleep." He looks at me curiously. "Did you sleep at all?"

"Yeah, a little. Thanks. Anyway, I'm just . . ."

"Sure. You know breakfast doesn't start for half an hour, right?"

"Right. I'm a bit . . ."

"I know. We all get like that."

That is the single best thing he could have possibly said. As I'm walking away, he calls after me: "Don't come here in winter."

I don't reply, because it is snowy, and that means it must already be winter, so what he said makes no sense at all.

Chapter Fourteen

"Yes, he says it's fine." Agi turns to me, and I pass her a bundle of money that is in my hand. She gives it to the man who is driving the minibus, and he counts it and nods. I follow her onto the bus and we sit together, Agi by the window.

You should always try to get a window seat. That is one of my rules, I think. If you get a window seat, you can tell exactly where you are. All the same, I can see out of the windshield.

We are the only two people on board. We are going on an outing, because Agi already had one booked, and at breakfast she invited me to go with her. I said yes, because it was exciting to be asked. I didn't recognize her at breakfast, but she knew me, and she sat down and asked about Drake. I pretended to remember her, and it seems to have worked.

We might be going to see polar bears. Drake might be out by the polar bears. I wonder if the driver has a gun.

• • •

The sun is shining. This place is beautiful. I don't think I have told Agi that I'm not normal, and so she is treating me like a real person. She is treating me like a friend who has writing on her hand. I am going to do my best to be normal, all day. That is my challenge to myself. I do not want anybody to guess the truth about me.

I look down at my left hand. I have written BE NORMAL on it. I see Agi looking at it too.

"I should also remind myself of this sometimes," she says, with a nod.

Today I have to find Drake. Otherwise my parents will notice I'm missing. Going out in a minibus is an excellent way to look for him. Mom has texted me and I have replied. I look at my phone. I have been saying all the right things to her.

The minibus stops at hotel after hotel, and each time more people get on. Agi and I are the youngest by far. Some of these people are old like my mom, and others are older. A woman leans across the aisle to talk to us, but she doesn't speak English and so she and Agi talk across me.

"She says this trip is the dream come true of her lifetime," Agi tells me, pushing her glasses back up her nose.

"Mine too," I say, and I smile at the woman, who gives me a thumbs-up.

When we get off the bus, the tour guide leads us across a metal walkway with railings, over some rocks, and out to a metal jetty with a rubber floor to stop you from falling over. A big metal boat is tied there: the word LANDØYSUND is painted on its side, in black. I spell it out and try to say it in my head: *Landøysund.* *Landøysund. Landøysund.*

I follow the crowd up the gangplank, smiling, trying to conceal my surprise at the fact that this is a boat trip. I had thought we were going to stay in the minibus to look for bears and for Drake. This boat is a huge exciting bonus. I kissed Drake on a beach, and now we are going out on the water. This is perfect. This will be the place to find him.

"How about this!" says Agi as we stand side by side. We are leaning on a white railing and looking out away from the town. Soon the boat will start moving. All we can see in this direction is a mountain ridge on the other side of the water, dotted with rocks and snow. It might be a hill, because it's not really tall enough to be a mountain, but it looks like a mountain. It runs on and on, beside the inlet. The stretch of water narrows to our right, and widens to our left. There is only one building visible across the water, and that is a cabin a little way up from the water's edge. I can just make out a figure pulling a rowboat up onto the shore, and watch as the person stands back to survey the scene. Then he turns around and walks up to the cabin and opens the door.

"Quite the home sweet home," says Agi. She is looking out across the water too.

"How could you live there?" I try to imagine it.

"How could you not? Don't you think it would be wonderful? Maybe not for your happily ever after, but for a year or two. In fact, I would live there for one year exactly. In the winter it would be so cozy. You'd just be there tucked away in the dark for months."

I shiver. "I would hate that."

"Yes. People say don't come here in the winter, but it makes me want to, more. We have dark winters in Finland. I like the cozy."

I shake my head. The figure has gone into the cabin and closed the door.

I write a note in my book, reminding myself not to come here in winter.

We stand quietly at the railing until the man in charge claps his hands and calls everyone over to him. I stand at the back of the group and half listen as he tells us about safety procedures and says where we will be going, which is away from the town and along the water into the wild. I have looked for Drake in the town, but I am going to find him in the wild.

"I cannot promise a polar bear," he says several times. "There is a mother and two cubs around the area at the moment, and we saw them on Thursday, but I cannot guarantee it by any means. OK? However, I do offer you seals and puffins. *That* is a promise."

He goes on and on, talking sometimes in English and sometimes in Norwegian, and I tune out. I look at my hands, which are white with cold. Today I am going to be brave and normal. To be normal is to be brave. I am going to sit quietly and listen to other people. I will ask them questions, rather than answer questions. I will stare at the mountains and the water, and I will breathe the cold fresh air and I will be quiet. I will leave this boat with nobody thinking there is anything odd about me. I will let everything happen in the way it is meant to happen.

I don't care where I am, or why. I am on a boat in another world wearing a warm coat. That, right now, is enough.

The engine starts up and we are away. The town vanishes, and the little cabin across the water is gone. The pace of the whole world slows down and almost stops.

I take a plastic chair from a stack of them and sit on the top deck and stare at the scenery going past. Every single worry that I have ever had—hundreds of shadowy ones that have blurred into a vague sense of dread—dissolves. There is nothing but this. The air is so pure that it almost hurts to breathe. The water is deeply blue, reflecting the sky, and its surface is silky. The boat sends perfect lines of tiny waves out diagonally behind it.

My head is clear. I take deep breaths and stare at the landscape, with its ridges and spikes, its snowy valleys and black rocks. There is nothing in the universe but this.

I smile. I do not talk to people. I just breathe and stare and exist. This is the Arctic. I am here. This is my present. This is my world.

I am a little girl. I am comfortable like that. I feel the world enfold me. I feel safe. I close my eyes and think about school and birthday parties and big brothers and the exciting day out we're going to have tomorrow at Flambards. I can't wait to go on the carousel with Jacob. I lose myself in happiness. I want to go to Flambards.

The water reflects the rocks as if it were a mirror. I am staring at a mountainous ridge and an upside-down mountainous ridge. I am on a boat. It is wonderful. I lean out over the glassy water and look at the face reflected below me.

It is not a ten-year-old's face. A woman is looking back at me.

Ripples distort her face. I stare until someone touches me on the shoulder.

"OK?" she says. "Am I disturbing you? You look like you're in a brown study."

I pull my eyes away from the hypnotic view to frown at this person in front of me. I am not ten. Years speed by. The person talking is a grown-up, and she is my friend. I work hard to catch up. I read my hand. BE NORMAL, it says. I make an effort, and try to do what is expected.

"A what?" I sit down in the chair next to hers. My hands are freezing. I rub them together.

"A brown study? I read it in a book of idioms. It was an old book."

"I'm not sure people say that." I am almost certain I have never heard anyone say they are in a brown study. I am Flora. I used to be ten, but now I'm not. Now I am much bigger. I have to act like a grown-up so no one knows that, on the inside, I am still ten.

"OK. I'll strike it from my list, if it seems weird to you. I will say, you seem thoughtful."

"Oh," I tell her, "I'm just happy."

"Me too. This is my biggest trip. I have been saving it up. A whole day out on the water. It's wonderful."

"Yes, it is. It's like magic. It's a different world."

"And you're warm enough in your lovely coat? Your hands are cold, no?"

"Yes, but I am warm. You?"

"My coat's normal, not lovely. But sure. I'm warm enough.

Here—take my gloves. Wear them for as long as you like. Did you buy your coat particularly for this trip?"

I take her gloves, which are shiny and quilted, and pull them onto my hands. I have no idea whether I bought my coat particularly for this trip, so I pretend.

"Yes. I thought it would be warm," I say. "Did you buy your coat for this trip? Do people do lots of shopping before they go away? Did you buy your gloves?"

"They do, but not me. Not for this one, anyway. I have this stuff, where I live. In Finland we need this kind of thing in winter. The coat. The gloves. The boots too. I have to go shopping if I'm going someplace with a beach and a hot sun."

"What's your life like, in Finland?"

"It's nice. I live in a town called Rauma. It's a beautiful place, I suppose. Lots of wooden buildings. It's on the water and everyone has a boat. If you don't have one, you would give an arm and a leg for a boat."

"Yes."

"That works? It's a curious expression. I would not really give an arm and a leg to have a boat. Sailing would be difficult with one arm and one leg."

"Yes, it would. It really would." I shake my head to make myself concentrate. I try to make the image of a one-legged, one-armed sailor leave my mind. "Have you always lived in that town?"

"No. I was born up in the north, in a place called Rovaniemi, up in Lapland. Some of my family are still there. Maybe that's what drew me here, to Svalbard. The northern thing."

My strategy of asking questions seems to work. I ask question after question about Finnish life, and traveling life, and life in general, and Agi answers all of them happily. Whenever she asks me anything, I smile and shake my head and ask what kind of animals they have in Finland, or what they watch on television. The boat goes on and on, chugging through the Arctic wilderness. I very much doubt that I have been happier than this in my life. If I am asking her the same questions again and again, she doesn't seem to mind.

I look at my hand from time to time, but there is nothing to read because my hands are warm and I am wearing gloves.

A long time passes. This new universe encloses me entirely and the old one melts into nothingness.

The man from the boat calls us all to the lower deck, and tells us that we have nearly reached the farthest point on our voyage. He has been talking to people for lots of the journey so far, but I have ignored him.

"We try to go to Pyramiden," he says, and he points directly ahead. "This is an old Russian mining town. It was very busy, but in 1998, the people all left. They knew there was no more money. It was very eerie. There were cups of coffee half drunk, food left on the tables. We can sometimes go there to look around, but today there is too much ice. So we go a little farther, and we stop for our lunch, and then we start the journey back. Look—here is a seal!"

I have a phone with me, and the phone can take pictures. I have to take my gloves off to use it, but I don't stop to read the words on my hand. Along with everyone else on the boat, which is twenty-two people, I lean over and photograph the big, lazy-looking seal with the comical face, who is lying on a sheet of ice nearby. He turns around, stares straight at us (he looks like a man with a mustache, his face orange around his mouth, his eyes droopy), and rolls straight off the ice sheet to go for a swim. I want to tell Jacob about him. Jacob would love him.

"He is quite the handsome fellow," says a woman behind me. She is an older woman with hair in a neat bun and pale pink lipstick.

"Yes, he is," I agree. "He doesn't look very pleased to see us, does he?"

"He looks like he's seen it all before."

I nod. I don't want to say any more, and I don't have to. I keep quiet.

The boat jolts and slows, and we are cracking a thin layer of ice and heading through it. This is exciting, and I take pictures of it. The town in the distance is strange; it is a cluster of redbrick buildings, iced in. I try to imagine that empty place, still with Russian miners' things in it, but I can't begin to picture it.

"Look!" calls someone from across the boat, and then the cry goes up: "Bear! Bear!"

We all turn to look. Sure enough, padding across the ice between the boat and the mining town is a big polar bear followed by two cubs.

I take some pictures, but then I put my phone away and look. These creatures are vicious: I know that because it is written on my arm, in my notebooks, everywhere I look. They are beautiful. They walk gracefully, in their own environment, and if they notice that there's a boat full of humans gawping at them, they don't bother to look twice. The cubs look cuddly and cute, though I expect they would be delighted to claw my eyes out and eat them.

And the mother would do anything to protect her cubs. Anything at all. She would tear anybody limb from limb, if they tried to take her babies away.

I hear a man in a big red coat asking our guide: "This ice would be too thin for them to walk across to the boat—am I right?"

"You are," says the guide. He raises his voice: "Guys! Just so you know, they won't get to us here. OK? We're perfectly safe."

There is a murmuring laugh of relief. We all stare transfixed at the bears as they make their way across the ice, turning toward the mining town and heading away from us.

I HAVE SEEN POLAR BEARS, I write on the palm of my left hand, because that is the only place that has space. Pics on phone, I add in tiny letters. I'm pleased that I'm not wearing those gloves anymore.

I see Agi watching me.

"Is this an English habit?" she asks, in a friendly way. "To write on your hand? I see you do it a lot. I don't see other English people doing it. Is it from your region?"

I think of all the different ways I could answer that.

"Yes," I tell her. "Yes, it is. It's what we do in Cornwall."

We have lunch, which is cooked on the lower deck on a barbecue, and which is pieces of cod and pieces of meat, and rolls and rice salad and normal salad. I get a plate, ready to accept everything that is offered.

"What is the meat?" I ask the woman from the coffee counter, who is dishing it all out.

"It's whale," she says. "You'd be interested to try it?"

Whales are big. I am sure you are not supposed to eat them. The fish looks nice, and so does the salad.

"No, thanks," I say. "Not whale."

"You're sure? Lovely local produce?"

Whales are enormous. The idea of eating slices of one is ringing alarm bells for me. I am certain that it is not a thing a person should do. I am sure that not eating whale is a rule.

"No, thanks. Just the fish, please."

"Sure. Suit yourself."

I take my plate back to my chair on the top deck, and look out at the ice and the Russian town and the retreating dots that are the polar bears. I take a few more pictures with my phone, because all the phone is now is a camera. It has no internet or phone reception.

If I could stay here forever, I would be perfectly all right. I would be happy.

Hours later, we are coming back toward the town, and I don't want to. I do not want to have to navigate the world anymore. I want to go straight back out on this boat, to go back to where the bears are, and the seal, and the little puffins who skitter along the surface of the water. I want to stay with these people, with the man who tells us that the bears won't catch us, and with the other people, and with Agi.

"Look," says Agi, taking my hand. "Look, these are the satellite dishes. You see?"

I follow where her finger is pointing. On the top of the hill, on the same side of the water as the town, is a row of what looks like tiny spheres. They are right on the horizon line, on top of a snowy hill. I realize that they are not tiny. They are far away.

"Satellite dishes?"

"Yes. You remember. We were talking about them when you told me about your boyfriend."

"My boyfriend."

I am ambushed by horror. I stare at my hands, but they mainly tell me to be normal, and about the bears, and that I am in Svalbard. They tell me to be brave, and when I push my heavy sleeve up my arm, the word DRAKE leaps off my skin and punches me in the face. I rub my arm, but his name is written on it in blood.

Drake works at the satellite place, and I am looking at the satellites now. I am looking at the place where Drake works, and he is the man I love, and I have just spent an entire blissful day on a boat when I should have been looking for him. I came here to look for him, and I have not done it at all.

I was on a beach with him. It is starting to fade away around the edges.

I want to lean over the railing and throw up.

"Flora." Agi has a hand on my arm. "Are you OK? What is it? Sorry if I said something wrong. I can kind of sense that things perhaps haven't gone so well with you and your Drake. You went to find him two days ago, but he's not with you."

I take a deep breath. We are nearly back on land. I want to scream and shout and fling myself off the edge of the boat and swim as fast as I can (which would not be very fast, if I can swim at all) to the satellite place and scramble up the mountainside and find him. But I won't do that. I won't do it because if I stay here, being calm and normal, I will be walking off this boat the normal way very soon indeed. I will walk off this boat, and stay calm, and then dash off and do everything I possibly can to find my Drake. I will find him if it means climbing these mountains on my own. I will find him if I have to fight past the polar bears. I kissed him on a beach, but it is starting to blur.

I close my eyes tight. I scour the inside of my head, pushing through memories of my childhood, of school and Jacob and Paige and my dad carrying me on his back, my dad piling stones up with me on the beach, my dad paddling in the sea with me.

I can see Drake and me on the beach, in my mind, but I can't hear what we're saying.

My phone starts to beep as we get back into reception. There are texts arriving on it, and I look at them quickly to see if there is one from Drake, but they are all from my parents. I don't read them.

I am the first off the boat, and I brush away the offer of the bus back to the hotel.

"I'm going to find Drake," I tell Agi, and I run away as fast as I can. It is too late. It is already too late.

Chapter Fifteen

I am sitting at the edge of a road. Drake is not with me. Drake is nowhere.

The inside of my head is out of control. It is on fire. It is snowing. It is a wild jungle. It is an Arctic wilderness. It is everything that has ever happened and everything that ever will happen, all at once.

Time is a random thing. It is the thing that makes us older. Humans use it to organize the world. They have invented a system to try to make order from randomness. The other humans, all of them but me, live their lives by hours and minutes and days and seconds, but those things are nothing. The universe would laugh at our attempts to organize it, if it could be bothered to notice them.

Time is the thing that makes our bodies shrivel and decay.

That is why people are scared of it. It doesn't affect me: I know I will never get old.

I am not like the rest of them. I can look out the window for a while, and in human terms I have missed a night. I can sit for hours and hours at the breakfast table on my own, staring at the bread and fish in front of me: I can sit there and stare and wait until a day and a night have passed and it's the next day's breakfast, and then the woman I like will come and sit down beside me and it will turn out that in human terms, only two minutes have happened.

I stride through days and nights. I do not need to sleep.

I am superwoman. I am here for Drake, so of course I will find him.

I am four and it is my first day of school. I am excited about it, and I walk to school holding my mom's hand. However, as we get closer to the building, I decide I don't want to go after all. I want to go home instead. I try to tell Mommy, but she laughs and says: "You'll be fine, my darling."

I tell her I don't want to go. I ask for Jacob, but Jacob has gone to his school, which is different.

"I'm going to big school," I said to him that morning.

"Well, I'm going to big, big school," he said. "I wish I could be at school with you, Flora, to look out for you."

Mom laughed. "Flora is going to be just fine, Jake."

"I know. She'll be running the place by Christmas. I'd like to be there to see it."

But Jacob's not here, and we are nearly at school, and I don't want to go anymore. I tug on Mommy's hand, trying to tell her, but she is not paying attention.

"Oh look," she says. "There's Yvonne. Come on, Flora. You can meet Yvonne's little girl."

I look at the girl, and she looks at me. Her braids are brown and mine are blond. We are both wearing red sweatshirts and gray skirts and white ankle socks and black shiny shoes. She smiles at me. I smile back, even though I feel so shy.

"Hello," I say.

"Hello," says the other girl.

"This is Flora," says Mommy.

"And this is Paige," says Yvonne.

I wake up and I have no idea where I am. This is a bed with pink sheets. I am crying but without knowing why. The bed has bars around it. I look at my hands. They have nothing written on them at all. I am too young to have lost my mind. I am too little to write. I am a normal child, crying for ordinary reasons.

I hear footsteps on the stairs. Someone is coming to take care of me. I cry harder and look forward to being held.

Even now, though, I am thinking of Drake.

I am in a metal box and I can't move. When I try to breathe, I choke. It is very hot on one side of me. No one else is here. I can't hear anything: there is just a ringing noise in my ears. It is so loud that my brain is melting away.

• • •

I am sitting in a bed with sheets tightly across me. Some people I don't know are sitting on the end of the bed and looking at me. I am very, very, very scared.

I am looking at some words on a screen. They say: You can't come over here, can you?

"I can!" I say to them. "Yes, I *can* come here."

Now I am in the snow, standing in the middle of a road, feeling the sun on my cheeks.

I run along the road in the direction in which I was facing. I just keep running. There is a creature standing on some snowy grass, beside the road. The tips of the grass are poking through the snow, and the animal, which has white and brown fur and antlers, is nibbling at it. I rush up to it, and it doesn't bother to look up.

"Where's Drake?" I scream at it. It lifts its head, looks me in the eye, and turns around and walks off.

I follow. I walk across the snowy grass, pleased to see that I am wearing sturdy boots. The reindeer (or reindeer-type thing) takes me to the edge of the scrubland, then stops and eats more grass. Ahead of me is a mountainside. The reindeer wants me to go there, and so I start walking up it. I yell, "Drake!" as I go, but I do not feel that I am likely to get an answer.

It is cold, and soon I am around a corner and out of sight. Something about this feels wrong, and I stop and push back the sleeves of my coat so I can read my arms.

Don't leave town! POLAR BEARS, it says on the inside of my left arm.

I stop and look around. I can't see any, so it's probably all right, but all the same, the reindeer might have been tricking me.

On the palm of my hand it says, I HAVE SEEN POLAR BEARS. Pics on phone.

I have seen them and it was all right. I am still alive. That is reassuring. I will not look at the pictures now, because I have to find Drake.

I very much doubt that I will find Drake in this direction. This is, of course, a test from a fairy tale. I am on a quest to find my prince, and I must not be distracted from it. There are rocks and sharp edges and drops, though I am not high up yet. I am not really on a path: I seem just to have scrambled over some rocks, and now I am standing on a stony slope, and I can go forward or backward.

I read my arm again. Don't leave town! That means I should probably go back. Although I feel that nothing could hurt me, a fight with a polar bear is probably not a thing I should seek out. If I have already seen them, there is no need for me to do it again.

All the same, the way ahead looks interesting. I could scramble up and up, and I would come to a ridge, and then I would go over it and see what was there. There could be anything: a magical city; the edge of the earth; Drake.

I will just walk up a little ways and have a look. Then I will go back down to the town, and I will keep looking. If I look in every single place, I will find him. I must just focus on staying in this reality for a while. I must not drift away to the past.

The waves are crashing on the stones in front of us. It is dark, and there is a streetlight somewhere, lighting us up. There is a flash of light. I am wearing a bright blue dress and chunky boots, and I am kissing Drake. I am kissing him and he is kissing me and I love him and he loves me and all around us there are smooth black stones.

I am on a ridge, shivering. In front of me there is a lot of landscape. It is jagged, with snow and rocks and scrubby grass in between them. There are no trees here; not a single one. There are no houses. There is no magical land. There is no Drake. Everyone is out to get me.

Something pings in my pocket. When I investigate, it is a phone, but it's not Drake. There are two texts from someone called Jacob. The first says: Please read your e-mails. The second says: Flora! Please.

I open them up. This phone, it seems, is full of messages.

Chapter Sixteen

I am in a café, reading the e-mails that are on my phone. There is a big milky coffee beside me, and when I notice it, I drink some of it. It is still hot, and delicious. There is a man nearby, a man who works here, and he sees me looking at him and walks over. He has hair all over his face and his head and a spot on his cheek.

I touch my cheeks. I have far more spots than he does.

"Is everything OK, with your coffee?" he asks.

"Yes, thanks. It's perfect." I smile and hope he thinks I am normal.

"Great. Look, Flora, are you OK? You were very concerned about your bag the other day."

"My bag?"

"Yes. Your bag. When you left it under the table. You remember?"

I nod, pretending.

"Yes," I say. "That's right. I'm OK, thanks. A bit . . ." I cannot finish the sentence because I have no idea which word to use to end it. A bit superhuman? A bit fearless? A bit alive?

"A bit confused. Yes. It happens to people here. It's an unusual place. When did you last sleep?"

I laugh. "I can't remember." I laugh a lot at that. I can't remember. I laugh until I cry, and then I see the way he is looking at me, and I try to get myself under control. "It's OK, though. I'm fine." This man is nice, and I would like to try to explain, but I don't know how to say it. "I need to give myself some help with remembering things," I tell him. I hold out my hands, push back my sleeves, but then I see that the word DRAKE is carved into my arm, so I push the sleeve back over it. "They don't stay in my head. They stay on my hands pretty well, though."

"You must try to sleep very soon."

"I'll try," I say, to humor him. "If I notice the night at all."

"Don't come here in winter. It's worse." I nod, to make it look as if I know what he means, and he carries on talking. "So, this boy you asked about the other day? Drake? I believe he came in here earlier. May I see the photo again?"

He picks up my phone from the table, which seems a little rude. I take it from him and find that the picture of Drake is on the screen already, even though I was looking at my e-mails, so it shouldn't be there. Drake comes to the front no matter what. He is written on my body, taking over my phone. He is everywhere except right in front of me.

I love Drake.

"Yes," he says. "Yes, this was the one. I said to him that there was a young lady looking for him. He was not expecting, I think, to be told this by staff of a café."

I stare at him. This man has seen Drake! Drake has been here, to this café. I have found him. I have come to the right place. He is here. I think about this very hard, trying to make it join my other memory. Drake is in this moment, so this moment can stay in my head.

"What did he say?" I ask.

"He said something along the lines of: 'Are you sure you have the right person?' I asked where you could find him and he said he was always around."

"OK." I feel the tears come back to my eyes and attempt to blink them away. When I look up, the man has gone to deal with another customer, so I let myself cry, just for a moment. It turns out that I just want to sit here and cry and cry and cry. I do it for as long as it takes, shaking my head and pushing away people who want to help me.

"I'm happy," I tell them, through my tears. "I'm happy."

When I stop crying, I sip my coffee, but now it is cold.

There are new e-mails on my phone. I forgot about them, and now I read them all, starting with the oldest one from Jacob Banks.

Oh, Flora. The only predictable thing about you is the certainty that you'll do something surprising. The Arctic? The bloody Arctic? I'm doing what I can to keep our parents off your case but it won't last. I nearly died, just to keep them here. Luckily for your adventuring, my health is so bad that they have to stay at my side, just in case. When I feel OK, I remind them that you're nearly eighteen, and you're with Paige, and it's my turn to be coddled. Your texts have just about been coming in at the right times and have been reassuring them just enough.

So. You brilliant, insane girl. I will only cover for you if you check in with me at least once a day. Preferably twice or more. I hope that if you find that boy he turns out to be worthy of your efforts. I'm going to tell our parents where you are in two days, so you have to find him by then.

The idea of your adventures is better for me than any of the "palliative" shit they're giving me, but I'm insanely worried about you too. You won't remember, but the last time you went off your pills you went through a manic phase before you settled down into your own kind of strange and lovely normality. I'm scared about you being out there. It's dangerous. If things get weird, GO TO THE AIRPORT AND BUY A TICKET TO PARIS. Write that on your hand right now. Please.

More when I've got a moment. Meanwhile, you HAVE TO call our mother and assure her that you're OK. If she wasn't beside herself at my disaster, then you would not have gotten away with this for one second.

You say you remembered me picking you up as a little kid. I did that all the time. You were brilliant. You are brilliant. KEEP IN TOUCH.

Jacob xx

Jacob does not seem surprised that I've run away. I write that in my notebook. Have I traveled somewhere before??

The next e-mail is shorter.

Flora? Write to me. Please. Tell me you're OK. That's all. Just check in. Otherwise I'm telling on you. Jx

The one after that is shorter still.

Flora! Jx

Then I see his texts. I know I need to write to him, this person who has appeared from nowhere and who is the brother in my head. I reply to his last e-mail first.

Sorry. I'm fine. I'm feeling amazing, in fact. I can do everything. Don't worry about me. I hope you're OK. Flora xxxxxxx
P.S. I haven't found Drake yet, but I'm very close. I'm in a café right now that he's been to! I am definitely on the right track.

Then I reply to his first e-mail, telling him everything I can remember. I pour my heart out, but as soon as I've sent it, I have no idea what it said. I send another message and ask him if I've run away before. I can't have. But if I had, I wouldn't know. Jacob seems to think I have, so I'll need him to tell me.

Then I send another e-mail asking question after question after question. I want to know everything about him, about myself, about our family. I want him to tell me all the things I have forgotten: that, I know, is a lot to ask. I do not know what I do not know; I only know that I want to know everything.

The phone starts to ring in my hand. The screen says MOM. I close my eyes and breathe deeply. Jacob told me I have to speak to her. He is right. I must answer it, but I must pretend to be in Penzance.

I am in Penzance. I only have a hazy idea of what Penzance means, right now.

I press the button.

"Hello, Mom!" I say, in the brightest and most cheerful voice I can manage.

"Why did it ring with an international tone?" she says at once. Her tone is sharp. I had no idea that her voice would make me feel like this. It melts me. I thaw into a puddle and drip onto the floor. I am twelve. I am nine. I am six. I am three.

I must focus. It is difficult, but I yank myself back into the present. I have no answer for her difficult question.

"I don't know" is all I manage.

"Are you in Penzance?"

"I live in Penzance," I say.

"Yes. But you're not there right now."

I don't say anything. I don't know what to say.

"Flora?"

"Yes."

"Flora—where are you?"

I take a deep breath. There was something in Jacob's message about my mania turning into lovely normality. I try to access that. *Lovely*, I remind myself. *Normality*, I add.

"You asked me to come to France," I say, in the most lovely and normal of voices. I have read that in my notebook. I hope it was true.

"I wanted to talk to you about the *possibility* of your coming to France. To make arrangements. And that was days ago. And you've sent a string of strange texts about . . . well, about wanting to go to Flambards."

I can't think what to say.

"I'm really fine," I tell her. "Stay with Jacob. I'm all right. I promise. We don't have to go to Flambards."

She is talking but I can't listen because I don't know what to do. I know that if I tell her I'm in the Arctic, she will call the police and they will come here, to this snowy place, and take me away, and I haven't found Drake. I need to find Drake, and then he will help me explain it all to everybody. I don't need to be afraid anymore. I can do anything. Mom doesn't understand that yet.

I don't know what to say, so I hang up. If they call the police in Penzance, they won't find me because I'm not there.

Drake won't believe what I've done to find him. But he will know that it means we will live happily ever after.

I kissed him on a beach. There is a blurry, hazy picture of it in my mind. I push myself onto the beach. I make myself go back there. The stones are black. I kissed a boy. But I can't keep hold of it.

I am in a metal box and my ears are ringing. Everything is going strange. We cannot go to Flambards.

Chapter Seventeen

My face is lumpy. I put on lipstick before I go out, because that will distract from the bumps. It is a nice bright lipstick that I can't imagine myself buying, but I'm glad I did. It looks practically new.

There is a woman with glasses waiting at the bottom of the stairs. I have prepared for this.

"Hello, Agi," I say to her, and she grins.

"Hey, Flora! You remember me! How are you doing?"

I stare at her. "Did I forget you?"

"It's OK. Don't worry, Flora."

"Sorry. I do . . . forget things." I wonder how to explain.

"I know." She puts a hand on my arm. "It's OK. I know about your problems. You showed me your notebook. Do you remember? No, sorry. You don't. On the boat you did well, but when you got off it, you went quite wild. We lost you, and then we found you sitting on the jetty trying to borrow a boat to row yourself to the satellite dishes. I was going to call an ambulance, so you gave me your notebook. You were sick when you were a girl and you have problems with memory. It's OK. I will be with you this evening, and if you forget things, I will remember you. If you try to go somewhere, I will at the very least go with you."

"*Remind* me. You'll remind me."

"I will *remind* you. And you will help me with my English! Thank you. Shall we 'shake a leg'?"

I nod.

"Let's go," I say. I don't know where we are going, but I am going to try not to tell her that. I will just walk with her and see what happens. I will not get distracted. I will not time travel into places inside my head. I will not visit memories, or things that might be memories. I will just walk with this woman—with Agi—and we will go to a place and do a thing. Drake will be part of it.

We set off down the road.

"How was your day?" I say. Those feel like normal words.

"Oh, it was interesting," she says. "After I put you into your bed, I went dog sledding. It was less fun than you might think."

"I don't think it would be fun at all." I try to imagine dog sledding. I don't even know what it would involve. Dogs, I suppose. Sleds. If I was sledding, I wouldn't want there to be a dog.

She put me into my bed. I try to decide whether I feel like I have slept. It is impossible to tell. I might have.

"Right. So it's even less fun than that. The dogs kept rushing into me. I tell you, I have bruises all down my leg. And it was cold. Obviously." She smiles. "Still! Never mind! I write it on my blog."

"I'd like to read that."

"Sure! I'll give you the web address again. I will write it in your notebook again for you."

"Oh. Sorry. I'm not usually . . ."

"I know. Because you don't have your pills. Don't worry. We are going to find your Drake tonight, Flora. It is very important for you. You have a friend here and we need to find him."

We keep walking and she talks to me, but I don't really listen. Then I do, because I hear Drake's name.

"Drake," she is saying. "Tell me about him. Tell me some more."

I grin at her. "I kissed him on the beach."

"Yes. You told me that. You showed me the photograph of him. He has those glasses, the look of the geek." She looks at my face. "I mean that in a kind way. He has geek chic."

"'Geek chic.'"

"So you still haven't heard from him?"

"I get a lot of e-mails and texts. They're from . . . people."

I would remember if Drake had written to me since I've been here. Wouldn't I? I am sure I would. I feel the phone in my coat pocket. I want to take it out and look at it right now, but I will try not to, because that would be weird and rude. I try to focus on my conversation with Agi instead.

I am looking at us both from high in the sky. I am wearing a fur coat. Where did I get a fur coat? No one else has one.

Agi, for example (Agi, Agi, Agi: I know her name)—Agi is

wearing a bright green zip-up jacket made from something much more factory-ish than fur. My fur, though, is not animal skin: it was probably made in a factory too. At least, I think it was. I hope my beautiful coat doesn't come from a dead animal because that would be wrong.

Agi is wearing a tight pair of dark blue jeans and a pair of snow boots that are a lot like mine. She has a bobble hat on her head. I have a hat on too, but it's bright red and made from wool, without a bobble. I have no idea where I got it. Agi is wearing shiny quilted gloves, but I am not, and my fingers are cold.

From the air, I watch us walking together, and I see that we are talking and I hope that whatever is coming out when I move my mouth is making sense, because even as the earth-me is speaking, the air-me is too far away to hear it. Agi is talking back, which makes me hopeful. Sometimes she laughs. Once or twice she touches my arm. I seem to be getting away with it. I think I am being normal.

I am on the beach with Drake. There is a flash of light. The stones are black. The water is black. The sky is black. I am wearing black and Drake is wearing black. Everything is black. I am with Drake and it is black and we are kissing.

I am in the cold place, and my feet are moving, one in front of the other, and I am walking down the road with the woman with the glasses. She is looking at me and I can see from the expression on her face that I have just done or said something weird.

"Sorry," I tell her. "Sorry, I just . . . drifted a bit. I didn't mean to."

"Hey," she says. "That's OK! Don't worry, Flora. I find you fascinating. I mean that."

"Oh. Really?"

"Yes, really! You are this amazing girl! You are so young and so pretty—"

I interrupt. "But my skin is horrible." I touch it. The pits and troughs are still there.

"That! I bet that's because you don't take your pills. How many years is it?"

"I was ten. Now I'm seventeen."

"So seven years. For seven years you have taken, how many pills per day?"

I shrug. I have no idea. "Some."

"So say it was three. A chemical going into your body, twenty-one times a week—albeit for good reason . . ." She stops. "'Albeit.' That is actually a word? I saw it on an old interview with your Princess Diana."

"'Albeit.' Yes, it is. One word, I think." I like the idea that I have a "Princess Diana."

"So albeit for good reason, you have been hooked on this medication. You don't know its name?"

"No."

"Or what it does?"

"No."

"Well, whatever it is, you may be going cold turkey. Or worse than that. I ought perhaps to call your parents after all."

She looks at me and I shake my head. "Please don't." I have no idea why she is talking about turkey.

"It must be to control things in your brain, which has clearly been damaged by your tumor. You don't mind me talking directly?"

I laugh. "No. I'll forget this conversation anyway, so you can say whatever you like."

"Yes. You said this yesterday also. And today. I think what you have—it's like Alzheimer's disease but for a young girl. It is very tragic for you. You only live in the here and now."

"It's not tragic. Not really. I love Drake. I kissed Drake."

"Can you find out the name of your medication? We need to get it for you, I think. I worry you won't be safe without it."

"I'll try."

"Thanks."

"I am seventeen. How old are you?" Is her name Abby? Ally? Ellie? Ella? It slips away, vanishing even as I reach for it. I don't call her anything.

"Me? I'm twenty-seven years old. Ten years more than you." She laughs. "An old lady, really. That's why I feel responsible for you."

"Thanks for helping me."

"You really are interesting, though. Are you sure it's OK for me to write about you in my blog?"

"Did you ask me that?"

"Yes. Perhaps we should write it down, to prove it. I don't want to upset you. We could write it in your book, our agreement."

"It's fine."

We have reached a square that feels like the center of something. There are a couple of restaurants, a supermarket on the far side, a hotel, a pub. I wonder whether we're going to the pub: I hang back and let my new friend take the lead. She gives me an encouraging glance, takes my hand, and sets off across the square, leading me. It is still brightly light, and the sun shines into my eyes.

"I very, very much hope that we will find your lovely Drake in here. The students, they drink here," she says. "Your friend will help us get your medicine. You need a friend. He'll know what to do. If we don't find him, then I'll have to . . ."

"I kissed him on the beach."

My friend pats my arm. "Yes," she says. "Yes, I know. And now you have come to Svalbard to find him. And tonight will be the night when we finally track him down."

"We shouldn't go to Flambards. We shouldn't go."

She looks very worried. I know that we need to find Drake right now. Otherwise everyone will try to make me go home.

Chapter Eighteen

There are empty glasses on the table. There is a full glass in front of me. It has beer in it. I don't think I should drink alcohol, but I pick up the glass and sip from it, and it tastes like the inside of my mouth already tastes. I take another sip. I don't like the taste, but the smell of it reminds me of my dad, and so I keep drinking it. Dad drinks beer. Mom drinks wine.

There is a woman beside me. She has glasses. I know her. She is talking to a man who has a beard and lots of hair and a brown spot on his face, who is sitting on the other side of our table. I don't think I know him.

"This is nice," I say, because I am in a pub, with people, and that makes me feel happy.

They stop talking and smile at me.

"Yes," says the girl. "It is, isn't it? Oh, Flora. You're drinking my beer. You're supposed to be drinking your lemonade. Here you are."

She pushes a different glass toward me and takes the beer away. I scowl at her.

There is a wall behind me, made of wooden planks. The tables are wooden. The place is hot, almost steamy, although I know that this is part of the cold place. They have made the inside hot because the outside is cold.

There are lots of people in here. They all have coats over the backs of their chairs. Their coats are different from mine. Theirs are made from new stuff and mine is made from fur.

I lean back and look around the room, staring into all the faces I can see. There are forty-two people in this room, and from what I can tell, nine of them are wearing glasses. Three of the glasses-wearers are women (one of them is sitting beside me), and six are men. Four of those men are noticeably old, so that leaves two men who could be Drake. One of them is sitting at the bar and has red hair, so he is definitely not my Drake. The other is sitting at a table, facing mainly away from me, and I stand up and walk between the tables, trying to get to the front of him, to look into his face, to check this man's face and see if it is, in fact, Drake's.

I hear someone saying "Flora?" behind me, but it's a woman's voice, and so not Drake's, and so I do not look back. I walk right to the other side of the room and turn to look at this person. This person might really be my wonderful, clever Drake.

"Drake?" I whisper.

He turns around to face me. I see immediately that this man is not Drake. It is, however, a dark-haired man with glasses (and with the wrong face), and I reach into my pocket, find my phone, and hold it out to him. He is probably the best person to ask.

"Excuse me," I say. "Do you know Drake Andreasson? He looks like this."

I show him the screen. It says 18 MISSED CALLS on it, so I make that go away so the photo comes back. The man frowns at me, shrugs, and says some things in a different language.

I am in the cold place. Not everyone speaks English here. I smile, hoping that it shows that I am sorry. I show him the phone again and try to look questioning.

He takes it and peers at it. He shrugs again and shakes his head while saying things I can't understand. I take the phone back and look around for my table. I see the word MOM come up on the screen, but the volume is switched off, and the phone doesn't make a sound. Since it is not really ringing, I do not answer.

A woman takes my hand and I follow her. She has glasses on and I know her. Her name might be Esther.

"There you go, Flora," she says. "You sit there. It's best if you stay with us, here. We're your friends."

"I know."

"Here. This is your drink."

"OK."

The man with the beard leans across to me. I don't know him.

"Don't worry, Flora," he says. "You'll be OK. You'll be OK with us and we will find your friend. Drake."

"You're helping me find Drake? Thank you!"

"That's OK. You remember me? Toby, from the café?"

I don't remember him at all.

"Of course," I say. He picks up his glass.

"Cheers," he says.

"Cheers."

There is a glass in front of me. I pick it up and take a sip. It is lemonade. I don't want lemonade. I am an adult and I want to drink beer.

There is half a glass of beer on the next table, and no people, so I check that neither of the people with me is looking, and reach over and grab it.

That is better.

Alba and the bearded man are talking. I wonder how they know each other.

I gulp down half the beer in one go. It makes me tingle. They are talking intently. It is getting boring. I am filled with energy. I want to go and do something. I am sick of being me. I can't bear to be the poor boring girl who doesn't understand for a moment longer. This is not me. This is not the real Flora Banks. I can be much better than this.

I tap Emma on the arm.

"Just going to the bathroom," I say, and I pick up the lemonade and drink a bit, to prove that I am behaving myself, as if these two people were my parents.

She turns to me. Her face is very kind. She wears glasses, like Drake.

"You will be OK? They're just over there. See the sign? Shall I come with you?"

I follow her finger and see the sign.

"No," I tell her. "I'll be fine. Of course I will. I can manage a trip to the bathroom."

She nods. "Of course you can. Sure. Sorry."

I make my way between the tables, which are far apart from each other, but which still keep getting in my way. The place is pretty full, but not completely. I am wearing jeans, and I check to see if there is money in the pocket. There is: there are some strange banknotes. There are some coins with holes in the middle and they say KRONE on them. Krone. It's strange that the cold place's money is krones, but I am sure the krones will buy me some beer. I have some coins with holes in the middle.

I go to the bathroom, because I know that woman is watching (Alice? Amber?). I sit on the toilet and roll up my sleeves and read everything I have written on my hands and arms, but the only part that makes sense are the words FLORA, be brave. The rest of it is things like superwoman and cold place is in my head and DRAKEDRAKEDRAKE and 5827 and a big DRAKE cut into my skin. I like that one the best.

On my left wrist, it says Agi. Friend. Glasses. That is the woman. Her name is Agi. I find the pen in my other pocket, where it always is, and write it in big letters above the word superwoman. AGI, it says. That should make me remember. If I knew that man's name, I would write it too.

When I come out of the bathroom, I look to check whether they are waiting for me. They are still talking to each other, and I walk quickly to the bar, which is long and wooden with lots of beer taps on it.

I am going to drink beer like a normal person. This, I think, is one of the things I need to do, before I am allowed to see Drake. I need to demonstrate to the world that I can act like an ordinary girl. I am seventeen and I kissed a boy on the beach.

"Can I have four beers, please?" I ask the bartender, as politely as I can. If I drink two of them quickly, I will catch up with the other people and be normal.

The bartender is tall with a grizzly gray beard and a black T-shirt with MOTÖRHEAD on it.

"Four beers," he echoes, looking at me with a suspicious face. "How old are you, my dear girl?"

I don't know what to say. I am pretty sure I am seventeen. Yet I want to give him the right answer, rather than the true one.

"Old enough?" I say, and he laughs.

"Fine—that'll do," he says, and picks up four glasses from a dishwasher tray and starts filling them. "You are on holiday?"

"Yes." I remind myself, fiercely, to be normal. "Do you live here? All the time?"

"My great-grandfather was a miner here. My grandfather too. My father moved away to Tromsø. I came back here nineteen years ago. We are four generations from Spitsbergen."

"Miners?"

He hands me the first glass. I sit up on a bar stool to watch him pour the rest and start drinking the beer while I wait.

"Yes," he says. "Coal miners. It was a terrible life they had. Where are you staying, may I ask?"

I frown. This doesn't seem like a good question; and more than that, I don't know the answer.

He laughs and puts his hands up.

"Sorry. I ask because some of the hotels used to be mining barracks. If you're at the Arctic Guesthouse, for example—those buildings up there are all the places where the miners used to live. They were not treated well, you know. It was a hellish life. They trekked to work up the valleys in snow and ice and blizzards, and darkness in winter. They were given a bucket of water to wash in once a month, 'whether they needed it or not.'" He laughs and looks at me. I laugh too.

"That's not very nice."

"No, it's not."

There are other people at the bar. I pay for the beers and carry three of them back over to the table I was sitting at. I seem to have already finished one.

"Here you are," I tell the woman (Agi! Agi Agi Agi—I read it on my arm), and the man who has a big beard and lots of hair that sticks straight up. They take the beers and thank me, but they look at me, and then at each other.

"Whether or not we find Drake this evening," says Agi, "we are going to contact your family tonight. Your parents. They will need to come and get you."

I shake my head. "No!" I shout. They can't do that. They can't. "When we find Drake, he can talk to them for me. He can explain."

I am scared by the idea that Agi could make a phone call and ruin everything. I stare at her. She looks at the man and makes a face.

"I'm not stupid," I say, my voice even louder. "I can see you looking at each other. Thinking how useless I am. You're not my mom and dad, you know. I am an adult. I came here, didn't I? However you get to this place, I did it and I have money in my pocket to buy you both a beer, and I've got a coat and some boots and all I need is Drake. Just Drake. I need Drake because he made me remember. I don't need you telling my mom. This isn't your place anyway. It's mine. You're only here because I imagined you."

I pick up one of the glasses of beer and drink quickly. It is horrible, but I force it down, gulp after gulp after gulp. It stops reminding me of Dad and makes me feel sick. I walk away from the table, stumbling, trying to be dignified. I don't know where to go, but I have a sturdy glass half-filled with beer in my hand, so I can't storm out of the room. I go back to the bar after all, and sit up on a stool so I can talk to that man again about the miners.

The room is perfectly quiet. Everyone is looking at me. They are not even pretending not to look at me.

I float off to the ceiling, because this is too difficult. From the ceiling I can see myself shouting. My voice is so loud that I can hear it too, even from far away.

"Stop looking at me!" I shout. "I'm fine. I'm normal! Normal! Normal! And we cannot go to Flambards! We can't. We can't."

Then I am crying and turning to the bartender. I ask him something and he shakes his head and comes around the bar to talk to me. A woman comes over from a nearby table, an older woman I probably don't know, and puts an arm on my shoulder. The figure that represents me turns into her shoulder and buries her face in it and cries.

"Don't cry, Flora," I whisper to myself, and I fly back down into my own body, and look at my hand. FLORA, be brave, it says on it, and I stare at it until I have absorbed its message. I am Flora. I have to be brave, or this will never get done.

I pull away from the nice woman, who smells like soap and cigarettes.

"Sorry," I tell her. I sniffle and wipe my face on a tissue that the bartender is holding out to me.

"My dear, that is quite all right," she says. "This place is hard. Never come here in the winter. You don't remember me, but I sold you those boots. You are a striking young lady."

I nod.

"Thanks for the boots."

I will probably still be here in the winter. Everyone says the winter is worse, but I don't know why. It can't be colder or snowier. Perhaps it becomes less magical in winter. Maybe it will stop healing me then.

"She's with us. Sorry," says a voice, and I look up, but it's the woman, Andi, Abigail, Anna. It's not Drake. The woman with glasses takes my hand.

"Come on, Flora," she says. "We'll get you back to your room and into bed. She should not have been drinking, I think."

The man with the beard and the hair is beside her, and he starts talking in that other language, and the bartender and the older woman reply in another language too, and they are all talking about me using words I don't understand.

The door is nearby. The bartender has gone back to the bar to serve some other person some beer. The beard and the nice older lady and Alphie are all talking about me. The other people have started talking among themselves. People are not staring anymore.

I ease myself off the bar stool. Nobody notices at all. I shuffle around until there is no one between me and the door.

When the path is clear, I move quickly, darting away and out. There is a flight of steps, going down, outside the door, and I was not expecting that, so I fall all the way down, but it doesn't hurt and I seem to bounce and it actually proves to be the most efficient way of getting to the bottom. Nothing hurts when I stand up.

I am in a square. There are restaurants and there is a hotel and a closed supermarket, and on the other side of the square there is a road. I run toward the road. I don't know whether to go right or left, so I go right, and I run and run.

It is starting to snow. Maybe it will get dark soon.

It never gets dark. That is the point of this place. It is light all the time, because it only exists inside my head. It is light all day and it is light all night. I must never come here in winter.

There is a figure at the end of this road, and I run toward it as fast as I can because even through the snow I can see that this man looks like Drake. As I get closer, he becomes more like Drake, not less. There is someone else with him. It is a woman. I ignore her and focus on Drake. He is my Drake. He loves me and I have found him. He made me remember and now he will make me remember again.

The man is wearing Drake's glasses. He is wearing Drake's jeans. He has Drake's hair. They turn and walk away from me because they haven't seen me, through the snow.

I kissed this man on the beach. I know I did. I know it because it is still in my head. I have to get to him. He will save me.

I haven't got my coat, but I am warm because I am running. I keep going, past buildings, and a few cars parked outside apartment buildings. I run past a couple of people walking my way and I don't stop, because these are not the people I want. I pass old bits of machinery that have pulleys and cables and huge rusty buckets, and I remember the man telling me about the miners and what a terrible life they led.

I remember.

I remember.

Drake is ahead of me, and I have remembered things. Drake makes me remember.

The snow is falling so thickly that I cannot see them anymore. I stop when I am beside a black expanse of water, with snowy mountains on the other side of it. There is a jetty sticking out into the water and a few boats are moored to it. The snow is blowing silently all around me, and as I stand and look around, the clouds close in and there is nothing at all. There is just me. I am here, in this place inside my head, and I am alone. Drake was here and now he is not.

Out on the water, I can see a faint light, and hear the *sloosh*ing sound of a boat being rowed away. I sit down on the jetty in the snow. I lie down and curl around myself. The snow lands on me. It starts to make me a warm white blanket.

I close my eyes.

When I open them again, I will be in a pink bed in an attic bedroom back in the normal place.

Chapter Nineteen

The pillowcase is cool under my cheek. I stretch out. My legs are bare, and my feet reach down to the bottom of the bed, where a sheet is tucked in. I explore sideways: I am in a single bed, and my head is pounding, and I don't want to open my eyes because I will be in Penzance and none of the things in my head will have happened.

I touch my face with my fingers. The skin is pitted and bumpy. I put my fingers to my temples and feel my pulse pounding.

I need to sleep.

There are words on my arm, huge words scrawled in black pen.

I SAW DRAKE, it says, in wobbly writing. IN A BOAT.

I saw Drake. In a boat. I want to remember it, but I don't. I don't remember it, but I believe it.

This is a room with two beds in it, and there is a person sleeping in the other one. This does not happen at home.

The person in the other bed is facing me, a narrow space between us, and she looks as if she is peacefully asleep. Her eyes are closed and her skin is nicer than mine. She has red cheeks and brown hair.

I should probably know her, or we wouldn't be sleeping in the same room. Perhaps she is Paige. Paige has smooth skin and dark hair.

There is a map on the wall behind her, showing some islands in lots of blue sea. Between us, on a little table, is a pile of books, but they are written in a strange language that I can't begin to read. One is called *Neljäntienristeys*. Either I have lost my ability to make sense of words or that is a different language.

I close my eyes again. I have no idea how long I have been sleeping for, but it's light outside, and so it must be daytime. I look up to the window, but the blinds are pulled down and all I can see is the sunlight coming in around it.

I look at my hands. One of them says FLORA, be brave and Drake, and the other says Agi and cold place is in my head and I SAW DRAKE IN A BOAT. Farther up my arm it says DRAKE in my skin. It is not written in pen. It is as if my arm were saying it to me by itself.

Agi is a woman with glasses. This woman does not have glasses, but she is asleep in bed, so she doesn't need them. People do not need to wear glasses when they are asleep. This seems sensible. I sit up and look around: on the bigger table at the end of her bed there is a pair of glasses, stretching out their limbs, looking at the door with their blank eyes.

Agi. This woman is called Agi and she is my friend. I know her. I am amazed with myself for knowing all of this.

That is why I love Drake. He kissed me on a beach and he made me remember.

I feel sane. I feel rational. I feel like I have slept for a long time.

I feel normal. There is no swooping around through time and space: I miss it but I am pleased, because I have work to do.

My machine is next to me. My phone. I take it out and look at what has been happening on it, then immediately wish that I hadn't.

Baby sister,

Imagine you're a mother with one child on his deathbed. You make sure your other kid, the one you usually look after, is OK and you go to the bedside of the one who's very sick. Then the other one turns out not to be safely tucked away at home with her friend, and when you finally track her down, she's at the North Pole, looking for a boy.

They figured out where you were in about two seconds, once they started looking. Mom has opted to stay at my deathbed, and Dad has just left to head your way. Beware: he will turn up in Svalbard in a day or so and will, I imagine, find you much quicker than you've found your Drake. He'll bring you directly to Paris, probably in a straitjacket.

They have, of course, called the police, and if there is a police officer on that island, he or she will be out looking for you just as soon as the right people pass on the right messages.

Paige told them about your liaison with Drake, and also that she never for one moment stayed in the house with you, and that she saw you on your way to the train station with a fur coat on and a suitcase and the word "Spitsbergen" written in big letters on your hand. She is quite the detective, though she actually believed you to be en route to Gay Paree, as you apparently told her that was what was happening. She thought the "Spitsbergen" was just a bit of an obsession. She says she never imagined you could actually go there. Our parents were not happy with her for abandoning you. She is terribly sorry and worried and has come to her senses: it seems that it was her poisonous mother who encouraged her.

And so they realized that you'd dashed off on an Arctic adventure to find the boy. Mom is as wildly, obsessively protective of you as any human being could possibly be, to the point where she doesn't accept that you have any rights of your own—I know you know that, on some level. At least, I think you do. She'll be even more desperate to keep you where she can see you from now on. You need to make the most of the freedom you have right now.

Time is running out for me. I hate it. I don't want to die. I am 24 years old and 24-year-olds don't die. It's not fair. I rage and rage against the dying of the light, but I'm forcing myself to shut up about that for a moment and think about you. Here are some things:

Do not let them get you back on those pills. Be yourself. If you're difficult or weird or strange or funny, that's OK. That's you, Flora. The person you are now, with all your imperfections and all your difficulties—the person who can be a total pain in the ass, who causes her parents to tear their hair out, who writes adorable wild e-mails, who fell in love with a boy on a Cornish beach and followed him to the end of the earth—that's you. That's my sister. You have amnesia, but you are alive. Live your life.

You asked why I ran away to Paris and cut off contact with our parents. It didn't happen as dramatically as all that, actually. I left home as a normal-ish teenager does, to go to college, and I came back to see you as often as I could. After a while, though, I couldn't stand the way they were treating you and I told them so one too many times. Keeping you dosed up placidly at home. Not letting you be yourself. I told them if they kept you on those pills (which you don't need—there's no medication for anterograde amnesia, as you don't have epilepsy, and all your pills are a tranquilizer to keep you quiet and pliable), I was going to help you get away from them. They told me to stay away, so I did. I've stayed in touch with you, though, my Flora. They blocked my number on your phone, but I always found ways to get to you. We've e-mailed, we've spoken, we've written letters. I sent you postcards often, but I never knew if you got them or not. I hope you did.

Until two weeks ago I barely contacted our parents beyond a card at Christmas, and I only saw them once and that was thanks to you. Then I got my terrible news, and everything changed, and I needed them again.

So that's the truth. I've told it to you before, and I wish I could keep on telling you forever, but I can't. You won't remember of course, but you have come off your pills before, and wild, wonderful things have happened. Our parents hate it, and you and I LOVE it. We have had some times together—I wish you could have those memories, my sweet sister. We've walked and laughed and been shopping and played hide-and-seek. We've watched movies. We've sat up all night talking. I love you.

I hope I get to see you.

If I don't—then thanks for everything. It's been a blast.

Jacob xxxx

I look at Jacob's message. I love him and he's going to die. I have amnesia. I have escaped before. Mom and Dad have been lying to me for years and years and I can't trust them. I cannot remember that I have amnesia, and I cannot remember anything else. I need to write it down: Don't trust Mom and Dad. I need to find Drake, and that is the only thing I can think about now because a police person is going to come here and find me and take me home, and if I haven't found him by then, then I never will.

Dad is coming. I write that on my arm. The letters come out wobbly.

There are loads of texts and e-mails from my parents, but I don't read them. I sit up in bed and watch the woman sleeping. I stand up, and sit back down quickly on the bed. My head hurts. I feel sick. The inside of my mouth tastes weird.

My stomach heaves. I am wearing shorts and a T-shirt, but the jeans on the end of the bed are also mine (my name is on the label), and so I pull them on as quickly as I can and open the door. There will be a bathroom somewhere nearby because bedrooms always have bathrooms somewhere nearby.

I run down the corridor, knowing that I have to get to a bathroom urgently. I try every door, including the ones with numbers on them, and the sixth door opens into a dark room that smells of shower gel and steam and other people's bodily functions. When I find the light switch, it turns out that this is, indeed, a bathroom.

I lock the door behind me and lean over the toilet just in time to be extraordinarily sick.

I had forgotten (of course) about being sick, but now I remember it from when I was small. My stomach clenches and convulses, and the bowl fills with a thin, foul liquid. I will definitely never drink beer again. As soon as I can, I will write that on my hand and later I will transfer it to a notebook. It is important that this becomes a rule for life.

I kneel and try to hold my hair out of the way until my stomach stops. There are tears in my eyes and I want to go back to bed and back to sleep. But the police are looking for me, and Dad is coming to get me, and although I do want to go to Paris because I want to see Jacob, I don't want to see the parents who tamed me to make me easy to manage. I want to see Drake. I cannot go without seeing Drake. I saw him in a boat. I know I did. I saw Drake in a boat.

Jacob is the only person I can trust and he is about to die.

It is all too much. I see that I am shivering.

Since there is a shower right here in this room, I strip off all my clothes and let the hot water wash away the trails of sick. I help myself to some shower gel and shampoo that are just sitting there, and get properly clean. There are things written on me and I try not to wash them off. I have, of course, no towel, so I dry myself as best I can with the paper towels that are beside the sink and put my clothes back on. It all feels slightly damp, but it will have to do. I brush my teeth using a bit of someone else's toothpaste on my finger. Instantly the inside of my mouth is cool and fresh, like snow.

It takes me a while to find the right room, but it turns out that

it is the only door that isn't locked, because I didn't close it properly behind me. The girl, Agi, is still asleep, so I take everything
that I think is mine, including the fur coat that says FLORA on
its label, and my bag, which has my notebooks in it, and sneak
back out. No one else is showing any signs of being awake: when
I check my phone, I discover that this is because it's ten past five.

I am sitting on a big black rock. I read my notes and then my
e-mail conversation with Drake. I am burning inside with love.
Drake is real. He kissed me on the beach, and then he wrote wonderful e-mails to me.

He wrote: I can't stop thinking about you.

He wrote: I spend more time than you might imagine thinking
of what you would look like naked.

He wrote: Your body is perfect. I know it is.

He wrote: I love you too.

I love him and he loves me. I want to go to him, to breathe his
air, to look him in the eye. I want to touch him with my fingertips. I want to touch his face, his hair. I want to smell his smell. I
cannot go home without doing that.

At eight o'clock the woman who works at the boots shop arrives
for work and finds me waiting on the doorstep of her shop.
According to my notes she was kind to me, and she sold me my
boots. I looked back through my phone and my notebook, discov-
ering all kinds of things, and I found the receipt tucked into the
pages. It had the shop's name on it, and so here I am, ready to ask
for her help. I have a fact sheet that I have just made for myself,
setting out everything I need to tell and to ask her.

She stops when she sees me.

"Flora," she says. She has kind eyes and long gray hair, and she is wearing jeans and a big red coat. "Come in, of course, but what on earth are you doing out here? I will call the guesthouse. They'll send Agi to come and get you."

"That's OK. I need your help with one thing. They're coming to get me anyway. A man is coming to get me. He's my dad. They called the police, but I don't want to see the police."

"Your father is coming to get you? Oh, that is excellent news. I am so pleased. And the police here are good people. Generally twiddling their thumbs. Not much happens. I'll give them a call when we've had a chat, and let them know you're here."

I follow her into the shop and sit where she indicates I should sit, on a stool behind the counter, while she bustles around doing things in her shop.

"Sorry," I tell her. "I should know, but what's your name?"

She stops, turns around, and looks at me. "Henny, my dear, Henny Osterberg. And you know what? I haven't said that to you before. So this is in fact not a thing you have forgotten. This is me telling you my name for the first time."

"Oh, that's good! Like a normal person."

"Like a normal person." She smiles at me with kind eyes. "A coffee?"

While she makes us a drink, I tell her what I need.

"Last time you told me to try the Polar Institute," I say, checking her face to see whether that's right. This is what it says on my fact sheet, and I have compiled it from my notebook. "To find Drake. I went there, but it was locked. He came here to study. He kissed me on a beach."

Two shadowy figures, kissing on a dark beach. I can see them, but I can't hear what they are saying. I used to be able to hear the words, and now they are gone.

"Right. So your father is coming and you want to give it one more go to find him while you still can? Your parents won't understand about the boy?"

"Yes. Right now. I think I saw him last night. In a boat."

"I don't really know your Drake, my dear. I told you to go to the Polar Institute because it and UNIS are in the same building and those are the places where the research happens." She hands me a mug. "Careful—it's hot. But. Now, Flora. He is here, so you are right—Toby met him in the coffee shop a couple of days ago and told him there was a young lady here looking for him, and he was a little alarmed as . . ." She stops and takes a deep breath. "Well. He has a girlfriend here. I'm sorry to say it, but it's true. Toby wanted to tell you, but he was nervous of upsetting you too much, far from home. But you have to know. A Russian scientist, older than him. Nadia Ivanova. Now, I do know Nadia because she has been here for a couple of years."

This makes no sense.

"Drake has a girlfriend?"

"I'm sorry, my dear."

"He does have a girlfriend. But it's me. It's not Nadia Ivanova."

Drake is my boyfriend. He was Paige's, but then I kissed him on a beach and now he is mine. I push Henny Osterberg's words out of my head.

"Where does Drake live?"

He became friends with a girl because he thinks I am in Penzance. He spends time with an older Russian scientist because he is lonely. They talk about science.

"Well, Nadia lives in a remote place, a house across the water. She works over there, and comes across in her little boat to the university. Drake spends much of his time over there, I understand."

"So I did see him last night! I did! In a boat!"

"Yes, Flora. It seems as though you did."

I sip my drink. I saw him. I did the thing I came here to do, and I found Drake. I walked around the town until I found him. I can hardly contain my delight. My face is grinning idiotically: I touch it with my hands to check. And now this woman is telling me where I need to go to find him.

"She lives across the water?"

"Yes. Apparently Longyearbyen is not remote enough! It's the only house across there: you can see it if you stand on the jetty."

"So Drake is over there right now?"

"No you don't, my girl. We'll call Nadia and arrange for Drake to come over here and talk to you face-to-face. If your father's coming to collect you, it's best you stay close for now. But I can see we need to make this happen before you go, or I think you'll just come back again, no?"

"Probably."

She sighs. "Have you had breakfast?"

"No. Shall I go and get something? For you and for me?"

Henny stares into my face. Whatever the test is, I seem to pass it.

"Go on, then." She hands me some money. "Go to the supermarket, across the road and in the square, opposite the pub. In the bakery section, get some pastries of some sort. OK? Could you collect some milk too? If you can get yourself here from England, I think you can get some food from the shop. I'm trusting you."

I write it on a piece of paper: Pastries and milk. Henny. Shop. Most of the writing has washed off my hand, so I write it there too.

"Thank you, Henny. You are very kind to me."

"You come straight back here, and then we'll see about getting Drake to come here to see you. I promise I'll make that happen. But, Flora, you must come right back here. OK?"

"Yes. I'll be quick."

I pick up my bag, tuck my notebook and fact sheet into it, and leave the shop. I turn right because that's the direction of the supermarket with the bakery, and I walk obediently along to the square. I cross the road. I walk right up to the supermarket. Then I carry on walking, back down the road parallel to the one with Henny's shop on it.

I break into a run. I feel bad about doing this because she is being so kind to me, but she has just told me where I can find Drake, and so I cannot do anything but go there before the police take me away.

I run back to the jetty. Today the sun is shining and the clouds are wispy and pretty and they are not about to snow. They are dancing across the sky on their way to snow later, somewhere else.

There are plenty of little boats down there, tied to the wooden jetty with strong ropes. A man in blue overalls is doing something on a big boat, and he smiles and holds a hand up in greeting. I wave back and quickly try to figure out what to do. I need to keep moving.

Henny said the house was the only one you could see. There is only one house over there, perched a little way up from the shore, across the water and to the left. I think I have noticed that house before. I sit down and get out my notebook and scrawl a quick note.

Sorry I have borrowed your boat. It is not stolen because I will be bringing it back. Here is some money for taking it.

I walk confidently to the smallest rowboat, moored at the corner of the wooden structure, and put the note and money under a stone next to it. I untie the boat's rope as if I have every right to do so. It is only wound around a metal thing on the jetty, so it's easy to do. I'm not sure what to do next, so I just fling myself and the rope into the boat, which rocks but doesn't tip over.

The oars are difficult to extract from their places, and of course I have no idea how to use them, but I manage to tuck them into the metal things that hold them.

In the bright Arctic sunshine I set off across the glittering water to find the love of my life. Whatever happens next, I will have found him, and that will change everything.

The man on the shore is shouting something, but I don't look around. I must have rowed a boat before, because my arms know what to do, and I am leaning back and forth and my oars are cutting through the water, using it to propel me forward as if it were solid.

This does not feel real, but I think that it is. I am on the water, plowing toward Drake, and the world has shrunk around me so that this is all there is. This is me, Flora, being brave at last.

The sun is over to my right, dazzling my vision on that side. As soon as the town and the boats and the man and the machines are behind me, I try to forget them. I don't think I have needed to try to forget things, until now. I think my mind has just done it without me telling it to. This thought makes me feel powerful. Drake was right. I am capable of more than people think. And now I am on my way to him.

Two birds swim alongside me for a while. They are tiny, and I recognize them from photographs but I don't know their names. They are smooth and shiny, black and white with beaks that are curved and striped in yellow and red. They skitter across the water to land, and bob along for a while, and then they take off again, using the surface of the water, somehow, as a runway. I like their black backs, their white faces, the red on their bills. They are my friends. I have seen them in books, when I was little.

I kissed Drake, and we wrote each other the most passionate, wonderful e-mails that anyone has ever sent, in this or in any other world. He loved me then and he will love me now.

I think I am rowing wrong. It suddenly occurs to me that I should have my back toward Drake, toward the cabin. I am rowing back to front, keeping my destination in sight. That doesn't work at all and now my arms are screaming at me. I maneuver myself and my little boat around until I am facing back toward the town, but I do not let myself see that there are now two figures waving from the jetty.

It is much easier rowing like this, and I wonder when I have done it before. It doesn't matter. I watch the edge of the town getting smaller as I leave it behind. More birds settle on the water near me, and a couple of them paddle beside me for a while, keeping me company.

"Thank you," I tell them. Puffins. They are called puffins. I am delighted with myself. "Thank you, puffins," I say. They tell me I am welcome.

Drake is ahead of me. I am rowing across this glittering water toward Drake Andreasson, the love of my life.

A boat is out of the water, resting on the snow-covered slope at its edge, and so I pull mine up next to it. My arms are burning, in a pleasurable way.

I stand still for a moment and stare up. The house is close to me now, just a little way up the hill, where the slope is still gentle.

I cannot stop to think or to worry about anything. The e-mail I read this morning from Jacob flashes through my mind. My brother tells me to be myself and to live my life. I inhale the words and imagine him beside me, encouraging me as I walk up to the cabin, and before I can stop myself, I knock on the door. I bang on it hard, four times in a row.

The house is made from wood, and it has a perfect sloped roof and a chimney. It is like a house from a fairy tale. The door is painted black. There are curtains at the windows, and they are closed. I stand where I am and wait.

My heart is pounding hard. Something is about to happen. I wait and wait and wait. I knock again.

The door opens slowly, but no one is there. I start to step inside, but then he is in front of me.

Drake Andreasson, the love of my life, is right there. There is no distance between us at all. I fling myself at him. This is it. Everything I have done has been for this moment. I launch myself into his arms, tears flowing down my cheeks. I smell the smell of him. I kissed him on the beach. I remember his smell.

He sweeps me up and kisses me on the lips.

He doesn't.

He steps forward and puts an arm on my shoulder and pulls me toward him.

He doesn't.

He says: "Flora. I can't believe you're here."

He doesn't.

Our eyes lock and something like love passes between us.

It doesn't.

He pushes me away from him and closes the door in my face. That is what actually happens.

Before he closes it, he says: "What the hell are you doing here? Flora? Jesus!" He puts his hands on my shoulders and moves me back, and he slams the door. I try to stick my foot in there to stop it from actually shutting, but I am too late, and the door is closed and I am standing in the cold on my own with my foot up against a shut door. I hear locks being turned on the inside.

I stare at the door. That was not right. People are shouting behind it. I can hear Drake's voice, and a woman's voice shouting back at him. I don't know what to do. I can't think or feel anything, so I stay exactly where I am and wait.

When the door swings open again, a beautiful woman is standing there instead.

"Hi," she says to me. Her voice sounds American. She has long straight hair and looks like a ballerina.

I look at her, but I have no voice to reply with.

"Would you like to come in?" she says. I hear Drake's voice somewhere behind her.

"She's not coming in!" he says. "She's a stalker."

The woman puts a hand on my arm and guides me into the house.

"Come on," she says. "Come and tell us what's going on." She turns to Drake. "She's not a threat, you idiot. Look at her. You can't slam the door in her face, Drake. What the hell is going on?"

Drake isn't looking at me. He is wearing his heavy-framed glasses. His hair is a bit longer and messier than it was when he kissed me on the beach. He is in his jeans, and a dark blue T-shirt, and his arms are more muscular than they are in my head.

"She's crazy," he says.

I try to pretend he didn't say that. I try to understand how everything could be going this wrong. I have done the thing I came here to do. I have found Drake. I remind myself that he kissed me and he wrote amazing words that are still in my head. I do not understand why he is being so horrible.

"Drake," I say to him. I am inside the house now. The woman closes the door behind me, and we are in a little hallway with two big coats hung up on a peg. It is warm. "I wanted to come and find you because . . ." I take a deep breath. This is the most important thing I have ever done in my life. "Because I love you and you love me. You kissed me on the beach. I remember it. You made me remember. You made that happen. I can see that . . ." But I can't finish my sentence because I don't know what to say. I wave a hand to let him know I can see there is a beautiful woman standing beside me. I touch my imperfect skin.

"Flora."

I look into his face. I gaze into his eyes, drinking him in. He looks into my eyes for a fraction of a second and looks away.

"Flora," he says again. He looks awkward. I am attempting to look into his eyes, but it is impossible while he is looking all around the edge of me and never into my face. "Look, I kind of heard you were in town. The waiter in the café said a girl had been looking for me, and when he described this girl, with blond hair and writing all over her hands, it, like, sounded like you. But I couldn't imagine for one second that it would actually, you know, *be* you. Not you. Not Flora Banks. Not Paige's friend." He winces. "Do your parents know you're here?"

"Yes. Drake, I came to find you because I love you."

"Flora. Look, I have no idea what you think is going on."

"You kissed me on the beach and wrote me beautiful e-mails."

He looks into my eyes for a few seconds. He opens his mouth. He closes it again, and turns and walks away. I turn to the woman.

"Are you Drake's friend?"

She nods her head. "I'm Nadia. Drake's girlfriend."

"You're a Russian scientist." My tone is coming out strangely because I don't know how to be. I need to say things as quickly as I can while the things are in my head, because I think that things disappear from my head. "This happened back home before he met you," I say. "Before he came here. When he was leaving Penzance, he had a party, and after the party I was on the beach and he came to sit beside me and we kissed. He said wonderful things. He gave this stone to me." I take it out of my coat pocket, where it always is. Drake comes back and I show it to them both. "This black stone." I know that the second one is there too, but this is not the time to give it to him. I will do that when everything has been sorted out.

"Flora," says Drake. "I did not give you that stone. That stone was in my bedroom. You went to my bedroom in Penzance and took it. I didn't give you a stone. You went to my room and took a load of my stuff. Aunt Kate said so. Paige was supposed to collect it all, but she didn't."

I shake my head and clear away the wrong words he is saying. "Then he left to come here, but he wrote me an e-mail. I replied to it and we e-mailed each other again and again and again. It was amazing. Nothing like that has ever happened to me before."

I turn from Nadia and look at Drake. "You said the most beautiful things. You made me feel normal. Better than normal. You made me feel . . . alive. Alive, and different in a wonderful way. Not a weird one. And I remember our kiss. You made me remember."

"Flora—"

"And then you asked me if I could come here. I read our e-mails all again just now, and so I know. They are still in my head. You can't tell me they didn't happen because I've got them right here. And I did come here, because you are the best thing in my life, because I can still remember kissing you on the beach. I can remember it. It is the only thing that doesn't fade away.

"And that's because you are the only person who's ever loved me for me, who hasn't wanted to try to make me ordinary, who hasn't thought that being ordinary would be better for me. You and my brother, Jacob. Everyone else tells me lies. I had to find you. Look—I've got your name on my arm." I roll up my sleeve and show it to them. Drake winces. Nadia stares.

She pushes him aside and puts an arm on my shoulder.

"Come and sit down, Flora," she says. Her English sounds American, but she is Russian. She is Nadia, the Russian scientist: I can remember Henny's words.

I notice that I am crying. Tears are streaming down my cheeks. I touch my face. It is not as lumpy-bumpy as I was expecting.

The living room is warm and cozy. The walls are painted dark red; the sofa and chairs are squishy and covered in cushions. There is a rug on the floor and two big radiators. In a corner is a desk with a computer and a lot of paperwork piled up beside it. Music is playing the background: it is crooning, tuney music sung by a gravelly-voiced man.

Nadia takes me to the sofa and pushes me down onto it.

"Come on, Drake," she says. "For God's sake. She comes here to find you. She's carved your *name* into her *arm*. Deal with this."

"But, Nadia," he says, in a quiet voice, as if that would stop me from hearing him. "I have, literally, no idea what she's talking about. She's Paige's friend. The one with no memory. I told you about her. Her parents try to keep her at home. They do lie to her. She's right about that."

I can't speak because I am crying too much.

"Well, if they keep her at home, they're not doing a very good job of it." She turns to me. "Who can we call?" Nadia is touching my shoulder. "I'll get you something to drink. You sit back. It's OK. You'll be OK. Drake, for Christ's sake, talk to her. She's not well, but she's not exactly dangerous. Be kind. She's young. I can't believe you just locked her out in the snow."

While Nadia goes to the kitchen, Drake sits next to me on the sofa. He tentatively pats my shoulder, and so I lean into his chest and cry and cry and cry. I can feel the material of his T-shirt getting wet with my tears and snot, but still I keep crying. He smells exactly the way I remember him.

"Flora," he says, when I pause for breath. "Flora. Let's talk about this for a minute. Can you calm down so we can talk?"

With an enormous effort, I slow myself down. I stop crying. I take deep, shuddering breaths. I want to spin away, to disappear into myself, to become three or seven, to wake up in a different time and place, but I make an effort and stay right here. I do not go to the ceiling. This is important. I am with Drake. I just have to say the right words in the right order, and it will all be perfect.

"Flora," he says. "I don't know what you think happened between us, but it really didn't. You were Paige's friend. But that's all. I never kissed you on any beach, Flora. I never asked you to come here."

I look into his dark eyes. His hair has fallen slightly across his face. He has disengaged from me, inched away across the sofa so we are no longer touching. I wish he would put his arm around my shoulders, but I know that won't happen.

He did kiss me on the beach. He did. I am not going to let him get away with this. I know he kissed me because I remember it.

"You did kiss me, I was sitting there and you came along. You said such nice things. Paige knows about it. That's why she's not speaking to me anymore."

"Yeah." He sighs heavily. "Yeah, this is where it gets complicated. Oh Christ. The last thing I expected was for this to follow me out here. Look. Paige sent me a bunch of furious e-mails when I left. Accusing me of sleeping with you. Telling me she knows it all. Telling me all kinds of bad shit about messing with someone as vulnerable as you, ruining your friendship, being a selfish bastard. That kind of thing.

"But the thing is, she's right to be mad at me. I did go to the beach in Penzance that night and kiss a girl. It was not my best moment. But, it wasn't you I kissed. I kissed Lily. She was at the party. Friend of my cousin's. She was there and I was drunk, and I was about to leave Cornwall forever, and . . . Well, one thing led to another, and it was stupid and I'm not a particularly nice guy sometimes, but I was leaving and somehow I was sitting on the beach with her and it was my last night in Cornwall and—yeah. I kissed her. But it was Lily, Flora. It wasn't you. But then I looked around and you were there, leaning over the railing, looking at us. I knew you'd tell Paige."

He is lying. I know he is lying. His face says he is.

"But I didn't think you'd tell Paige I'd kissed *you*. I'm sorry that it messed with your head that much. That you think you remember it. OK? I'm sorry. Truly I am."

Nadia is in front of us. I'm not sure how long she's been there. When I look at her, I see she is perfectly made-up, and she is wearing tight jeans and a diamanté-studded black top. She does not look like someone who lives in a remote cabin in the cold place. She hands me a glass with some dark liquid in it.

"Drink it," she says. "It's brandy. I'm sorry you are feeling this way. I think you are very brave and I think Drake is an idiot."

"He's lying," I tell her. "I know he kissed me. I can remember it. I know the things he said to me." I take a deep breath. "And then there are all the messages he sent. He wrote the sweetest e-mails. He was different in them from the way he's being now." I stare at him. "Completely different. I know he wrote them because I read them all this morning."

"I swear I did not send you an e-mail. I have never sent you one single e-mail in my entire life." He looks at Nadia. "That is a fact," he says. "Seriously."

"I sent you a text." I saw that on my phone. I know I sent him a text.

"You wouldn't have my number here. My old British one doesn't work. If you did send a text, I didn't get it."

I reach for my bag.

"I have the e-mails right here." As I reach into the bag, I know that there is a high chance that I will have done something else with them, that I got them out to show to Henny or that I threw them into the cold sea. However, they are there.

"Look."

I am not sure who to hand the stack of papers to. I give them to Drake, because they are his. Nadia squeezes next to him on the far end of the sofa, so I move over to make room. Drake does not shift into the gap I have opened up in the middle: Nadia comes to sit there instead.

My Drake, the love of my life, does not want me anywhere near him.

Drake skims his own words, looking uncomfortable, then pushes the bundle of papers at Nadia and stands up, pacing the room. I cannot look at him anymore. I don't know what to think. I have no idea if there was a woman named Lily at the party, or if he is just saying whatever he wants because he knows no one in the world would believe me over him.

Nadia is reading every word.

"Look," Drake says. "That e-mail address you've got there— it's not mine. Those e-mails are sent from DrakeAndreasson@ hotmail.com. My e-mail address is"—his eyes flick to me and then away—"a Google one. I don't think anyone uses Hotmail anymore, do they?"

"It's true," Nadia says to me gently. "This is not Drake's usual e-mail address, but"—she looks hard at him—"but perhaps he has one I don't know about. Drake—if you did write these, it's OK. I *really* don't care. I do care if you're messing with a sick girl's head. Now, that I would care about very much."

"I didn't write them. I mean—you know I've never been to the satellite dishes, don't you? I didn't write a word of this."

"Then who did?" I demand. I knock back the brandy that

Nadia put in my hand and stand up. I am furious. "Look at them. They exist. I came here, to this cold place, because of these messages. They mean everything. They changed my universe. I came here to find you. You said: 'If you were here things would be different.' Well, I am here. I know you don't want to see me, but you can't just lie and lie and lie to my face like that. Everyone lies except Jacob and it's going to stop. These messages are real. Look. I'll show you. I'll show you them in my e-mail account. In my inbox."

I walk over to the computer. I am propelled by absolute fury. My fingers are shaking. I sit down at the chair, which is some sort of special chair without a back on it.

I am on the ceiling, watching myself. My fingers pound on the keyboard. Nadia stands up and comes to stand behind me, with Drake. He reaches for her hand, but she steps away from him. She does not look friendly toward him.

He looks at the screen. He freezes.

She looks. She freezes.

I am back in my body, and I too am looking at the screen. I am trying hard not to freeze like them.

"See," I say, although I know something is very wrong. I hear the wobble in my voice. "See—here they are. The messages. Right here."

I am looking at the inbox on the screen, but all the messages in it come from Flora Banks. This cannot be the inbox of my e-mail account. I have done something wrong.

I look at the top of the screen. This e-mail account belongs to DrakeAndreasson@hotmail.com. These are all the messages of our correspondence, all of them.

"You've got this account on your computer," I say, but my voice trails off.

"Flora," says Drake. He is angry. "You logged into it yourself. You did this, yourself. You wrote the messages. You created this. And then you came here. Somehow. You stalked me, when you should never have been allowed to leave your house. Ever. I'm calling the police, right now, to come and take you home. You . . ." He stops and blows the air out through his mouth.

I stare at the screen. My fingers have just done this. They have taken me straight into Drake's e-mail account. This cannot be true. I try to think of a different explanation, but I can't find one.

I wrote the messages.

I cannot have written the messages. I received the messages. I cannot have written them as well.

"Stop it, Drake!" Nadia is saying. "Listen to yourself, for God's sake. This girl is not well. She needs help. She needs us to look after her. But we should call the police, because they'll help us help her."

"Don't," I tell them. I am on my feet. "Don't call anyone. Don't do a thing. Forget it. Forget all of it. I'm going."

I grab my coat from a chair and run out through the front door. Neither of them tries very hard to stop me.

"You're just . . ." Nadia is saying to him as I leave. She continues talking, but I run away.

I cannot go back, so I run the other way, instead. The two little boats are on the shore ahead of me, but I go up the steeply sloping hill behind the cabin. The sun is shining. The hill gets steeper as it goes. Little rocks poke up through the snow. Something that looks like a fox runs away from me, in the distance.

I am at the top of a hill, and although I know I have done something terrible, I have no idea what it is.

A minute or an hour ago I knew, but it has vanished from my mind, and I didn't have time to write it down, so now it is lost. I know that I need to stay away, but I don't know what I am hiding from.

I am standing on the ridge of a mountain in an impossibly beautiful icy place. Far below me on one side is a stretch of water, with two rowboats pulled up on the shore beside it. On the other side there is nothing: mountains stretch as far as I can see. The sky is the deepest blue, the sun dazzling. There is light snow on the ground, but I am hot because I am wearing a big fur coat. This is a bright, snowy place. It cannot be a real place. I am in a place inside my head, hiding.

When I look back, I see that there is a hut far below me, down near the boats: I have scrambled away from it, up the hill, away from whatever is inside it. I should not be out here on my own because I know that there is something dangerous.

I will take my chances in the wild rather than face the thing that is in the hut.

As there are no trees, I must cross the ridge before I can hide. As soon as I am over it, I will be in the wild. There will be just me and the mountains and the rocks and the snow.

I stand on the ridge and take two smooth stones from my coat pocket. I don't know why I am doing this, but I know it is essential. They are black, and together they fit neatly into the palm of my hand. I throw the stones, one after the other, as hard as I can, as far as I can. They disappear among the snow-covered rocks and I am pleased.

Soon I will be out of sight. I will find a place to hide, and I will not move until I remember what it is that I have done. I don't care how long it takes. I will probably stay here, in this cold place, for the rest of my life.

Chapter Twenty

"Flora!"

In the distance someone is calling my name. I can only half hear it. I don't know who they are or what they are doing: I do know that I don't want to see them.

I want to disappear, to swoop away through time and space. I want to float up into the sky. I want to leave my body behind.

I have already done that. I am on my own, in the cold place. This isn't real. None of it is real. I can stay here, sitting in the snow in this cold place with its blue skies, forever.

I kissed a boy on a beach. I push my sleeve up. I carved his name into my arm. I don't want to see the letters and so I pick up a handful of snow and rub at the word to make it go away.

When someone sits beside me, I don't look at him.

"There you are! Jesus Christ."

It is a man I don't know. It is a not-Drake man. This man has hair on his face and his head, and I edge away from him. I have made an assassin to come and finish off this part of me that is sitting in the snow.

"Hey," says my killer. "Come on. Up you get. Everyone is out looking for you."

He stands and yells something down the hill in a strange language. He reaches out a hand to help me up, but I don't take it. He looks around, and then sits down next to me and puts a hand on the sleeve of my coat. He has a brown spot on his face. He is gentle, for a killer.

"Come on, Flora. You can't sit out here. It's not safe. You don't want to die, do you?"

I shrug.

"Well, OK. Perhaps you do, but I don't and neither do the other people who are out looking for you. Come on. We need to get inside."

I don't move.

"You remember me?"

"No." There is no point in pretending.

"I'm Toby. I've sold you lots of coffee, though usually I don't ask you to pay. I've seen you every day for the past four days."

I shake my head. "I'm staying here."

"You had too much to drink last night, and that's our fault. Mine and Agi's. But that's not a reason to do this. Your life is difficult. You got emotional. People do. It happens all the time. Come inside and talk. Please. People care about you."

The man has a kind face, and he is saying nice things, but I don't want him here.

"Tell them to go away."

"Look, Flora. You have to get indoors, because out here you're in danger, and so is everyone who's looking for you."

"I will not."

"You will." He looks around, clearly hoping for someone to come along and help him. "Look, if I have to, I'll just pick you up and carry you. There are bears out here. There are terrible stories. I'll take you if you won't come with me."

"I am not a little girl."

I am a little girl. I have been a little girl all my life. People pick children up and carry them when they refuse to do as they're told.

I am seventeen, but I am unwinding, becoming younger. Soon I will cease to exist at all.

"I've thought you were amazing, Flora, from the first time I met you. I could see you were different. You got yourself to Spitsbergen to find the boy. You kept on and on telling me about him, about how he made you remember, about how you had to find him quick before your parents came. You are someone who gets things done. You found the boy. You can't give up now. You have amnesia, but you are alive. You can live your life."

Someone else has said those words to me, too.

"I can't," I say. "Please go back."

"It's not safe out here, Flora. I have a gun."

"Are you going to shoot me?"

"No. It's because we're on the bears' territory."

"Have you ever shot a polar bear?"

"No. I had to learn to use a gun so I could go cross-country skiing. But terrible things do happen, and you must never go out alone like this, unprotected. It's worse in winter because you can't see anything. Can you imagine the winter here?"

"This must be winter. It's cold."

He smiles. "The height of summer. You know how it never gets dark?"

"I thought that was in my head."

"In summer it never gets dark. In winter it never gets light. It is, I promise you, as dark as night from the start of November until the end of January, when sunrise starts to arrive. In March the first rays of proper sun hit the town and it's party time. It's much easier to be happy in summer. Don't come in winter."

I shiver. "I won't."

I take out my pen and roll my bundle of sleeves up as high as they will go, and write on my arm in thick pen: DON'T GO TO SVALBARD IN WINTER. That can become one of my rules.

He indicates with his head.

"So. Now we'll go back."

I shake my head. I try to say "I can't," but it turns out that I cannot speak. He puts an arm around my shoulder, and because I am surprised that he is a real warm human being, I lean into him. I force myself to stop crying before I have really started.

"I'm useless," I tell him. "I can't do anything. I'm not really a person because I don't know what's happening. I have no idea what I'm doing here. I kissed Drake on a beach."

I look at him for validation. I can remember kissing Drake on the beach. Somehow that has brought me here, to the snow, on my own.

The sun is dazzling me. It is shining right in my eyes. I am looking straight ahead because I cannot look this stranger in the eye while I am saying these things. I don't care who I am saying them to: I just need to speak the words.

"I am not human," I say. "I just exist, like an animal."

"Well, if I may say so," the man says, in his careful voice, "I think you're talking shit. You think we don't all feel like that? Like we're crazy, like we're not a real person, like we don't exist? Everyone feels that way sometimes. I can remember talking to you when you lost your bag. So what? You can't remember and that's not a bad thing. It doesn't make me better than you. I'm a stranger to you, but here's what I see:

"I see a girl who has suffered a terrible damage to her brain. Someone who, it seems, is shut away by her parents to keep her safe. But inside there is a vibrant person, a traveler, and her memory of this boy Drake has propelled her into action. I think, Flora, that you came here not to find Drake but to find yourself. It wasn't Drake—he's an unlikely romantic hero, really—it was you. Didn't you come here, perhaps, because you heard him talking about the place he was going to, and it called to you?"

I don't know what to say. I don't say anything.

"I come from Oslo, and Svalbard called me, even though I'm not really the rugged adventurous type. Like you, I had to come. Some of us are meant to be here. We need this place." He sweeps a hand around at the jagged horizon, the rocks, the snow, the wilderness that goes on and on. "We need to be small specks in wild nature, by the pole. The midnight sun. The midday darkness. The northern lights. It called to you, Flora, and you answered. You overcame everything, and you came here, alone. You are the bravest person I've ever met."

I look at him. "You're just being nice."

"I mean it. I respect you. You're better than what you call 'normal' people because you have so much to overcome, and you've done it. But now, please stand up and walk with me very slowly and carefully back down to the cabin, because there is a polar bear with cubs two ridges away from us and they can run fast. We must go immediately."

We reach the door and the man, whose name I don't know (at least, I think I don't) pushes me inside, then turns around, ready to head back up the hill.

"Drake's house," he says. "In you go. There are five other people out looking for you, and a mother bear with cubs is protective. Wait right here, inside, by the door. Every time someone comes back, make sure the door is closed properly behind them. I'll go and find the rest and tell them you're safe."

He is brave, this bearded coffee man.

I stand in this house, paralyzed. He called it Drake's house. Does that mean Drake is here? If anyone is killed by a bear because they're looking for me, I will find the bear and feed myself to it too. If the bear is shot, it will be my fault. The bear is doing nothing wrong. It's just being a bear.

I hope I haven't made anyone die by doing stupid things before. I might have. The fact that, if I have, I wouldn't know about it chills me. If this bear rips anyone apart because of me, I'll forget it and carry on as usual, and no one will ever tell me.

After a few minutes, the door flies open and two women come in. I stare at them. I don't know them.

One of them, who looks like a ballet dancer, puts a rifle carefully away in a safe behind the door and locks it.

"Flora! You're back," says the other one, who is wearing glasses. She gives me a hug. "Oh, thank goodness, Flora. This is wonderful. Oh, Flora. I'm sorry we didn't look after you as well as maybe we should have."

I am supposed to know her, but I don't.

"There's a bear," I tell her.

"Yes," says the other woman. "Sit down. It's OK. Toby and the others know what they're doing. I promise—he'll get everyone back. He's tougher than he looks."

She looks nervous.

I sit on the floor beside the door. I want to see people coming back. The woman with glasses sits beside me and takes my hand.

"It's me," she says. "Agi. Your friend."

Agi. I try to put her name into my head.

The next person to come through the door is Drake. My heart leaps at the sight of him: he is my Drake. I kissed him on the beach. I love him. There is a woman with him, an older woman, but all I see is the boy I love.

It is Drake. I stumble as I get to my feet. Drake! I have come to Svalbard to see Drake, and now he is here. I walk toward him, scarcely able to breathe. He is going to heal my mind and make everything better.

"Drake!" I whisper.

He looks at me, and I see that he is scared of me. Something has happened.

"Drake," I say again.

He puts a hand awkwardly on my arm and leads me into a different room. There is a rug on the floor and a nice sofa. He sits me down. The woman who looks like a dancer is standing by the window, but when we come in, she leaves the room.

"Flora," he says. "You don't remember, do you?"

I shake my head. I don't remember.

"You kissed me on the beach," I say. "I remember that."

"You didn't kiss me on the beach. You think you remember it but you don't. You think I wrote you e-mails but I didn't. You wrote them to yourself. It all came from your head. I'm sorry, Flora. But I'm very glad you're safe."

I do not look at him. I cannot. I make a muttering noise in the back of my throat and try to move away.

"I feel really bad about it," he says. "When you came here, a little while ago, I wasn't very nice to you. I'm sorry. You ran away and when we saw you hadn't taken the boat, we had to call Henny to get people over to find you. I thought you'd gone forever. That would have been my fault. I'm really glad you're OK."

I cannot bear the sound of his voice. A switch has flicked inside my head, and I am not in love with him. Now I cannot imagine it. I do not love him. I do not know him. He is a stranger and I cannot think of a word to say to him. I did not kiss him on a beach. I wouldn't want to kiss this boy, and he wouldn't want to kiss me.

I will miss having feelings. I will miss thinking that I had a real memory. I will not miss Drake because this boy is not the Drake in my head. I made him up—every bit of him.

"It's OK," I say. I rub the inside of my arm where I know his name is on my flesh. "Really."

"Yeah?"

"Yeah. I had two stones. I threw them away."

"I used to pick up nice-shaped stones. In Penzance. Just because they were there. That's what those were. You got them from my Aunt Kate's house."

"You didn't give one to me?"

"No. You went to Kate and Jon's place. They told me. You were going to go back and get all my stuff, but I guess you came here instead."

"I went to their house?"

"Yep."

"Oh." I am glad I threw the stones away. Nothing is what I thought it was.

The woman who looks like a dancer is a Russian scientist called Nadia and this is her house. She makes coffee for everyone, and then passes out a warm dark drink that Agi says is brandy. I drink everything they put in front of me. Drake disappears into a different room, and I am glad. I thought I knew Drake, but he is a stranger.

I will have to write myself a big note about that, just in case I make a fool of myself again and again and again. It is vital that I remember to stop looking for him. I must put it in my notebook urgently. I look around for my bag. It is in the corner. I run to pick it up and sit back down on the sofa.

"How long have you known Drake?" I ask Nadia, as if time means anything at all.

She shrugs. "Not long. Things work differently out here. He mainly stays over, but it's not exactly . . ." She looks as if she's going to say more, but stops herself, and in fact I don't want to know.

We all sit in silence. Someone else is still out there, with the man named Toby who makes coffee and knows how to shoot a bear, and who was nicer to me than anyone has ever been aside from Jacob, and I don't know who it is. I feel as if everybody I have ever met in the Arctic is in this room already.

I shut my eyes. I want to leave my body, to float away, to drift back up the ridge and to look at the bear, the people, at Toby with his gun. I hope the bear won't have to die. I try and I try, but I stay right here, drably in my own body. I take a pen and a notebook from my bag, and write: I DID NOT KISS DRAKE ON A BEACH AND HE DID NOT WRITE ME ANY E-MAILS. I cannot forget this. Then I start to read my most recent words.

There is a gunshot outside. It cracks out and echoes around. I jump and drop the notebook. Everyone tenses. I feel it, but I do not look at anyone because I don't want to see their faces.

I pull my knees up to my chin and put my head on them. Blood will be smeared on the snow. A bear, living in its natural wild habitat, smelling food, going after it, has been shot because of me. I want to disappear. I want to go back out into the snow, where I belong. I want to find the bear's body. Toby said it was a mother with cubs. I wonder what will happen to the cubs now.

The door flies open. Two men fall in through it and slam it behind them.

"Look!" shouts Nadia from the living room, and because everyone is here now, and because of the tone of her voice, I run to see what she is looking at.

Through the window, we can see a polar bear, walking calmly away from the house, back into the wild. Two little bears are following it.

Its fur is yellowy white. Its body swings from side to side as it walks. It is huge and it is terrifying. It lopes along calmly, its legs thick, its feet huge. Its babies are close behind.

I turn and look at Toby.

"Was there another one?"

"Just this one." He smiles. "These three. I scared her. It was a closer call than I would like."

I burst into tears and hug him. He strokes my hair and pushes me away.

"There's someone here to see you," he says, and turns me around, to face a man I know.

"Enter, pursued by a bear," says the man. "Oh, Flora. My Flora." He is wearing a nylon coat and has just unzipped it, and under it he has on a patterned knitted sweater. His hair is all messed up. I have seen him lots of times before, but I have never seen him here. He has never been in the cold place.

I cannot believe it is him. I don't dare to say the word. I look at both my hands. I roll my sleeves up to look at both my arms. On the inside of the right one, in shaky letters, I have written: Dad is coming.

I look at him. The word seems to fit.

"Dad?" I say. I know my dad. I have always known my dad. I do know my dad.

He nods. Of course it is Dad. I have known him all my life. I run into his arms and hope that he will hug me forever.

. . .

We sit on the sofa and I lean on him.

There is one thing I have to know, and he is the person who will tell me. If I made up the e-mails from Drake, I must have done the same with the ones from Jacob. I have just read about Jacob in my notebook. He appeared, writing to me, just when I wanted him to. Drake wrote me wonderful messages telling me exactly what I wanted to hear. When he stopped writing, Jacob took over, sending me encouragement and answers and support from afar. I want Jacob to be real, but I am scared to ask.

"Is Jacob real?"

"Jacob?" Dad is looking at me, taking me seriously. "Yes, Flora. Yes. Jacob's real. He's your brother. He's twenty-four and he lives in Paris. He won't be with us for much longer, I'm afraid. I've had to say good-bye to him before I came here."

"But is he . . . would he write things like this?" I pick up my bag and feel around inside it for my phone. I find the e-mail from Jacob and put it in front of my dad.

"This," I say. "Would he have written this? Does that sound like actual him? Did he write it, not me?"

I watch my dad's face as he reads it. He nods, breathes deeply, seems to calm himself.

"Oh yes," he says as he gives it back. "Yes. That's your brother. He hasn't changed. So you two have been in touch throughout. I should have known. He never told us. Not even when we were desperately trying to track you down."

"But it's him."

"It's him. Absolutely."

Jacob is real. I screw my eyes tight shut and think about him.

"Will you tell me, Flora?" Dad says. "Will you tell me every-thing that you can?"

I look around the room. Agi is talking to Toby. I watch them for a second, and see that they look as if they're going to kiss. Drake and Nadia are arguing in a different room: I can hear their voices but not their words. The older woman is on the phone.

I start to tell him anything I can, talking as quickly as I can before it melts away from the inside of my head. I know it is coming out jumbled, and there are things I am sure I am getting wrong, but I read it just now and I feel that most of it is still in my head.

". . . and then I got here," I say, in the end, my words falling over themselves. "And Drake told me, just now, that I didn't kiss him. I watched him kissing someone else instead. I didn't kiss him myself. Only in my head. I remembered it but it was wrong." I hate saying these words, but I have to explain and so I keep talking. "And all the e-mails. He didn't write them. I wrote them. But I didn't know I was doing it." It is hard to get the words out.

Dad takes my hand. "I bet you wrote better e-mails than he could ever have."

I look into his pale eyes and see that he is crying too.

"I did!" I tell him. "I really did." I laugh, in spite of every-thing. "I think I wrote the best e-mails ever."

"I don't know the young man," he says. "And I could be mis-judging him. But it seems to me that he's not really a person who's ever likely to send anyone 'the best e-mails ever.' He should be thanking you for making him a million times more interesting. He doesn't really seem the Casanova." Then he sighs.

"Flora," he says. "So you're not taking your pills."

"No."

"And you're yourself. You're Flora. My Flora. You've made a load of friends and come to the North Pole and found the boy. You're alive. You're lucid. You're capable. I suppose we need to let you be this Flora. Real Flora. I guess I knew that last time, really, but now you're grown up. I'm so sorry, darling. You're not a child to be protected from everything, are you?"

"No. Not really. Am I capable?"

"You are a million times more capable than we've ever allowed you to be. And now I'm afraid I'm going to have to take you back home. And . . ." He takes a deep breath.

I can feel things starting to fade away at the edges, and I try to hang on to them.

"Your mother," he says, "is very protective. She adores you. She does it out of love. We both do. It's what drove Jacob away, exactly the way he said. We have lied to you. He's right. You've been away before. This is your third trip, and I'm sure you'll do it again. Maybe we need to be thinking about your independence. But, sweetheart, all we've ever wanted is to keep you safe."

He stops talking and swallows. He runs a hand through his sticking-up hair.

"I can understand that you probably don't want to leave, sweetie, but I have to take you back. The three of us will have a lot to talk about when we get home."

I replay what he just said. This is my third trip. I am capable. I travel. Dad believes in me. I write better e-mails than Drake. They are going to think about my independence. I haven't been taking pills but I'm all right.

Henny hands me a drink. It is hot and steaming. I take it and wrap my hands around it.

This is all too much to think about, and so I sip my drink and cuddle up to my dad.

Part 3

Chapter Twenty-One

I have no idea where I am.

I cannot think. In my mind, words come and go, but nothing fits together.

I have no idea.

No idea.

No ideas.

A woman is crying. She is crying and crying and crying. I don't like it.

I can smell something I like. A drink is on the table in front of me. If I reach my hand out, I will pick it up. If I pick it up, I can drink it. I must not spill it.

I stare at it. The cup is pink and white. I stretch out a hand and touch it. It's hot. I take the handle. I lift it. It spills on the table. I put it down. I lean my head back and close my eyes. There were some words on my hand.

I open my eyes. There is a cup on the table in front of me. I won't try to pick it up.

There are people somewhere in this room, talking. I try to make sense of their words.

"She's *fine*."

"She is not fine. You should have seen her. I can't bear to look at her like this. It's not right. It's not fair. She's in there."

"She's alive. She's safe. Oh God, I know, Steve. I do know. But it won't be like this forever. It's just for now. Just to get her anchored back here. I can't lose her. I can't let her do it again. Better that she's like this, than . . ."

"She's breathing. She's not alive. They're not the same thing."

I close my eyes.

There is a TV on. A man and a woman are on the screen, talking directly to me, saying, "The kitchen renovation." It suddenly stops and the words HOMES UNDER THE HAMMER appear on the screen.

I don't know why homes would be under a hammer.

I am in a comfy chair in the living room, watching TV. I close my eyes for a moment.

"She should know about him. At least that she *had* a brother."

"She doesn't need to be upset like that. It's better this way."

"She'll remember him at some point."

I am sitting at a table, and there is food in front of me. I stare at it. It is pasta and vegetables and things.

"What's this called?" I ask.

"Vegetable lasagna, darling," says a woman. I look at her face. She has red eyes. She has been crying. There is no food in front of her. She is my mother.

The man is sitting opposite me. He has a plate of vegetable lasagna too, and he is eating it in huge forkfuls. He looks up and smiles, though there are big black bags under his eyes. He has sticky-up hair. He is my father.

"Eat up," he says.

"Do I like this?"

"Very much."

"And you love garlic bread," says my mother. "Go on. Have some."

I take a piece of it, even though it is yellow inside with green dots and doesn't look very nice. I take it to make her happy.

I try the vegetable lasagna. It is fine.

I look at my hands. One of them says FLORA, be brave. Nothing else is written on them at all. I look all the way up both of my arms. I don't really know why I'm doing it, but there is nothing there except a little bandage on the inside of one of my arms, stuck down with Band-Aids. I start to pick it off.

"Don't do that," says my mother. She turns to my dad. "I'm going to see about getting that tattoo removed," she tells him. "She doesn't need her own body telling her to be brave every time she looks down."

"Really?"

"It might give her ideas."

I have no ideas.

No idea.

. . .

Things get clearer, bit by bit.

Both of my parents are dressed in black. They are serious. I can tell from my mother's makeup and perfume that they are going somewhere.

"Where are you going?" I ask.

"Nowhere. It's time for bed, Flora."

"I don't want to go to bed," I say. "I'm not tired."

"Come on, darling. Take your medicine."

She leads me upstairs, and up again, into my bedroom with its walls that are completely pink, and its pink duvet and white furniture and pink curtains and a board with photographs of people. There are pictures of the man, the woman, and me. There is a box of Legos, and there are dolls and teddies.

"Why don't you get into your pajamas, sweetheart?" she says. While I get changed, she counts out some pills and produces a glass of water from somewhere. She hands me the water and gives me pill after pill. I swallow them all, one by one, a gulp of water with each of them.

"Now into bed." I climb in under the duvet and put my head on the pillow. She puts a teddy bear into my arms. "You'll sleep now, darling." She kisses me on the forehead and whispers: "I'm so sorry, Flora. So sorry. I know this is wrong. Your dad's right. But I cannot lose you too. I can't."

I close my eyes and sink into darkness.

I wake up and there is daylight coming in around the curtains. For a second I think that I am in a place that never gets dark, not even at night; a place that has daylight coming around a blind even at three in the morning. But it always gets dark at night, and so that place cannot exist. The daylight probably means it's daytime.

There is a notebook on the pillow beside my head. I pick it up, open it, and begin to read.

You are Flora Banks.

You are 17 years old and you live in Penzance in Cornwall. When you were ten, doctors discovered a tumor growing in your brain, and when you were eleven, they removed it. Part of your memory went with it. You can remember your life before the illness, but since then you have not been able to make new memories.

You have something called ANTEROGRADE AMNESIA. You generally keep things in your head for a few hours (sometimes less), and when you forget them, you are confused. Dad and I help you by reminding you of who you are and what is happening.

You can still remember how to do things (how to work the shower). You remember us, and you sometimes remember people you used to know up until you were ten. You forget other people, but that's OK because the people here know you and they understand.

You can never live anywhere but Penzance, and you'll never want to, because this town is mapped in your mind, and it is your home. We lived in this house before your illness, so you know it well. You will always live with us, and we will always

take care of you. You can never go anywhere alone: you don't
want to and you don't need to.

You are very good at reading and writing, and you like
watching television.

We will always make sure you have everything you need.
You take medication twice a day, and you always will.

We love you very much.

Mom xx

I read it through twice, until the information sinks in. I live
here. I never go out. That is good. I could not imagine going out.

I stand up and feel dizzy. My vision starts to go black, and I sit
down quickly on the floor. From here I can see under the bed.
There is a box under there. I reach across and pull it toward me.

It is empty. There is an empty shoe box under my bed. I think
it should have things in it, but I don't know why I think that. I
don't know why it would have things inside, and I don't know why
it would be there, empty.

I walk downstairs. There are letters on the doormat, and I
walk over to them and pick them up. I stumble as I walk. Nothing
feels real.

There are three letters. Two are typed ones in white envelopes
addressed to Mr. and Mrs. Banks, and the third is a brown one,
also typed, and addressed just to Mrs. Banks.

"What are you doing?" My mother takes the letters out of my
hand and looks through them—one, two, three—and puts them
aside. "Why are you looking at the letters, Flora?"

I shrug. I don't know.

"I don't know," I tell her. "They were on the floor and so I picked them up."

"Because that's what people do?"

"What people do," I echo.

She smiles. "OK, darling. Sorry. I'm sorry."

I am sitting up straight on the sofa, a bit nervous because my dad has just told me that I've got a visitor and I have no idea who would come to visit me.

A girl walks into the room. She has long hair that is dark and curly, and she is wearing a pair of denim shorts and a pink-and-green T-shirt.

"Flora!" she says. "Oh my God. Flora. It's amazing to see you. Oh God."

She is next to me on the sofa. I look at her.

"It's me," she says. "Paige. Remember? Paige. Your friend."

She is familiar. Paige had her hair in braids and we met on the first day of school.

"Flora?" she says. "Flora. Say something."

"She's OK," says my dad. "Just give her a few minutes. She's getting better. Thanks so much for coming to see her, Paige. Can I get you a drink?"

"Oh, no, thanks," she says. "I'm fine."

"I'll leave you to it, then," he says, but he doesn't leave. Instead he says, "I know this is shocking. It's just for now. Right at this moment, after Jacob, Annie needs to know that she's safe. You understand?"

"Right. Sure, of course I do. OK. Look, we'll be fine. I'll just talk to her a bit and make sure she knows we're friends again."

"Don't tell her you weren't." He puts his hand on my shoulder. "Nothing about any of that."

"OK. Sure. I promise. Honestly, you can leave us."

"Of course. I'll close the door. Let you chat." He smiles.

The moment the door is closed, the girl, Paige, changes completely. She takes my face in her hands and stares into my eyes.

"Flora," she says urgently. "Flora, look at me. Try to focus. Flora, it's me. Oh my God, I can't believe what they've done to you."

She grabs my arm and pushes up my sleeve.

"Look at that! That's not your arm. This is not your hand." She picks up my right hand, which has the words FLORA, be brave on it. I lick my finger and scrub at them, but they don't come off.

"Be brave. If they'd give you half a chance, you'd be the bravest person in the world. I bet the tattoo won't be there for much longer, will it?"

I have no idea what she's talking about. I pick at the edge of the bandage on my other arm. She takes my hand away.

"Look," she says. "I don't know how much of this you can understand, but I'm going to say it anyway. I am so sorry, Flora. So, so sorry. I was awful to you. I took it out on you, when the only person to blame was Drake. Flora, you are my hero. You're amazing and, Flora, listen to me: *Drake lied to you.* You *did* kiss him. You remembered it and that memory was real. He is an absolute bastard for telling you it didn't happen. I can't believe he'd stoop to that. We don't care about him anymore." She raises her eyebrows. "You've forgotten him, haven't you? And I've got a new boyfriend. But you. You went to the bloody Arctic! You did it. You got yourself there by writing yourself notes about everything. You went to the North Pole because you are amazing. Flora, I'd give anything to be as strong as you and that's why it breaks my heart to see your mother keeping you like this. Everyone wants you out of here and it's going to happen. I feel sorry for your mom, and I know she's having a breakdown of her own right now and clinging on to you, but she can't do this and your dad's doing what he thinks is best. He hates it. I can see that. But he's doing what your mom wants because of Jacob. Oh God, I'm so sorry. I should have gone out there with you. We should have confronted Drake together."

I am staring at her, and trying to form some words. I went to the bloody Arctic? I have not been anywhere. I don't know what "the bloody Arctic" means. Her words are noises.

I sit and look at her. She is Paige. She is my best friend.

"I'm going to come and see you every day. OK? Where do they keep your pills? Are they in the bathroom?"

I see the pill bottles often. Mom is always giving me pills.

"Kitchen." That is the word for the place where they are. That, I am sure, is the word. "Kitchen renovation," I add, frowning because I don't know why I said that.

"Kitchen. Are you sure? That's going to be tricky. I'll have to make a plan. We have to do this. You wouldn't believe the things your brother said he was going to do to me if I don't. But you have to trust me. Can you do that?"

I have no idea. I nod.

"OK."

I see that she is thinking hard. "OK. Today we're going to keep it normal. I'm coming back for your birthday. We'll do it then."

"We'll do it then," I say.

She looks into my face. "God, Flora. They've lobotomized you. Jacob said they would. Jacob said this would happen." She takes my face in her hands and stares into my eyes. "Flora. You are an amazing human being. You are wild and wonderful. Your spirit is like nothing on earth, because it shines through everything they try to do to you. And you're drugged up *to the eyeballs*. Beyond the eyeballs. They've made you into a zombie. You've got no idea what you've done or what you are capable of doing. They've killed you."

I stare back at her in dismay. They have not killed me because I am alive. Am I alive? I am not sure.

"Oh, sweetie. Sorry, but I have to tell you something else. You had a brother who *adored* you. Who disowned your parents because they drugged you—not this badly, but badly enough. He looked out for you from a distance. He was brilliant. But now that he's gone, it's up to me."

I gaze at her. I hate these things she is saying. Jacob is gone? Jacob is my brother. I painted his toenails. He picked me up. A tear rolls down my cheek. She hugs me tightly.

"You kissed Drake, OK, and even though he was my boyfriend, I'm happy that you did. You kissed a clever, handsome man. And then you remembered it. All the bad stuff about that is on him, but I blamed you and I'm really sorry."

"I kissed Drake?" I will try to remember this, if it is important, if I remembered it before. I can't imagine myself kissing someone.

"Yes. I can't believe he pretended you made it up. Just to make it seem that your whole adventure wasn't his fault, even though it was. I know you kissed him because *I have a photo.* Lily took it. I didn't believe her, so she sent it to me. Here." She holds up her phone and I lean in to peer at the screen.

I see a picture that is black around the edges, with a strip of stones that are too brightly lit. The bright stones lead to two people, who are sitting down. The boy has his back to the camera. He could be anyone. The girl has blond hair. She is wearing a white dress that is glaring in the light. She is leaning toward the boy and kissing him. I stare at her.

"That's you." Paige is touching her with a finger. "And this," she says, "is Drake."

"That's me?" I hold the phone closer, trying to work it out. I didn't know I looked like that.

"It is. Look."

Paige uses her fingers to make the girl in the picture bigger. It goes a bit fuzzy. I look around for a mirror, and when I see that there's one on the wall, we both go and stand in front of it.

"See?" says Paige. She turns my head to the same angle as the girl's in the photo. I look at myself, and when she holds the phone up, I look at the picture.

"Yes," I say. Yes, that is a photograph of me, kissing a boy, on a beach with some very bright stones. I stare at the boy. That is Drake. I kissed him on a beach, but I don't feel anything about that.

Paige leads me back to the sofa and sits me down.

"Drake knows *exactly* what I think of him," she says. "We've exchanged some messages. He says he feels terrible. He claims he acted in the spur of the moment, and he assumed you'd never remember, so that would make it safe. He said he'd never tried to hook up with you before, but I'm not sure I even believe that. God knows. The implications aren't great. But anyway. Forget him. Here's the thing: Do you want to get out of here and live a life again?"

She is looking at me in a way that tells me that this is a very important question. I can see she wants me to say yes, and so I nod. Of course I want to live a life. I am confused by her words, but I'll ask her to write it down so I can figure it out later.

Then my parents are there, and Paige changes completely, and tells them that she has to leave now.

"I'll come and see you again tomorrow, Flora," she says. "If that's OK, Mrs. Banks?"

"Annie. And yes, of course it is. It's nice for her to have your company. I know that nothing that happened was your fault. We do very much appreciate how good a friend you are to her, you know."

Paige gives my mother a smile and hugs me at the front door. I don't want her to leave. I want her to explain things until I understand them. "See you soon," she whispers. "I promise I'll help you. I love you."

Chapter Twenty-Two

"Come on, Flora," says my mother, a big smile on her mouth but not in her eyes. "Blow them out."

"Blow them out," I repeat. There is a cake on the table in front of me. The curtains are closed and the room is pretty dark, though there is daylight coming around the edge of them. Perhaps this is a place where it is always light, even in the middle of the night.

"Go on!" says my dad.

I look around. Paige is sitting beside me.

"Want me to do it with you?" she asks. She takes my hand and squeezes it. "Come on. We'll blow out your birthday candles together. One, two, three . . ."

The candles are in front of me on a cake. There are lots of them. Lots and lots of tiny flames. I copy Paige and puff at them, and they flicker and go out, most of them. We do it again and all the flames are gone.

My parents clap. I look at them, from one face to the other. They are both looking at me and smiling. I look down at myself. I am wearing a white dress—a party dress—and a pair of yellow shoes.

"Now you need to cut the cake," says Dad, and he picks up a knife to hand it to me. Mom leans over and takes it from his hand just as I am reaching for it.

"I'll do that," she says. "Flora doesn't need a sharp knife."

Paige is still holding my hand. I feel her tense up at my mother's words.

There is music playing. A man is singing about a hearts club band, but I don't know what that means. I don't know what anything means.

I stare at the light coming in around the edges of the curtain. For some reason it makes me sad.

"Don't cry, Flora," says Paige, softly. Mom hands me a little plate, which is white with gold around the edges. There is a slice of cake on it. I take it and stare at the cake. It is brown. It is chocolate cake. There are brightly colored circles on the top. It looks nice but I don't want it.

I look at my mother. She is watching me, and when she sees me looking, she makes her face into a smile.

"Eat up, darling," she says. "You're eighteen now!"

"An adult," says Paige, and I see her give my mother a look.

"Yes," says my mother. "An adult. In your own way."

Nobody says anything. The singing man says he'd like to take us home with him.

My mother says, quickly, her words falling over themselves: "I'm sorry. But I'm not losing her too, Paige. I'm just not. She's all I've got left and I am keeping her safe. I'm taking care of her. I cannot bear to do anything else. I'm her mother and she stays with me and I will look after her every need. She is completely fine. I'm changing her dosage, now that she's used to being back home. She just needs . . . not to think of running anywhere. Ever. For her own safety."

"Dr. Epstein sent her a birthday card," says Paige. "She *is* eighteen now."

"That man is not getting anywhere near her."

My father starts talking quickly. He looks as if he's on Paige's side, not my mother's, but I know that can't be right.

"Maybe we should get Flora out for a bit this afternoon? Since it's her birthday. And such a nice day. Maybe we could walk down to the beach?"

"Why don't I take Flora to look at the sea?" says Paige. "She always liked that. I *promise* I'll look out for her. It'll be nice. Or I could even take her to the movies. A birthday treat. She's allowed to leave the house sometimes, isn't she?"

"That's a very thoughtful idea, Paige," says my father. "It would be nice for Flora to go out with you."

"I swear I'll take care of her."

Everyone looks at my mother. She is looking down at her glass. I notice that she and Paige are both drinking something with bubbles in it out of a tall thin glass. My father is drinking something orangey colored in a thicker glass. I stare at his drink. I know something about that.

"Beer!" I say, pointing.

Paige bursts out laughing. My dad smiles. My mother frowns.

"That's right," says Paige. "That's beer."

I look at my glass. It has lemonade in it. There are two cubes of ice and a slice of lemon. This is good.

"I must not drink beer because it makes me sick," I say, not knowing where the words are coming from. I don't know what I am saying.

"That's a good rule," says Paige, after a few seconds.

"Yes," says my father. "Yes, it is. Well done, Flora."

My mother says nothing.

They all talk among themselves, and I stop listening. I make myself eat a bit of cake because it is my birthday. I drink my lemonade. I listen to the music. I look at my hands. FLORA, says one of them, be brave.

"Come on, then!"

Paige is standing at the front door. My mother puts a hand on my shoulder. It makes me jump, because she is standing behind me and I forgot she was there.

"Just down to the beach and back again," she says. "That's it. Promise?"

"Of course I promise, Mrs. Banks. We'll be fine. You know it'll be nice for her to get some fresh air."

"Yes. You're right. OK. A birthday outing. But promise you'll have her back by four thirty. It's four o'clock now. Thirty minutes is the absolute limit."

"Sure. When we come back, she can open my present."

"Yes. That would be great. We've got a couple more things for her too. I've tried to spread it out throughout the day so she keeps getting the joy of opening something all over again."

Paige smiles. She puts her arm through mine and leads me out, through the porch, which has nothing on it at all, down a path, and onto the pavement.

The sun is shining. The sky is light blue. The air smells of flowers and lovely things. Paige leads me out of the garden and takes me across the little road to the park.

"We'll go through here," she says. "You like going through here."

I let her lead me down paths, past leafy green trees, past a pond. She takes me to a bench and sits me down on it. Then she changes. She takes my face in her hands and stares into my eyes.

"OK, Flora," she says. "Today is when we start to get the real you back. You're coming off your pills. The pills you're taking now won't do anything. I switched them when I was sticking the Smarties onto the top of your cake. All the bad pills are in here." She takes a little brown bottle out of her pocket and rattles it.

"The bad pills are in there," I say.

"Yes. The ones your mom is going to give you now are placebos. You're off the bad stuff. It might be hard, but I hope not too hard because you haven't been back on them for that long. Your skin will go strange again. You'll start waking up. You'll go to different places and times in your mind. You'll want to start writing things down. Your mom will notice, so we haven't got long. I'm going to be around you as much as I possibly can. You won't remember me saying this, and we haven't got much time. I'm going to give you a letter, OK? It's really important that you read it, on your own. I have to get you back by four thirty, so you can't read it now. I wish you could, so I could talk you through it. But you're going to have to read it, and keep it, and keep reading it again and again as you start to get your mind back."

She puts a hand on my knee and squeezes it.

"Don't worry," she adds. "I know you're not taking this in. I know you couldn't possibly. I still need to tell you. Maybe some of this will stick. Take care, Flora. We're going to help you. Now, can I have your arm?"

I hold out my arm, with no idea what she wants it for. She pushes up the sleeve of my cardigan and takes a pen out of her pocket. High up on my arm, above a bandage, she writes: Lock door. Take Jacob's letter from bra & read it.

I frown. "Read it?"

"Yes. I've got a letter for you and we're going to put it in your bra so your parents won't notice it." She takes a folded piece of paper and sticks it under my bra strap and rearranges my clothes. She squints at me and nods.

"That'll do. OK. Now we'll quickly go to look at the sea, and then I'll take you back home again."

I am leaning on a railing, beside Paige, who is my friend, and we are looking at the sea. The water is halfway up the beach. There are stones on the beach. Most of them are gray and black. There is a picture of a cat tied to the railings.

I love the smell of the air. I love to lean on a railing and look at the water. Some birds are flying, high in the sky. They are shrieking. I want to lean on this railing and breathe the fresh air and look at the sea all the time.

There is a bandage on my arm. I pull my sleeve up and pick at the edges of it. When I look under it, there are letters cut into my skin. I don't understand, and I don't like it, so I push the bandage back down.

There are cars going past, behind us. Lots of people are on the beach. Many of them are lying down without many clothes on. Children are running around. People are swimming. They are eating. They are reading. They are living.

"Oh, Flora. I know you want to stay here, but we can't. I'm so sorry."

I look around. "Why can't we?"

"Not today. I have to get you back. Don't worry, though. It's not for long, and we're going somewhere better than this. Come on." She takes my hand, and we stand together on the pavement and wait for a gap in the traffic. I let her lead me across the road and up the street toward the house in which I spend all my time.

They give me presents. I open them and say thank you. My parents have given me a teddy bear. It is a big one with a bow around its neck. I hug it tightly to my chest.

Paige gives me a new bag. It is white with red flowers on it, and lots of things would fit into it. I open it. There are bottles of things inside it, things that smell nice. There is a lipstick. There are necklaces and scarfs. There is a brand-new notebook and there are a lot of pens.

I love it. I love everything inside it.

"Thank you," I say to her, over and over again.

She laughs. "You're welcome, Flora! You really are. Very, very welcome. I'm glad you like it so much."

. . .

We are standing at the front door. Paige is leaving.

"Don't go," I say. I long for her to stay with me.

"I have to. But I'll come back tomorrow. I promise. Maybe we can go for another walk."

She looks at my mother, who nods.

"Of course," she says.

"It was nice for Flora to get out today," says my father. "Thank you, Paige, and thanks for spending her birthday with her. We appreciate it, and I know Flora does too."

"Flora does too," I say, and I really truly mean it.

He laughs. "See?"

Paige hugs me good-bye. She pulls me in close to her and whispers: "Go to the bathroom right now and read your arm." Then she says loudly, "I'll be here at eleven tomorrow, if that's OK?"

"We'll see you then," says my mother.

I go into the bathroom right now and read my arm.

Lock door, it says, above a bandage. Take Jacob's letter from bra & read it.

I lock the door. There is something folded and pointy in my bra. I take it out and open it, and I sit on the bathroom floor and start to read.

Chapter Twenty-Three

The first sheet of paper is small, and says, in loopy writing:

Chère Flora,

Here is Jacques, boyfriend of Jacob. Jacob spent many days writing this for you. I promise to post it. He care for you very much. Please write me soon.

Grosses bises,

Jacques

I have no idea what this means, but something inside me is urging me on. I put that note carefully aside and start to read the letter. I read it slowly, because my brain does a terrible job at processing the words, and I barely understand a quarter of it.

My little Flora,

If you're reading this, it means I'm gone. I'm sorry, my darling. It's not fair, but it's true. Being a ghost might suit me—I've been a ghost in your life for years now anyway. I'm trying to look on the bright side now that all other avenues have been exhausted.

I'll do my best to keep an eye on you. Look around you now. Give me a smile. Kiss the air and I'll be in it. Will I? Who knows? Maybe.

I'm sending this to your former friend Paige, who will be viciously haunted by me for the rest of her days unless she steps up to get you out of the drugged-up fog our mother will undoubtedly impose upon you. And she knows it.

OK. Basics first—

You are Flora Banks. I'm your brother, Jacob Banks. I am seven years older than you are and I wish I could be around to have you live with me, now that you're grown up. I lived in Paris with my boyfriend, Jacques, who's going to keep an eye on you as best he can.

Our mother and father have lied for seven years about your memory loss. Clearly it's my job to tell you the truth, so here you go. This is our story:

When you were ten, you and I, and our parents, were all in an accident. They have always pretended you had a brain tumor because they can't bear to talk or think about the accident, ever, and they didn't want you asking about it every five minutes.

We were in the back of the car together, on our way to Flambards, which is a theme park. Imagine it, Flora. You, a normal, gorgeous ten-year-old, excitedly asking about the rides. You'd been looking forward to it for weeks. All you would say was: "I want to go to Flambards," over and over and over again. Me, a grumpy gay seventeen-year-old who had decided to come along for the day because you were so excited, and because I was secretly looking forward to it. Our parents were sitting in the front listening to the radio and talking about their usual boring shit.

We were at a traffic circle just before we got there when a truck went straight past the yield sign and plowed into the side of the car. We flipped over a few times, went straight up into the air, and landed upside down. Our parents were both unscathed, physically at least. You had horrendous head injuries because you'd taken your seat belt off because we were almost there. And I—well, I didn't have your sort of injuries, because I was still buckled in, but I didn't get to walk away easily either. I was the only one stuck in the flames when the car caught fire—you'd been taken out, and Mom and Dad had jumped out for help immediately, but I was still inside. Believe me, facial scarring and plastic surgery are not what a self-conscious teenager wants.

I got to keep my mind, while you got to keep your looks. Between us, we could have made up a functioning human being.

Mom was driving. That's why she's always wrapped you in cotton wool. It's why she's never driven since. It's why she's had a breakdown that's lasted seven years, and counting. That's why you've had to resort to such subterfuge to escape whenever you can. She was driving, we were both hurt, and she has always blamed herself. Everything she's ever done has been to try to protect you. To make sure nothing like that can ever happen again. To this day, I think she suffers from PTSD, and one of the reasons I had to see them before I die was to tell Mom, again, that it wasn't her fault.

You only have solid memories from before the accident. You don't have much of a short-term memory. You remember things for an hour or maybe three, and then you forget. This sort of amnesia can often get better over time, because the brain is a mysterious and wonderful thing that finds new pathways, but for a long time yours didn't. Recently, I've suspected it could have been improving (not least because of your memory of kissing that boy—it was the memory that was the momentous thing about that, not the kiss, and you knew there was something amazing going on and ran straight off to the North Pole to see if Prince Charming could make it happen again).

As our mother has kept you on the pills, it's been hard for anyone to tell, particularly you, whether you might actually be getting better. But you started talking all the time about going to Flambards, and that meant something was breaking through. As you can imagine, you asking to go to that particular place has not been easy on Mom.

As I said in one of my e-mails, the reason for my estrangement from our parents until now is because your personality changed slightly after the accident and our parents felt it was a problem. You were impulsive and wild beforehand, though—that was why you were so brilliant. It was what made you you. But after the accident and because of your amnesia, they felt that when you were "better," you behaved too dangerously. You'd climb out of upstairs windows to sit on the windowsill and talk to the birds. You'd run off and find you had no idea where you were. You'd paint huge crazy pictures of the inside of your head. You'd tell strangers about your journeys through time and space. And Mom decided (for your own safety, blah blah blah, and because she couldn't handle the guilt of any more accidents) to tame you.

I couldn't bear it. It was worse than the injury.

They made the decision to put you on a drug that would dull your senses, stop your moods, make you malleable and easy and controllable, on the grounds that "you were a danger to yourself" otherwise. Mom has never been her real self since the accident: she never wanted to risk anything happening to you ever again, and I mean that literally. She never wanted anything to happen. They decided to keep you on mood stabilizers, calling it your "medicine," and you became pliable and "good," and they kept you at home, as safe as safe could be. They buy them from the internet, because no doctor would allow that kind of long-term dependency. In time they added an antidepressant, because too many pills can bring a girl down. There's no real medication for amnesia: you don't actually need to take pills at all. They fogged up your brain because you were easier to manage that way.

The worst thing is, there's a neuropsychologist named Joe Epstein who's been wanting to get his hands on you ever since I contacted him years ago. He would help you, or at least assess you. He's tried to see you, and Mom has always said no. Not out of vindictiveness, but because she's scared. She wants to keep you ten years old and take care of you. I would say she wants to look after little Flora forever, to assuage the guilt she feels for not having taken better care of you for that split second.

When they said no to Dr. Epstein the first time, I hated them. I moved to Paris and learned to speak French properly, and worked and lived and made my life. I came back from time to time until Mom made me stop, and then I kept in touch with you as best I could, with cards and letters and e-mails and calls, and it was always wonderful to get the tentative contact from you, calling a number I'd left for you, not at all sure what was going on, ready to have it all explained again.

Where was I? Yes. It turns out there's no crushing my little sister. The first time you left home, you got on a train one day and went to London, on your own. You were thirteen and they were beside themselves. The police found you and you were returned to Penzance, with your dosage firmly upped. Then, together, we got you a passport, and soon after that you turned up here in Paris to see me. That was last year, and you were a gorgeous, confused sixteen-year-old. You already had your name on your hand: you wanted something to remind you to have adventures, so we went to a tattoo parlor together and had the words "be brave" added. I admit, getting you that was a massive "screw you" to the parents on my part. We spent four days together in Paris, and I showed you the Eiffel Tower, the Musée d'Orsay, the Luxembourg Gardens, and all the sights, and introduced you to the joys of red wine and afternoon movie screenings and long lunches.

You've achieved all this by writing to yourself. You have used the written word to circumvent some of the work your neural pathways should be doing. You've made your notebook your external memory, your memory stick. You are brilliant.

Then, this year, you kissed a boy, and remembered it, and chased him to the top of the world. To rewind a tiny bit, I had been feeling ill and not getting any better, and after putting off going to the doctor for much longer than I should have, I ended up with the fucking awful diagnosis of stage-four kidney cancer. There was no coming back, so I asked Mom and Dad to come over when I realized that this was it. I am being glib because I have to be. They were so panicked by my news that they left you with Paige, but as the boy you kissed was her boyfriend, she decided to leave you to fend for yourself. The amazing thing is that you remembered kissing him and so you booked a flight to the Arctic Circle to find this boy. You had a hell of a lot of adventures, came right off your medication, just about became real Flora again, and nearly got eaten by a polar bear.

I don't know for sure what will happen next, but I would bet everything I own that by the time you get this, they'll have drugged you into a vegetal state, and that you're never allowed to go anywhere. I bet they want you to sit nicely watching TV.

I have e-mailed with Paige and got her on our side, and learned from her that you really did kiss the boy, that she has a photo of you doing it. Jacques is going to send this to her house. She's going to give it to you and make sure you read it alone, and she's also going to swap all your medication for sugar pills, which J and I have ordered from the internet to be delivered to her. We've ordered them in every format, and she assures me that your medication has always come in little bottles, so she's going to replace them with the correct size and shape of pill. Take the pills you are given, and pretend to be a zombie. Not the brain-eating kind. Pretend to be incapacitated, passive, obedient. Lie on the sofa and watch the TV and drool a little.

Paige will visit every day and when the time is right, she will break you out of there.

Be careful about what you write down. I know you have to write things down, but you must not keep anything under your bed because they know about it and they always have. Paige will help you find a new hiding place.

I've set up a bank account for you, and Paige has the details. I want you to travel and have adventures. You met a load of people in Svalbard who were all spectacularly fond of you, because you are adorable.

The moment you're eighteen, you can decide what to do with your life. You can talk to Dr. Epstein yourself and see what he has to offer. You can make some decisions and take control. But none of that will work unless we get you off your pills.

I've been writing this for ages. I fear I must go now.

If there is any form of afterlife, I will be looking after you as best I possibly can.

Live your life. FLORA, be brave.

Your brother,

Jacob xx

I stare at the letter. I will need to read it again because there is too much there for me to understand. I pick up the next sheet of paper.

Dear Flora,

This is Paige. I know you've just read Jacob's letter and you must be overwhelmed, but please, please read this too. I need to tell you a couple of things.

First: we did fall out, you and me. Drake was my boyfriend. I said this to you before and I am going to say it again until you're able to take it in. YOU DID KISS HIM ON THE BEACH. He succeeded in convincing you and everyone else that it never happened, to get himself off the hook (probably more for his new girlfriend's benefit than anything else), but I know it happened, and the reason I know is because Lily saw you. You won't remember Lily, but she was one of Drake's friends in Cornwall. She followed him out of the party to the beach, probably because she wanted to be the one kissing him, to be honest. She saw him walking over to you. She said he sat down beside you and kissed you. I wouldn't have believed her, but she took a photograph, with her phone, and I've seen it. You'll probably have seen it too, by the time you read this. It's a picture of the back of his head, and your face. It's definitely you. It's definitely him. You kissed.

I was furious with both of you and decided never to talk to either of you ever again.

You were insanely vulnerable, and he is a bastard, and neither of us will have reason to speak to him again now that I have had it out with him over e-mail. I assume he thought he'd get away with it because you would forget about it. So that's nice. He panicked and told you he kissed Lily, who took the picture. He is not worth a fraction of you, Flora, or a moment of your time.

So, don't worry about that. This is the thing to take away from it: You have kissed a handsome, clever boy, on a beach in the moonlight. You have. That happened. And you remembered it, which is an amazing thing.

You met some nice people while you were looking for him. Your friend Agi has written about you on her blog (using all kinds of interesting English idioms) and it is getting quite a following. Everyone is asking about you but your parents won't let anyone in. Dr. Epstein has been in touch again. Your mother will never budge, and your father goes along with her, because he knows that she will fall apart if he doesn't. Though he's subtly doing everything he can to get me close to you, and I think we might actually have a very quiet ally.

I have finally been allowed in, just because I have been your best friend for years. They do not imagine I will ever try to take you more than half a mile from home. They're wrong.

Jacob is right: I am dumping your medicine and putting the

exact same number of sugar pills in the bottle. That will buy us a few days to bust you out of there. Be ready.

Put this in the box on your mantelpiece. DO NOT put it under your bed. If you write something on your arm, write it high up where your mom won't see it. Flora, your mom is not a bad person—she is very caring. She is suffering terribly and I feel so sorry for her. But you're an adult now and you get to decide how to live your life. Maybe you'll stay in Penzance. Maybe you'll never go back on your meds or perhaps you'll find something else that lets you be your wonderful self. Whatever you decide, it has to be your choice.

I've got your passport. I stole it from the study a few days ago when I went upstairs to the bathroom. Jacob told me it would be in there.

See you soon.

Paige xx

There is too much in my head. I stare at the sheets of paper. I lean back against the bathroom door. Mom is calling my name from downstairs. It seems I am crying.

Chapter Twenty-Four

"Flora!"

The man is looking at me, smiling broadly, shifting from one foot to the other.

"Flora," he says again. "We meet again. How are you feeling?"

He is bald and quite old, and he is wearing a shirt with rolled-up sleeves, and trousers, and a tie.

"I'm feeling OK," I tell him, and I am. I am actually feeling excited. Feeling things is, in itself, exciting.

Paige is beside me, holding my hand. We are standing on the beach, below the road, out of sight of anyone passing by unless they are on the beach too or passing in a boat. The wind is blowing our hair all over the place, and the water is choppy, in a million little peaks.

There is a poster tied to the railings of the steps we have just walked down that asks if we have seen a cat that has no ears. If you find a cat with no ears, you should take it home. That should be a rule.

"I'm Dr. Joe Epstein. I'm a neurologist. I've been interested in you for many years, Flora. We first met in Paris when you were over there and your brother contacted me—and I'm very sorry to hear the news about Jacob. Very sorry indeed. It's a tragic terrible waste. He was a complicated and fascinating young man. Now you're an adult and so I wonder whether you would be interested in letting me try to help you with your memory issues."

I hesitate.

"I don't know you." I don't know if I like this man. He is talking about Jacob. I don't really understand what's happening.

"I'm sorry. Look, I have something on my phone to show you. To vouch for me, to prove what I'm saying."

I have no idea what he is talking about, but I watch him tapping his screen.

"Are you ready?" he says. "Here. This is to prove to you that we've met. We made it last time, so you'd know. Look."

He comes to stand right next to me, and holds out the phone so Paige and I can both see the screen.

I gaze at it. The doctor man is on the screen. I am there too, and so is a boy with a big red blotch down one side of his face and features that make me cry, because this is my big brother, the person I love most in the world, the boy who let me paint his toenails—but here, he is not how I remember him. Here he is grown up and scarred.

The red side of his face is shiny and stretched, but he looks happy.

"Hello, Flora," Jacob says, and the sound of his voice makes me smile. "This is me, your brother, Jacob, in Paris, where I live. Look." Some houses appear on the screen and a river with boats on it.

"You're here, Flora. You've come to visit me and we are having the best time. I love having you with me. We're with Dr. Joe Epstein, who knows all about memories like yours. Here he is. We're making this, and keeping it on my phone and his, so you'll know you've met him before."

The doctor appears on the screen. He looks like he does now, except on the phone he is wearing a blue checkered shirt.

"Hello, Flora," he says. "Like Jacob says, I'm Dr. Joe Epstein. Jacob and I have been in contact for quite some time. Your mother doesn't want me in your life, as she didn't want me writing papers about you or producing you at conferences. And I absolutely respect her right to make that decision."

"But I don't," says Jacob. "And you'll be an adult in a couple of years, so it'll be your decision, not hers. Joe's a brilliant neurologist and he wants to help. I think we should give him a chance. As soon as you're eighteen, you can come and live here with me if you want."

The me on the screen nods at that. I gaze at my brother in the video, and also now, on the beach, with absolute love. As I watch it, I shiver. I want to see Jacob.

"So when we meet again, Flora," says the doctor on the screen, "this is who I am. I hope this makes sense to you and that we will be able to talk."

The film stops. I look at the real doctor.

"Where's Jacob?" I say. I see the doctor and Paige looking at each other.

"Flora," Paige says, and she puts an arm around my shoulders. "Flora, Jacob died. I'm so sorry. He got sick, and then he died. I'm so, so sorry."

I close my eyes. I want to forget that. I want it to delete itself from my head. Paige nods at the doctor. "We're very short on time," she says.

"Flora," he says. "It seems you've had what we call an 'island of memory' recently. A clear and, as far as we know, accurate memory stayed with you. There are many reasons this could have happened, but it could be the beginning of your amnesia lifting. You've had it for an unusually long time. I'd be beyond delighted if you'd spend some time with me. Your case is unusual and fascinating and I would very much like to try to help you as much as I can."

I look at Paige, totally out of my depth. She squeezes my hand.

"It's OK," she says. "We can talk about this some more before you agree to anything. You can watch the video again, if you want to. You can watch it as much as you like. Dr. Epstein's sent it to me, so we've got it on my phone now too."

I nod. She turns to the man.

"Thanks, Dr. Epstein. We'll be in touch as soon as we . . ." I see her look at me. "Depending, of course, whether you want to, Flora. We can get you away from here. If you want to. You don't have to. You're not taking your pills anymore. You can just tell your parents that you're leaving. Or you can go and leave them a letter."

It is a hot day. I push my hair back from my forehead. I cannot imagine being away from here, but I am desperate to do things, to have things happen. I have been to Paris. I have just seen a film of myself, in Paris. Paris is the capital of France: I know that from school. If I can go to Paris, I can go to other places too. I can do things. There is a world out there.

"Can you actually help me?"

"I would like to try."

I take a deep breath.

"Then yes," I say.

I am hazy about exactly what I am agreeing to, but I know that I want to do it. Over the past indeterminate amount of time, I have started to wake up, and realized that I live a life of staring at the TV and sleeping.

I feel sorry for that cat with no ears. I would like to find it.

"You're absolutely sure? This is going to take a lot of input from you, and you can't write much on your arm for the moment, so you're going to have to trust me," says Paige.

"I trust you."

"And Dr. Epstein."

"Yes. Because Jacob said so."

"We can go away and have an adventure. But only if that's what you want. I'm not going to kidnap you. You get to make a choice."

"I kissed a boy on a beach. I remember it."

"You did. You kissed a boy on a beach. And now you're eighteen. You're an adult, and you have options. Dr. Epstein will meet us in Paris again if you want to see him properly. They can't keep you here anymore."

I smile at her. Although I don't know much about anything,

I know that I have a story. I know that it is not over. There are shades and shadows of adventures and people and wild new places. Whatever Paris might turn out to be, and whatever Dr. Epstein is able to do, I want to be there to find out.

"Yes," I tell her. I look down at my hand. I read the words written on it. I look out to sea and say them aloud.

"FLORA, be brave."

Flora's Rules for Life

1. Don't panic, because everything is probably all right,
    and if it's not, panicking will make it worse.

2. Always try to get a window seat so you can tell
    exactly where you are.

3. Be brave.

4. Do not stray into polar bears' territory.

5. Live in the moment whenever you can. You don't
    need a memory for that.

6. If you have bad skin, lipstick will stop people from
    noticing it.

7. Don't eat whale.

8. Do not drink beer because it will make you sick.

9. Don't go to Svalbard in winter.

10. If you find a cat with no ears, you should take it
    home.

Turn the page for an exclusive bonus chapter from the author about when Flora visits Jacob in Paris.

I step off the train with everyone else. They all know what to do, so I do the same. We get down onto the platform and start walking in a big group down toward the station. As I pass it, I read the sign. I don't know what it means, but I am sure it's the right place, because I have come to find Jacob and PARIS GARE DU NORD is the place where he lives.

I look at my hand. FLORA, it says, and underneath that I have written Paris. Find Jacob. Look in your pocket. I know, because I saw it on the train a few minutes ago, that in my pocket is a piece of paper with the place Jacob lives on it. Get a taxi, I have written. Give the driver this piece of paper. Pay with the French money. There is French money with the note. I can do this.

The station is huge. I have to stop for quite a long time and just look at the people walking past. It goes a bit fuzzy. I don't know what I'm doing here. Someone stops and talks to me, but I don't understand, so I smile at them and say I'm fine.

I sit down on the ground and read my hand and then the piece of paper in my pocket. Jacob is the person I want to see most, and I can see a sign that says TAXI, so I stand up and follow it, and then I'm in a taxi and on my way to the address from the piece of paper.

I sit back and look out of the window.

There are people everywhere, and cars. The sky is cloudy, and everyone has big coats on. They have their heads down, and they are walking fast, to their Paris places. I like the tall buildings. I like everything. I like going past it in a car and watching it all. I am in Paris. This, right now, is my perfect place.

We spend quite a lot of time in traffic jams, but I don't mind because I can look at the people and the shops and the buildings for longer. In the end the driver pulls up and points to a building and says something to me. I hold out my money and let him take the right amount from it, and even though I don't really know what he's saying, I say "thank you very much," and then he laughs and says "for nothing."

This is where Jacob lives. I hold onto that fact. Jacob lives here. He lives here, but there are lots and lots of doorbells, and I don't know which of them is his, because they have numbers next to them instead of names.

I look at my piece of paper again. I look at the numbers on it. I look again at the numbers on the doorbells. I cannot possibly get this far and then not be able to find him because I don't know which button to press.

One of the numbers on his address is 13, so I press that, but nothing happens. I press a few more, and a voice crackles through the wall, but it's not Jacob, and so I say "sorry" and sit down on the doorstep to wait.

It's very cold, but I'm wearing my coat. I can just sit here and see what happens.

"Flora! What the fuck?" He laughs. He holds out a hand to me.

I blink a few times. I have no idea.

"Flora. You're actually here? It's me, Flora. Jacob."

I look at him. He doesn't look like the Jacob in my head. This Jacob is older, and he has bright red scars all over his face. I hate that, and I start to cry. He sees me looking and touches them.

"Yeah. I know. I'll tell you about it. Don't cry, darling. It's OK. Shit, you're freezing. Come in."

I stand up. He's right. I am freezing. I let him, this not-quite-Jacob, lead me into the house. He opens the front door with a key and we walk across a bit of floor and get into a tiny little elevator. I am trying to work it all out. Jacob is wearing very tight trousers and a red shirt. I like his shirt.

He looks at me as the elevator doors close.

"You're in Paris, Flora," he says. "I'm Jacob. I hurt my face, but I'm still Jacob. You're sixteen. I'm twenty-three. You have just turned up out of the blue, but I kind of hoped you'd do this one day. I left you money and instructions with your passport. Come on. You're all right. You've done everything right. I'd better make a call to Penzance."

His flat is small and not at all warm. I'm still shivering, but that doesn't matter because it smells of Christmas and food, and that makes me think that I'm very hungry. We go into a tiny kitchen that has twinkly lights going all around it, and posters on the walls. I stare at one that is orange and swirly, that says VERTIGO on it. I love that.

I see a photo of myself. Actually there are quite a lot of them. My face is on the walls of Jacob's flat. There's a picture in a frame of the two of us together, when I was small and Jacob's face was the way it used to be, without the scars. I sit and stare at everything. There is a picture of Jacob with another man. There are lots of Christmas cards, and I wonder whether one of them is from me. I hope so.

Jacob switches on the oven and all four gas rings and straightaway the room is a tiny bit warmer. He pulls a wooden chair up to the window, and I sit there and look down at the street, far below, while he wraps a blanket around me. I watch the cars going past, but I can't hear them. The cold air comes in around the edges of the window, and I don't care: I just pull the blanket more tightly around me. After a while he gives me a cup of hot chocolate with marshmallows floating in it.

There is snow starting to fall. I watch it drifting past the window. The flakes get bigger and bigger until they are like feathers. I hear Jacob on the phone saying: "I promise she's safe. I promise she's fine. Let me have her here for a few days. I promise I'll look after her. I'll bring her back for Christmas." I know he's talking to Mum, because he's talking about me, and because he said he was going to call Penzance.

I sip my hot chocolate. I look at my big brother and want to mend his face. I smile at him as he puts his phone down on the table.

"You were very brave to do this," he says.

"I like being brave."

"You're always brave."

"Can I come and live with you in Paris forever?" I say. I like Penzance, but I love Paris.

He laughs. "Yes. You'll have to wait a few more years, but when you're an adult you can move here and I will always, always look after you. I promise."

The door opens and another man comes in. He's the man from the photograph but with more hair. He laughs when he sees me.

"Flora!" he says. "*Bonsoir!* Good evening!"

"This is Jacques," says Jacob, and he is so happy that everything around him glows. "Jacques will always look after you, too."

I believe them, and this feels important, so I take a pen from the windowsill and write it on my hand.

) +) will always look after me.

Acknowledgments

This book would not exist without a number of fantastic people. On the publishing side of things, the following have been incredible to work with, and I feel extraordinarily lucky:

Lauren Pearson, Steph Thwaites, Liza Kaplan, Talia Benamy, Camilla Borthwick, Ruth Knowles, Tig Wallace, Annie Eaton, Tash Collie, Clare Kelly, Wendy Shakespeare, Rebecca Ritchie, and Emma Bailey, and the rest of the teams at Penguin Random House and Curtis Brown.

Kate Apperley donated to CLIC Sargent as part of their Get in Character auction for children with cancer, and thus became Drake's aunt.

Dr. Kevin Fong helped with the medical side of things and gave me papers to read about amnesia: all mistakes and exaggerations are mine. Dr. Oliver Sacks also helped unknowingly by writing such inspiring reference books.

Practical support of all kinds came from, among others: Adam Barr, Charles Barr, Nigel and Bridget Guzek, Lucy Mann, and Kevin Ashton.

Emotionally, I could not have written this without the support of Craig, my partner in life, writing, and everything, and without the wonderful distractions provided by Gabe, Seb, Lottie, Charlie, and Alfie.

Questions for Discussion

1. Though Flora's memory remains finite, she manages to grow as a character throughout the novel. How does she mature, and what has she gained by the end of her story?

2. The memory of kissing Drake is both pleasurable and painful for Flora. How does Flora grapple with these feelings?

3. Flora may never have "come-of-age" in the conventional sense, but describe how, despite having no memory of becoming an adolescent, she still conducts herself like an average seventeen-year-old.

4. Do you think Flora's bravery is a product of her memory loss? In other words, does she push herself to take risks she might not if her memory were intact?

5. Flora is able to remember parts of her childhood before the accident. How does this change her current perspective on the world and the people she meets?

6. How does the repetitive nature of Flora's story affect the reader's experience in relation to character and plot?

7. Flora follows Drake to Svalbard, believing he's the key to restoring her memory. In your opinion, does Flora have other reasons for making the trip?

8. To an outsider, Flora's life may be considered restrictive, as though she was a prisoner of her own mind. Are there parts of her circumstances that are liberating?

9. Due to her memory's limited scope, Flora is only able to convey her story in small pieces. How do the book's supporting characters aid and supplement Flora's storytelling?

10. Do you think the setting of Svalbard had a particular effect on Flora? How might her experience have been different had she traveled elsewhere?

Flora be brave

Flora be brave

Flora be brave

Flora be brave

Flora be brave

ra be brave

Flora be brave

Flora be brave

Flora be brave

lora be brave

Flora be brave

Flora be brave

Flora be brave

Flora be brave

Flora be brave

Flora be brave

rave

Flora be brave

Flora be brave

Flora be brave

Flora be brave

Flora be b

ra be brave

Flora be brave

Flora be brave

Flora be brave

Flora be brave

Flora be brave

Flora be brave

Flora be brave

Flora be brave

Flora be brave

Flora be brave

Flora be brave

Flora be brave

Flora be brave

Flora be brave

Flora be brave

Flora be brave

Flora be brave

Flora be brave

brave

Flora be brave

Flora be brave

Flora b

Flora be brave

Flora be brave